## The Sound of Death

At first Clint could see only three bodies. Then he spotted the woman, bound hand and foot and tied to a tree near the horses.

Satisfied that she was out of the line of fire, he walked into the camp, his rifle ready before him. A short, gap-toothed warrior was the first to discover the sinister visitor. He sat up, childlike in his attempt to brush the sleep from his eyes. The peaceful night was shattered by the crack of Clint's rifle as a .44 slug smacked into the warrior's chest.

In rapid succession, Clint leveled the Winchester to pump a fatal shot into each of the other two as they sprang from their blankets. It was all over in a matter of seconds, and the peaceful night was quiet again except for the frightened sounds from the horses. . . .

# LAWLESS PRAIRIE

Charles G. West

A SIGNET BOOK

SIGNET
Published by New American Library, a division of
Penguin Group (USA) Inc., 375 Hudson Street,
New York, New York 10014, USA
Penguin Group (Canada), 90 Eglinton Avenue East, Suite 700, Toronto,
Ontario M4P 2Y3, Canada (a division of Pearson Penguin Canada Inc.)
Penguin Books Ltd., 80 Strand, London WC2R 0RL, England
Penguin Ireland, 25 St. Stephen's Green, Dublin 2,
Ireland (a division of Penguin Books Ltd.)
Penguin Group (Australia), 250 Camberwell Road, Camberwell, Victoria 3124,
Australia (a division of Pearson Australia Group Pty. Ltd.)
Penguin Books India Pvt. Ltd., 11 Community Centre, Panchsheel Park,
New Delhi - 110 017, India
Penguin Group (NZ), 67 Apollo Drive, Rosedale, North Shore 0632,
New Zealand (a division of Pearson New Zealand Ltd.)
Penguin Books (South Africa) (Pty.) Ltd., 24 Sturdee Avenue,
Rosebank, Johannesburg 2196, South Africa

Penguin Books Ltd., Registered Offices:
80 Strand, London WC2R 0RL, England

First published by Signet, an imprint of New American Library,
a division of Penguin Group (USA) Inc.

First Printing, February 2009
10 9 8 7 6 5 4 3 2 1

*For Ronda*

# Chapter 1

"Ballenger, Washburn, Conner—stables!"

Clint Conner looked up in surprise when he heard his name called. This was the second time this week he had been assigned to the horse barn to clean out the stalls. It wasn't a bad job. It was better than working in the broom factory behind the prison. He tossed the last slug of coffee down his throat and put his cup and tray on the table beside the door, then walked over to the opposite wall to join the two prisoners already standing there. *Ballenger and Washburn*, he thought to himself as he waited for the guard to secure the short chain between his ankles. Of all the inmates in the forty-cell prison, he couldn't think of any two he'd less like to work with.

*What the hell?* he thought, reminding himself that the only way he could prevent his mind from rebelling against imprisonment was to cling to the belief that his mind and spirit were someplace outside these stone walls. With those two as partners, he would probably do most of the work in the stables, but he didn't care. Working made the day move faster. The more he thought about it, however, the more curious he became. How did a convicted killer like Clell Ballenger manage to get himself assigned to stable detail?

Ballenger was already sentenced, and a hanging date had been set for a week from yesterday. A prisoner sentenced to hang was not usually sent to work in the horse barn. That job was typically given to men with lighter sentences, because of a temptation to attempt escape. The prisoners mucking out the stalls were accompanied by only one guard, so the job was routinely assigned to short-timers and trustees. As a rule, men sentenced to be hanged were confined to their cells until execution day. Clint had to assume there had been a payoff to somebody, and he would bet that Nathaniel Boswell, the warden, knew nothing about the arrangement. Boswell was a hard-nosed former U.S. marshal with a reputation as a stalwart enforcer of the law. He would hardly approve of assigning a dangerous man like Ballenger to the stables.

Clint barely glanced at the smirking face of Clell Ballenger as he waited for the guard to finish locking his chains. He knew the notorious outlaw by reputation only. There had been a great deal of talk about the man supposedly responsible for the murders of twelve people during a spree of bank robberies over the last two years. Ballenger's repute made him somewhat of a celebrity in the recently opened Wyoming Territorial Prison, and he was the cause of much talk and speculation among the prison population. A big man, though not unusually tall, Clell Ballenger possessed an aura that tended to cow other men. With black hair, long and heavy, resting on the back of his collar like a bushy broom, a flat nose, dark eyes set deep under heavy eyebrows, and an almost constant scowl on his lips, the notorious outlaw was thought by some to be Lucifer himself. Ballenger had never sought to discourage that speculation. His hands were unusually large with fingers thick and powerful. It was rumored that he had once strangled two men at the same time, although those present on that occasion would tell you that it was actually a Kiowa woman and her infant son.

There were some, like Clint Conner, who had little use for him, or the man standing beside him for that matter. Bob Washburn was a brainless dolt, doing time for the assault and rape of a thirteen-year-old girl. He had eagerly assumed the role of Ballenger's personal servant.

Clint had made it a point to avoid the two of them up to this time. He had no fear of either man, or the combination of the two; he just didn't like their kind in general. He thought about the day the guards had brought Ballenger into the cell block. They seemed to purposely walk him by every cell in the prison to exhibit the notorious killer to all the inmates before locking him in next to Bob Washburn. It was a regular circus parade with four guards escorting the smirking outlaw. But for the most part, instead of demonstrating the punishment coming to those who broke the law, the parade only served to inform everyone that the new prison was now graced by the presence of a famous person. For many of the prisoners, Ballenger was someone to be looked up to for being feared by honest folk throughout Wyoming and Kansas. As far as Clint Conner was concerned, men like Clell Ballenger were little more than scum on the slime of humanity.

Some might be inclined to infer that the kettle was calling the pot black. Clint didn't give a damn what others might think. He knew the man who dwelt inside his young, muscular body, and he was at peace with him. He had made a mistake as a brash eighteen-year-old, and now, three years later, he was still paying for it. Although the confinement threatened to bring him down at times, he was determined to fight against the longing to escape to the prairies and rugged mountains he loved. Halfway through his sentence, it was getting harder and harder to persevere. Thoughts of escape seemed to visit his mind more frequently with each new sunrise.

"All right, boys," the guard said, breaking Clint's reverie, "let's get moving." Holding his shotgun up before him, he motioned toward the door with the barrel, then stood watching until the last of the three prisoners filed out before him.

Once they reached the barn, the guard nodded toward the tools propped in a corner of the tack room. "Conner, fetch them pitchforks and a broom." Clint did as he was told. "Now," the guard continued, "give one of them pitchforks to Washburn, and you take the other one. Give Mr. Ballenger there that broom." He cracked a knowing smile. "I expect you'd rather have one of them pitchforks in your hand, wouldn't you, Ballenger?"

"I might at that," Ballenger replied, displaying a grin of his own.

"What are you doin' on this detail, anyway?" the guard asked. "You ain't supposed to be on any work details at all this close to gettin' your neck stretched."

Still displaying a wide grin, Ballenger said, "I ain't one to lay around doin' nothin' when I could be helpin' you boys out." He glanced over at Washburn and winked, causing the simple man to break out in a foolish grin.

Not entirely without suspicion, the guard said, "You musta paid somebody off to get sent to the stables today. Nobody shoulda sent you to work here where there ain't nothin' between you and the open prairie but this here shotgun. But let me tell you, this shotgun is enough."

"Ah, come on, Williams," Ballenger said. "What's wrong with a man gettin' a little bit of fresh air and sunshine before they hang him? You wouldn't fault a man for wantin' one last day outside before they put him in the ground, would you?"

"*Mr.* Williams," the guard corrected. "It ain't up to me. I didn't set the policy. I just know there'll be hell to pay for somebody when the warden finds out." He motioned toward one of the stalls. "Get to work with that broom, and just keep in mind that this here shotgun has got a hair trigger, and I wouldn't mind savin' the hangman a little trouble if you took a notion to run."

"Why, *Mr.* Williams," Ballenger replied in mock indignation, "I wouldn't have no idea of cheatin' the territory outta hangin' me. Hell, I'm lookin' forward to it. See what kinda saloons they got in hell."

"I'm sure there's a place down there for murderin' skunks like you," Williams said. "Now get in there and clean out that stall." He waited to see that Ballenger did as instructed before turning his attention toward the other two prisoners. He gave Clint only a brief glance upon seeing that the young man was already at work, and paying little attention to the conversation he was having with Ballenger. Washburn, however, had to be told to put his pitchfork to work.

The morning progressed without cause for concern while Williams made sure he remained alert to any funny business. He was sure, however, that it was risky letting a desperate outlaw like Clell Ballenger work this close to the wide-open prairie behind the barn. He planned to return the notorious killer to his cell when he marched the three-man detail back for the noon meal. Glancing at his pocket watch, he muttered to himself, "Eleven fifteen." Still an hour before dinnertime. He looked up to see Ballenger leaning on his broom handle and staring at him as if amused about something. He was about to order the insolent prisoner to get back to work, when he heard the distinct sound of a pistol's hammer cocking. He abruptly turned to meet the muzzle of a Colt .45 only inches from his face. It was too late to react.

"Mornin', Yancey," Ballenger drawled, his cocksure smile still in place.

"Clell," Yancey acknowledged, his dark eyes focused intently upon the guard's frozen stare as he slowly reached for Williams' shotgun.

With no choice but to yield or die, Williams made no move to resist, releasing the weapon. Stunned by the suddenness with which the sinister outlaw had appeared, the guard could hardly believe their brazenness in carrying out this confrontation in broad daylight, no more than fifty yards from the main prison. "You must be crazy," he finally managed to stammer as Washburn grabbed his keys to unlock the shackles. "There could be guards comin' in here any minute."

"It'd be a sorry day for 'em if they did." The statement came from the back door of the barn when another man stepped inside. "What about them?" he asked, nodding at Clint and Washburn.

"Howdy, Skinner," Ballenger responded, then motioned toward Washburn. "This here's Bob Washburn," he said. "He's in on it." Then turning toward Washburn, he instructed, "Bob, throw a saddle on one of them horses in the corral." Then he looked at Clint. "I don't know about him. He just happened to catch stable duty today." He said to Clint, "I reckon it's just your tough luck, young feller, unless you're wantin' to join up with us. I ain't plannin' on leavin' no witnesses."

"Wait a damn minute," Washburn said, quick to protest. "He ain't in on this deal." He turned to Ballenger in appeal. "I'm the one that stuck my neck out for you. That son of a bitch ain't never given either one of us the time of day."

Washburn's jealous outburst brought a trace of a smile to Ballenger's face. It amused him to see his simpleminded lackey get his hackles up at the threat of a new man moving in. He looked Clint directly in the eye and spoke. "Bob's right, you never did have much use for me or him. Whad-daya say about that?"

It was a lot to think about in a few seconds' time as Clint looked from one gun to the other, both pointing at him now. Ballenger's statement promised a death sentence for the guard, Williams, and for him as well if he didn't throw in with the escape.

"Well?" Yancey demanded, turning to face Clint. "We ain't got all day."

"I still ain't got a helluva lot of use for either one of you," Clint responded. "But you're holdin' all the cards, and I want out of this place, too." Thinking of the possibility of saving the guard's life, he said, "We ain't but about fifty yards from the main building. If you go shootin' off those pistols, you'll have half a dozen guards up here in no time."

"He's right," Ballenger said. "Better use a knife."

Clint was trying to think fast, but ideas for saving Williams' life were not coming very rapidly. There wasn't much time to come up with something. He glanced at the fright-stricken eyes of the guard as Williams, realizing Clint was his only hope, silently pleaded with him for help. "Yeah," Clint finally said, "best done with a knife." He turned to Yancey then. "Give me your knife. I'll take care of the guard, and the rest of you can get a head start. Leave me a horse and I'll catch up."

Ballenger didn't respond at once. He just stood there staring at Clint, trying to determine whether he was attempting to fool them. Up to that point, he wasn't even sure the young man wanted to join them, but he couldn't deny he was amused by Clint's response. After studying Clint's face for a long second, he turned to Yancey. "Give him your knife." Turning back to Clint, he said, "Now you can cut the bastard's throat, but we ain't goin' nowhere till we see the job's done."

Clint took the long skinning knife from Yancey, and looked at the quivering guard. Williams, seeing no hope for his safety, took that moment to bolt for the barn door. "I got him!" Clint exclaimed, and immediately took off after him. He caught him before he could reach the door and tackled him to the ground. Yancey started to go after them, but Ballenger, still finding the situation amusing, caught his arm and said, "Let's see if he can do it."

Wrestling with the desperate man, Clint, with desperation of his own, managed to pin the guard to the ground. With his lips close to Williams' ear, he whispered frantically, "If you wanna live, you better damn sure play dead. I'm gonna have to hurt you." Sitting on the guard's back, he suddenly jerked Williams' head up and made what he hoped was a convincing show of pulling the knife across his victim's throat. The slash, though not deep, was enough to cause Williams to cry out, and was sufficient to immediately bring blood. Realizing then that his life was hanging in the balance, Williams ceased to struggle and lay still. Clint wiped the knife blade across the guard's shirt and got to his feet.

The others started toward him to confirm the kill, but stopped when Clint warned, "There's a couple of guards lookin' this way." He stared out the open barn door as if watching them. "He's dead," he stated, anticipating the question forming in Ballenger's mouth. "Let's get the hell outta here while we've got the chance."

Ballenger hesitated for just a moment, giving the guard's body another look. "All right," he finally decided, "let's get goin'. You'll be needin' a horse. You'd best be quick about it."

Like it or not, the die was cast for Clint Conner. To refuse to escape with Ballenger and his men would mean a death sentence. And although he had no desire to accompany the small band of outlaws, neither did he have any wish to defy them when the odds were four to one. He had gone to sleep many nights dreaming about escaping his imprisonment, but he never intended to actually attempt it. Now the decision had been made for him. He grabbed a bridle from the tack room and ran into the corral to pick a horse. The only saddle left, after Washburn took the best one, was a well-worn single-rigged model. The last rider to use the saddle was evidently short in the legs, but Clint didn't waste time adjusting the stirrups. Climbing aboard a mousey dun gelding, the best of the lot of poor choices left in the corral, he could not deny a feeling of freedom to be on a horse again. Ballenger held the gate open for Clint while he waited for Yancey to bring his horse from behind the barn. When all had mounted, the five fugitives left the prison grounds at a fast lope, riding on a line that kept the barn between them and the main prison until crossing a low hogback that offered concealment. Veering south then, Yancey led them toward Colorado, the daring daylight escape a success.

Clint rode last in the single file of riders, his knees bent like a jockey's in the short stirrups, a hailstorm of conflicting thoughts swirling in his head. He had never considered himself an outlaw, but he was damn sure one now. He could turn around and hightail it back. Ballenger might shoot at him, but probably wouldn't chase after him, and maybe he could square things with the warden, explain the situation as it had occurred, leaving him no choice. The guard, Williams, would surely vouch for him. The problem was, running free again across an open prairie, he didn't want to return to the stone walls and his tiny cell for another three years. The three he had already served were killing his soul day by relentless day until he had come to the point where he feared he might one day explode.

*I've given them enough of my life*, he decided as he followed the outlaws down a grassy draw and across a shallow stream. Three years was enough for the crime that he had committed. His thoughts then went back to recall the reason he had been sentenced to six years in prison. His troubles all started with the purchase of a horse—six horses, actually. Clint's father had made an especially good trade for the horses with a Texas cattleman who sold off his remuda after a cattle drive. Among the six, the most valuable one was an Appaloosa gelding that caught young Clint's eye at once. He worked with the horse every day, and a bond between horse and rider was soon created, as Clint spent every second of his free time training the spirited mount.

Clint's eye was not the only one attracted to the handsome gelding. Judge Wyman Plover, who owned a stable of fine-bred horses, spotted the unusual breed when Clint rode into town one Sunday morning. Immediately coveting the horse, the judge wasted little time before riding out to Arthur Conner's ranch, determined to own the Appaloosa. Arthur Conner was not a wealthy rancher, and the offer Judge Plover extended was too much to pass on— even knowing it would deeply distress his son to lose the horse.

Clint understood his father's position, and tried to make the best of it. He resigned himself to the loss of the Appaloosa until he happened to witness the treatment the horse was subjected to at the hands of Plover's foreman. Clint tried to tell the brutal foreman that the horse responded to a gentle touch. "I'll gentle the son of a bitch with an ax handle," the foreman responded, and ordered Clint off the property.

Clint, concerned for the horse, went to see the judge to protest the foreman's rough treatment. "Mike Burke has been training horses since before you were weaned," the judge said. "I expect he knows better than you how to train a horse."

"Not from what I saw today," Clint had responded heatedly. "He's gonna break that horse's spirit."

His patience with the young man having run out, Judge Plover dismissed him abruptly. "Well, at any rate, I don't see that it's any concern of yours, so I'd advise you to mind your own business." When Clint turned on his heel to leave, Plover called after him, "And don't be coming around here anymore."

"You ain't fit to own a horse," Clint had muttered in parting.

During the past three years, he had often thought about the price he was paying for his rash actions that followed his confrontation with the judge. He earned his conviction as a horse thief when he removed the Appaloosa from Plover's corral. And he added the charge of assault when he broke an ax handle across the foreman's back when Burke tried to stop him. The only satisfaction Clint enjoyed was in knowing the Appaloosa gained his freedom. *Hell*, he thought as he guided the dun after the four riders preceding him, *I'd do the same thing if it happened today.*

Bringing his thoughts back to the present, he considered the situation in which he now found himself. One thing he knew for certain was that he must extricate himself from Ballenger and his friends at the earliest opportunity. However, he was reluctant to strike out on his own without weapons and supplies. It might be necessary to ride along with the men until there was some way to equip himself to go it alone. He had to consider himself a real horse thief now, since he was riding a horse stolen from the prison barn. But at the moment, the dun was his only possession. He had no gun, no clothes other than the prison-issued garments he wore, no supplies, and no money. There seemed little chance he could acquire these things lawfully.

As the riders slowed their horses in order to file down

through a rocky draw, Clint glanced over at Washburn to catch the brooding simpleton glaring back at him. *What in hell did I do to make an enemy out of him?* Clint asked himself. *I'm liable to have trouble with that one before this is over.*

# Chapter 2

Pete Yancey stood for a moment, thoughtfully watching the last-minute addition to their small party as Clint adjusted the stirrups on his worn-out saddle. He commented to Ballenger, "I don't know about that one. Maybe we shouldn'ta brought him along. I got a funny feelin' about him." He stopped short of telling Ballenger why he had this feeling about the quiet young man who had immediately volunteered to slit the guard's throat. Yancey never confided in anyone about the one fear that had haunted him since he was eighteen. Shortly after joining the Confederate army to escape a prison sentence, he had been visited by a black angel in a dream one night. In his dream, the angel had told him that he could not be killed by anyone but one man, and then that man had appeared. Yancey could still see the man's face clearly after waking. It was a broad, youthful face, and it was distinctive in that a single lock of light brown hair hung down on the assassin's forehead. In the dream, the killer pointed his pistol directly at Yancey's head, and Yancey could see the bullet coming straight at his eye as if suspended in flight, deadly and certain. It had seemed so real that he had determined it to be a prophecy. After the dream, he had survived several major battles without a scratch while men were falling all around him, reinforcing his belief that he could not be killed except by that one man. The critical thing for him was to always keep a sharp eye for that man, and kill him before he had a chance to fulfill the prophecy.

But now this familiar face had appeared unexpectedly, looking very much like the face in his dream. He might not have thought that much about it except for the single lock of hair that fell across Clint's forehead when he removed his prison cap. Coincidence, he told himself, but the man worried him. He decided to keep a close eye on him.

Ballenger shrugged indifferently after Yancey's comment. "Hell, I expect he's in the same boat as the rest of us."

"Whaddaya know about him, anyway? What was he in for?"

Ballenger reached for the coffeepot resting on the coals of the campfire. "Horse thief is what I heard," he answered. "Don't know much more. I didn't have that much to do with him." He paused to consider what he had just said, then added, "Like Bob said, he didn't have much to do with anybody. Just kept to himself mostly."

"I reckon we'll find out when we get to Fort Collins," Yancey said. "Might be better if we run him off before somebody spots him in that getup, though."

"Might at that," Ballenger allowed, turning to gaze at Clint again. There had been no plan to bring along two extra men on his escape from prison. He had gotten word to Yancey that there would be one other, Washburn. Consequently, Yancey brought weapons and clothes for Ballenger and Washburn only. Now he was looking at Clint in his prison stripes and wondering whether Yancey might be right. There was no sense in advertising the fact that they were escaped convicts.

"Hell," Yancey cursed, becoming more convinced that Clint's presence might bring them bad luck, "we can't ride into that town with him in that damn jail suit. Somebody's likely to shoot on sight." The plan, known only to Ballenger, Yancey, and Skinner to this point, was to hit the bank at Fort Collins. Yancey figured that Washburn would be included since he had supplied part of the bribe that got him and Ballenger on stable detail. He was wondering now what use the extra man might be, especially since he didn't even have a gun. The more he thought about it, the more he was certain he wasn't going to agree to a five-way split on the bank job. "We got one more man than we need," he said to Ballenger.

"I expect you're right," Ballenger replied. "We'd best get rid of him." They didn't know that Bob Washburn was already working himself up to take care of their problem.

In Washburn's mind, Lady Luck had placed him in the cell next to that of Clell Ballenger. To Bob, it was the answer to a longing to be associated with greatness. Clell Ballenger was a living legend among outlaws. At least that was his picture of the notorious murderer, and he was honored to have been the one inmate allowed close contact. He was avoided by the other inmates because of the crime for which he was sentenced. And now, when they referred to him at all, they called him Ballenger's lackey. But he didn't see himself as Ballenger's lackey. He thought he was Ballenger's friend and confidant. After all, wasn't he the only inmate privy to the famous outlaw's escape plan? Now the presence of Clint Conner made him fear that his status as Ballenger's friend might have suffered.

The more thought he gave it, the more he suspected Conner's intention of moving in to take his rightful place as Ballenger's right-hand man. Why, he wondered, had Ballenger let Clint kill the guard? *I coulda done it*, he thought. That would have proved to Ballenger and Yancey that he was worthy of their respect. Maybe they thought that because he was imprisoned for raping a child, he didn't have the nerve necessary to kill. He needed to prove to them that he could.

Suddenly everything about Clint made Washburn angry, and his resentment toward Clint swelled up inside until he felt about ready to burst. When Washburn could stand it no longer, he approached Ballenger with a suggestion. "I don't think we need that son of a bitch, Clell." Washburn spoke in a low tone, all the while eyeballing Clint coldly. "He ain't no good to us, and he's gonna draw attention to us in them prison stripes."

Ballenger looked mildly surprised. "Why, me and Yancey was just talkin' about that. We was sayin' we got one more man than we need. We're figurin' on hittin' that bank in Fort Collins, and four's an easier split than five—and four of us is plenty to take that little bank."

"I knowed it!" Washburn exclaimed. "I figured Clell Ballenger would have a job all picked out!" Like a child, Washburn could not conceal his excitement at the prospect of robbing a bank with Clell Ballenger. He then jerked his attention back to the situation with Clint. "Why don't I take care of Mr. Smart-ass Conner for you?" he suggested. "We don't want him around messin' up our plans."

Ballenger grinned. "Why don't you do that, Bob? Do us all a favor." He glanced over at Yancey and winked.

Seated at the edge of the creek where they had made camp, Clint looked up to notice that three sets of eyes were focusing on him. He glanced over his shoulder at Skinner, who was evidently taking the opportunity to get a little shut-eye. Looking back again at the other three, he sensed that something was about to happen, something that involved him, and he didn't like the feeling. Being the odd man, he had already given thought to the possibility that he might be eliminated. He was anxious to take his leave of the four, but not this way.

He put aside the saddle he had been working on when Washburn took a couple of steps in his direction. There was a smug expression on the simpleton's fleshy face and he walked with an exaggerated swagger. Never taking his eye off the three outlaws, Clint casually reached behind him, feeling around until his hand rested on a sizable rock. Then, after another fleeting glance to make sure Skinner was oblivious of it all, he waited, watching Washburn carefully. Whatever the play, it appeared that it was to be Washburn's alone, for Ballenger and Yancey seemed content to hang back and watch the show.

The only weapon he had was the rock his hand rested upon, not much to rely on when facing the six-gun riding on Washburn's hip. He was thinking that it could amount to a swift execution if Washburn had brains enough to simply pull the pistol and shoot him. He was gambling upon the notion that the bumbling child molester would want to gloat over his position of dominance to satisfy his jealous ego.

Clint was accurate in his judgment of the man. Washburn swaggered up to stand a couple of yards from him. His feet spread wide, his hand resting on the handle of his holstered pistol, a mocking smile quirked slowly across his broad face. After taking a few moments to enjoy the situation, he spoke. "This here's the end of the line, Mr. Smart-ass. It's time for you to cash in your chips." He took his time pulling the revolver, to give Clint plenty of time to think about it. Unable to understand why there was no desperate look of fear showing in Clint's face, he thought he had to explain what he was about to do. "You dumb son of a bitch, I'm fixin' to shoot you."

"I figured," Clint replied calmly. Another quick glance

confirmed that Ballenger and Yancey were spectators only. His fingers tightened around the rock.

Disappointed to the point of dismay that his victim showed no signs of fear or panic, Washburn took another step closer and pointed the pistol at his head. "Damn you! I'm gonna put a hole in your head. How do you want it? Sittin' there, or standin' up?"

"Well, if you're givin' me a choice, I think I'll take it standin' up."

Washburn took a step back to give himself room, still baffled by the victim's calm acceptance of his execution, but he misjudged the quickness of the man he sought to kill. Clint's moves were slow and deliberate until he rose to one knee. From there, however, he sprang up in a fraction of a second, hurling the heavy rock into Washburn's face. The startled man could not help but flinch when the stone smashed his nose. It was all the time Clint needed to clamp down on the wrist of Washburn's gun hand and jerk back on his arm with such force that the man's shoulder popped out of joint. Washburn's scream of pain brought Skinner up from a dead slumber. "Let 'em be!" Ballenger yelled at Skinner as the confused man drew his weapon.

With his right arm useless, Washburn was unable to hold on to his weapon. Clint easily wrestled it from him and cracked him upside the head with the barrel. Dropping to the ground like a sack of potatoes, Washburn lay still, his eyes glazed, his mind a jumble of confusion. Clint backed away, far enough to gain a field of fire that could include the two men on his left and Skinner on his right. Aiming the pistol toward Ballenger and Yancey, he waited for them to make a move.

Still grinning, Ballenger held up his hand. "Take it easy there, son. Ain't nobody gonna shoot ya." He walked over beside Washburn, who was still lying on the ground. Still talking to Clint, he said, "I like the way you handle yourself, young feller."

His head clearing somewhat, Washburn struggled up to his hands and knees. "Damn, Clell," he whined, "I think he broke my arm."

"That don't matter none," Ballenger replied. "You ain't gonna need it." When Washburn looked up, still confused, Ballenger explained, "Like I said, we got one too many." With that, he pulled his revolver and put a bullet in Bob's head. Looking back at Clint, he said, "Looks like you got yourself an outfit. You can shuck them clothes offa him. I shot him in the head so's not to put a hole in his shirt."

With no display of emotion on his face, Clint replied, "That was damn thoughtful of you."

Ballenger threw his head back and chuckled. "You're a cool son of a bitch."

Although maintaining a calm exterior, Clint could feel the cold pocket of sweat that had appeared under his arms, left by the tense moments of uncertainty when he was waiting to see whether he was about to meet his Maker. His unruffled demeanor convinced Ballenger that it was a good trade-off when he rid himself of the clumsy Washburn. He figured any man who exhibited such cool nerve when facing a .44 with nothing more than a rock in his hand would prove to be damn handy in a bank holdup.

"I'm cuttin' you in for a full share of a little job Yancey's lined up in Fort Collins," Ballenger said. "We're plannin' on hitting the bank there day after tomorrow." He then deferred to Yancey and Skinner. "That all right with you boys?"

Skinner merely shrugged. Yancey answered, "I reckon it don't make no difference to me. We'd already planned on a four-way split," he said, although still not sure it wouldn't have been more desirable to have had the threat of the dream killer eliminated.

"Whaddaya say to that?" Ballenger asked Clint.

"Sounds all right to me," Clint replied. This was not the time to tell them that he wanted no part in anything the three had planned. Admittedly, he was a fugitive and on the run, but he had no intention of going the way of many an ex-convict. He was not a bank robber or murderer, and he was determined not to become one, no matter how desperate the situation. He had no choice but to seem to play along with them for the moment, however.

"Good," Ballenger said. "We'll strike Fort Collins by tomorrow afternoon and look the job over. Yancey says they ain't got much of a sheriff, but it don't matter much. The four of us can handle anything they got."

Clint nodded and returned the smile Ballenger aimed his way. At least, his main problem had been solved. He immediately busied himself with the removal of Washburn's boots and clothes. The clothes were not a good fit, but they would do. His luck was better when it came to the boots. They were a size larger than Washburn had needed, but just right for Clint. He strapped the gun belt on and then pulled the Winchester from the saddle sling, checked the action, and made sure the magazine was loaded. Satisfied, he turned back to the campfire, feeling a great deal more comfortable.

"Now that you got him skinned," Yancey remarked, looking at the corpse lying there with nothing but his underwear remaining, "drag him on outta here. He didn't smell too good *before* he was dead." He watched as Clint grabbed the body by the ankles and pulled it away from the camp. "You can pay me for them guns and clothes outta your share of the bank money."

"I reckon," Clint answered, looking the ferret-faced outlaw squarely in the eye. He backed toward a shallow gully, dragging the dead man over the rough ground, Bob Washburn's sightless eyes staring wide up at the sky, his head bumping drunkenly along the rocky stream bank. *The world ain't lost much with him gone*, Clint thought as he dumped him into the gully.

Echoing Clint's thoughts, Clell said, "I never cared much for that boot-lickin' turd," as he walked over to his horse to get some tobacco from his saddlebags.

Clint studied the three men he was now associated with. There was no doubt that Ballenger was the leader and Yancey was his lieutenant. Skinner seemed little more than hired help. The ranking had been obvious even in the line of travel, with Ballenger leading astride a chestnut Morgan with a white star on its face. The horse was probably no more than fourteen hands high, and looked even smaller carrying Clell's bulky figure. Yancey, by contrast, rode a splendid palomino with a white race on its face, and the lean, rangy man rode slumped over in the saddle as if trying not to have his head higher than his leader's. Knowing his place, Skinner seemed content to ride along behind the other two.

It was early afternoon when they rode into the town of Fort Collins, close by the Cache la Poudre River. Judging by the look of it, Clint surmised that Fort Collins was a thriving place to live, with a church and a school, several stores and saloons, and a bank. On the way in, they had passed a few farms as well. The town seemed to indicate a welcome atmosphere. Clint couldn't help feeling remorse, knowing what lay ahead for the citizens with money in the bank. It was a helpless feeling as well, for he struggled with the question of whether or not he should try to warn the sheriff, or the manager of the bank, so that they might ready themselves for Ballenger's visit. It was a dilemma he would wrestle for the balance of that day, for there were several sides of the problem to consider. He truly desired to prevent the holdup of the town's bank, but he planned to be long gone from Fort Collins before tomorrow dawned. Also to be considered was how the sheriff would react if he warned him of the planned robbery. Since he was an escaped convict, the sheriff might deem it his responsibility to hold him, and Clint had no intention of returning to prison now that he was out. His only desire was to leave the territory and possibly head north to live free in the mountains and prairies of Montana Territory, lose himself somewhere. How was it his responsibility to warn the town, anyway? It would be in his best interest to simply slip out of town that night, and let the sheriff and the bank take care of their problem themselves— the same as if he hadn't been with Ballenger at all. *Damn!* he swore to himself, knowing he had to make up his mind.

"God damn," Skinner exclaimed when they rode past a saloon. "That's what I'm lookin' for. I swear, my throat's as dry as a corncob."

"We'll take care of business first," Ballenger said. "I need to take a look at that bank. Then we need to get some supplies. I wanna be ready to ride when that bank opens in the mornin'. After we get everythin' else ready, then we'll all have us a drink." There was no argument. There never was when Ballenger gave orders.

Making a concerted effort to appear ordinary, even though everyone who chanced to glance their way knew they were strangers, the four riders split up into pairs and took a casual walk—Clell and Yancey down the alleyway behind the bank—Clint and Skinner on the boardwalk in front. When they had surveyed the streets and alleys around the building, Clell went inside to get a look at the tellers' cage and the bank vault. Satisfied that it would offer no real problem, they left the bank then and went to buy supplies.

Using the dun gelding Clint had ridden for a packhorse, they bought food supplies to last them a good while, mainly salt, sugar, coffee, bacon, flour, tobacco, and extra cartridges. That taken care of, Ballenger and Yancey wanted to get rooms in the hotel for the night. Skinner preferred to sleep in the stable with the horses. Seeing it as his only chance to get away, Clint volunteered to sleep with the horses, too.

"Suit yourself," Ballenger said. "Me, I'm gonna sleep in a bed tonight. Ain't a bad idea for you two to sleep in the stable, though, so's you can keep an eye on all them supplies we bought today. Let's put the horses away and go get us a drink."

Yancey was not the only one to have dreams. But instead of dreams forecasting death by a stranger's hand, Ballenger's dreams were of fancy hotels with the best whiskey and women to do his bidding at the snap of his fingers. And the only road he could see to that end led through one bank after another until he hit a big enough payday to quit.

# Chapter 3

Deputy U.S. Marshal Zach Clayton walked along the west bank of the tiny stream, studying the tracks leading away from the ashes of a campfire. The trail he had followed to this point had generally led south, toward Colorado. It was an easy enough trail to follow, five horses and riders. They had made good time, but evidently felt no pressure to ride through the night. Standing near a clump of willows where the tracks left the water, he paused and gazed out toward the open prairie. The hoofprints led to the west, but he was confident they would turn south again—Fort Collins, most likely. Clayton had spent enough years tracking fugitives from the law to know how to anticipate their actions. He had gained enough experience over the years to know the typical thinking of an outlaw on the run—and of this one in particular. Clell Ballenger was probably the meanest, most cold-blooded killer he had ever hunted. But Ballenger was also possessed of a fun-loving nature. He loved his whiskey and his women, and he had a passion for gambling. For that reason, Clayton felt certain that Fort Collins would likely be Ballenger's first destination, instead of heading for the wild country in hopes of disappearing altogether. A patient man, Zach Clayton was in a position to know Ballenger better than most. He was the marshal who dogged Ballenger's trail until he ran him down near Scotts Bluff in Nebraska and brought him to trial. Clayton had a personal interest in Ballenger's recapture, and he had been vocally critical of the inmate's ridiculously easy escape from prison.

Crossing the stream again, he returned to the campsite where his horse, a broad-chested sorrel with three white stockings, stood patiently waiting with reins on the ground. Before mounting, Clayton walked over to the gully once more to reassure himself that the underwear-clad corpse was the inmate named Bob Washburn. Based on the description given him by the warden, he was pretty sure of the identification. He knew it wasn't Conner, for Conner was a much younger man—and he certainly knew what Clell Ballenger looked like. So he figured he could mark Washburn off his list. The poor bastard had evidently exhausted his usefulness.

So he was now trailing four men, two of whom he couldn't identify. But if he had to guess, it wasn't a stretch of the imagination to assume they were two of Ballenger's old gang. Pete Yancey came to mind. He had ridden with Ballenger from the beginning, and was damn lucky to have escaped when Clayton had surprised Ballenger in a whorehouse.

Of curious interest was the young horse thief, Clint Conner. According to the prison guard, Williams, Conner saved his life by pretending to cut his throat. Clayton considered that as he prepared to step up in the saddle. It just proved the man was not a murderer, but he was still a horse thief and an escaped prisoner. Clayton's job was to bring him in, along with Ballenger, and if he was lucky, the other two who arranged the escape. That thought triggered another, and Clayton shook his head when he recalled how astonished he was when told that Clell Ballenger had somehow drawn stable duty, a job usually performed by trustees and short-timers. Warden Boswell was still fuming about that. Clayton snorted half a chuckle when he pictured the angry warden. "One of my guards has just come into a little extra money," he had said. *Well, that'll be the warden's problem*, Clayton thought. *I'd best get about mine.* Anxious to close the distance between himself and the fugitives, he struck out across the stream at a lope. He was still betting on Fort Collins as the first place the four would light. If he wasted no more time, he should reach the town sometime after dark.

"I need another drink," Clell Ballenger snorted. "Go get us another bottle." He gestured in Clint's direction.

"I don't have any money," Clint replied.

Ballenger laughed. "Give Mr. Conner some money, Yancey. I need another drink. I need somethin' else, too," he added with a wink, and nodded toward a well-endowed woman talking to the bartender. Perceiving Ballenger's obvious interest, the buxom lady sent a smile in his direction. The smile more closely resembled a sneer, but it contained the proper message, and Clell motioned for her to join them.

"It's a good thing we're makin' a withdrawal tomorrow," Yancey uttered under his breath, "'cause we're spendin' it like it warn't nothin' tonight."

"That's right, partner," Ballenger replied, his eyes remaining upon the woman approaching the table. "I got a lot of catchin' up to do." He reached over and dragged a chair from the table next to theirs. "Set yourself down, darlin', and have a drink with us." While she settled her generous backside in the chair, Ballenger poured her a drink and slid it over toward her. Making lewd reference to the lady's overabundance of breasts, he joked, "Don't slide that glass too close to her—she won't be able to see it." He roared with laughter for his joke while Yancey looked at him, puzzled, having missed the point.

Upon closer inspection, the woman, who introduced herself as Violet, exhibited the obvious signs of hard winters and rough riding. But through the magical powers of alcohol, she was transformed into an innocent dove in Ballenger's drunken eyes. Sufficiently under rye whiskey's spell, Yancey found himself likewise affected, and asked if she knew of another virgin like herself. Clint slowly nursed a drink while watching the negotiations between the worn-looking lady of the evening and his two *partners*. Although Skinner seemed to show no interest in joining the party that was being planned in the hotel, he was obviously no less inebriated. Skinner, Clint surmised, was a dedicated drunk, interested only in drinking himself into a stupor and sleeping it off.

Finally, at around eight o'clock, the drinking party came to a close. Skinner was already nodding drunkenly in his chair, and Ballenger and Yancey had settled their price. Ballenger got to his feet and pushed back his chair. "Come on, Rose," he said to Violet. "It's time for beddy-bye." He grinned foolishly at the puffy-eyed woman, who by then was too drunk herself to remember which flower she was named for. Turning to Clint, he said, "You don't look as drunk as I feel. Good thing, I reckon, 'cause I ain't sure Skinner can even find the stable on his own."

"I'll take care of him," Clint assured him.

"All right," Ballenger announced. "Let's go, then." For a moment his smile faded. "Keep an eye on them supplies, and go easy on that bottle. Tomorrow's a workin' day."

Clint was happy to see that Skinner was to be no problem as far as his escape was concerned. It was all he could do to keep him on his feet long enough to reach the stable. As soon as they got there, Skinner curled up in a pile of hay in the corner of a stall, hugging a half-empty bottle of whiskey to him as a child hugs a teddy bear. Clint spread his saddle blanket over him and could see that he was out for the night.

In no hurry now, Clint saddled the horse Washburn had

ridden and then helped himself to extra ammunition and supplies. After taking another look at Skinner, he led the horse
out of the stable and climbed in the saddle. He rode out into
an empty street, the town having gone to bed except for the
hangers-on at the saloons up at the far end. Walking the horse
slowly, he went past the sheriff's office, looking it over carefully to make sure there was no one there. Satisfied that the
sheriff and his deputies were home in bed, he pulled up in
front of the office. About to dismount, he realized he had
nothing to write with. He hesitated, trying to decide whether
to just forget it or not. His conscience got the best of him, and
he turned his horse toward the hotel beyond the saloon.

There was a night clerk behind the counter, fast asleep in
a chair tilted back against the wall. Clint considered waking
him, but decided against it, preferring to help himself to pen
and paper. Tearing a back sheet from the guest register, he
wrote a simple note. *The bank is fixing to get robbed this
morning.* Thinking that was warning enough, he walked quietly out of the hotel and returned to the sheriff's office, where
he slid his note under the door. Satisfied that he had done his
part for the people of Fort Collins, he climbed back in the
saddle, and under a full moon, slow-walked his horse back
toward the road he and the three outlaws had taken into town.

With no particular destination in mind, he started back toward Wyoming, undecided about stopping on his way north
to visit his father. It might be a risky thing to do. His father's
little ranch might be the first place the law would look for
him. He decided to think on it while he rode north. This
would most likely be the last chance he could have to see his
father again, because he planned never to return to his home
once he reached Montana.

Zach Clayton caught himself nodding off in the saddle as
his horse plodded slowly along the road leading to Fort

Collins. He tried to shake the sleep from his head and stood up in the stirrups to stretch his legs. He and the sorrel were tired of traveling and both looked forward to something to eat and a bed. With the light of a full moon, he could almost read the time by his watch, but not quite. One thing he knew for sure, however, it was getting on toward bedtime. He wondered whether it was too late to drop in on his friend Jim Popwell.

Jim was the sheriff in Fort Collins, and he had worked with Zach before on a few searches. Zach knew he would be welcome to stay with him overnight, so he decided he'd ride straight through town to Jim's place on the river.

He reached in his saddlebag and pulled out a piece of beef jerky to quell the demands of his empty stomach. A mile later, he saw the faint lights of Fort Collins. Maybe it was later than he thought, for the town showed few signs of life on the north end. One lone rider was the only person he saw, traveling to meet him on the dark road. *Probably ran out of drinking money and heading home*, Clayton thought as the rider approached.

"Evenin'," Clayton offered as the rider rode past him.

"Evenin'," the rider returned with a nod of his head.

Neither man bothered to look back as the distance between them increased to the point where they faded into the moonlit evening. Clayton cast little more than a glance toward the sheriff's office as he walked his horse up the middle of the lonely street. It was obvious that there was no one in the office. *Must not have anyone in jail*, he thought. At the far end of the street, he found the only signs of life in the sleepy town, as the saloons were still going strong. He thought about taking a look inside in case he spotted the men he trailed, but decided to wait until he talked to Jim.

"Who is it?" Popwell demanded from the other side of the closed door of the simple frame house.

"I'm bringin' the word of God to save all the hard sinners," Clayton replied. "And somebody in town gave me your name."

"You what?" Jim sputtered. "Who the hell sent you out here?" he demanded as he opened the door and thrust a lantern up before him to reveal the grinning face of the deputy marshal. His deep frown turned instantly to a wide grin. "Zach Clayton!" he roared then. "What in the hell . . . ? Come on in, man!" He threw the door open wide. "You're a sight for sore eyes, and the last son of a bitch to save anybody's soul."

Clayton grabbed his friend's hand and pumped it enthusiastically while slapping him on the shoulder with his free hand. "Good to see you, Jim. Glad to see you're still standin' up. I thought somebody mighta shot you by now."

"Hell, man, Fort Collins is a peaceful town. We ain't got no trouble here. What are you doin' down here, anyway? You chasin' somebody? You're ridin' mighty late at night."

"Yeah, I'm on somebody's trail, and it looked like they were headed your way, but I ain't sure." He hung his saddlebag over a chair back. "Thought I'd drop in on you for tonight, if it's all right." He paused to look around the tiny room. "You ain't took up with a woman since I last saw you, have you?"

"Hell no," Jim replied. "I ain't found one that'd stay for more'n a night, and had to be paid for that." He pulled a chair back from the table. "Set yourself down, Zach, and I'll put on a pot of coffee. You hungry?"

"Well, I could eat, if you've got somethin' handy. Let me take care of my horse first."

Popwell carved a couple of slabs of meat from a haunch of venison he had butchered that afternoon, and while Clayton was eating, he filled him in on the reason he was in town. "Well, no, I can't really say," Jim answered when Zach asked whether he had seen anyone resembling the four men he was after. "Like I told you, I took the last two days off to go huntin' since everything's been so quiet. But we can take a look around in the mornin'."

"These are some bad fellers," Clayton said, "Clell Ballenger and a couple of his boys."

"Ballenger?" Jim interrupted. "I thought they hung him."

"They were goin' to in about a week, but the son of a bitch broke out with two other prisoners. I found one of 'em dead yesterday, and the rest of 'em headed this way. They might not have wanted to be seen in town, but I couldn't find any sign that they left the road into Fort Collins. I can't say for sure they *didn't* go around, 'cause the last several miles before I got here I was ridin' in the dark."

"If there had been any trouble, my deputy would most likely have rode out here to tell me," Jim said. "He lives in a little room back of the Palace Saloon, so he pretty much keeps an eye on things in town. We can check with him in the mornin'."

The two old friends sat around the kitchen table reminiscing a little longer than Clayton would have preferred, since he was already sleepy and tired when he arrived. But it had been a while since he had seen Jim Popwell, and the quantity of strong coffee that was consumed served to keep his eyelids up way past time when they normally would have dropped. As a consequence, they didn't get the early start they had planned, and it was half past eight when they left Jim's place and headed to town.

Jim only gave his office a glance to confirm that his deputy was not there as they rode past. "We'll ride on down to the Palace and rout Grady out," Jim said. "He could be eatin' some breakfast at the hotel, though. We'd better look there first." He turned his horse toward the hotel next to the saloon. "I don't think you know Grady—Grady Jacobs—I

believe I hired him since I saw you last." Clayton replied
that he didn't know the deputy. "Good man," Jim continued,
"young feller, his daddy's the Baptist preacher."

Just as Jim had suspected, they found Grady Jacobs hov-
ering over a plate of potatoes and eggs and a generous slab
of bacon.

"Mornin', Sheriff," the young man greeted Jim when he
walked in the back door of the hotel kitchen. He paused
briefly a second time when he saw the stranger following behind Jim, only mildly curious. "Did you have a good hunt?"

"Fair," Popwell answered. "I passed up a shot at a twelve-
point buck and took one of his ladies instead. I was looking
for meat, and a nice doe is a little more tender than an old
buck." He glanced at Clayton and smiled. "Me and Zach ate
a good portion of it last night." Catching an impatient look
in Zach's eye, he got down to business.

After introducing the deputy marshal to Grady, he filled
him in on Clayton's reason for being in town. "I'm lookin'
for four men," Clayton told him. He produced a sketch from
a prison photograph of Clell Ballenger. "This is one of 'em.
He's with three other fellers." Before Grady responded,
Zach read the recognition in the deputy's eyes.

"I seen 'em!" Grady exclaimed. "They was here! There
was four strangers settin' at a table in the saloon last night.
I asked Ernie if he knew 'em, and he said he'd never seen
'em before." He took another look at the picture on the
Wanted poster. "That feller was one of 'em, all right."

Clayton took over. Checking with the dining room staff,
he learned that a man resembling the sketch and another
man had come down earlier for breakfast, but there were
only the two. A few minutes later, the three lawmen talked
to the desk clerk and were told that the two *gentlemen* had
already checked out of their room. "I'd best run by the office
and get a couple of rifles just in case," the sheriff said.

"I need to find out which way they headed," Clayton said. "You and Grady meet me back here. I'm goin' down to the stable. They musta had their horses there. Maybe I can find out where they went." He hurried back to his horse, a real sense of urgency driving him now that he knew he was so close behind the fugitives and might have just missed them. He told himself that he should have checked the saloons before going to see Popwell.

Charging down to the stables at a gallop, Clayton pulled the sorrel to a sliding stop at the stable door to be met by the perturbed owner. "Yeah, there was four fellers here. They got their horses early this mornin', at least three of 'em did. One of 'em snuck outta here last night without payin' for board or grain. I got my money outta the other three, but they wouldn't stand good for the other feller. Said they didn't even know him—the lyin' bastards. I shoulda knowed they was outlaws."

"Which way did they go when they left here?" Clayton asked.

"Hell, I don't know," he retorted in disgust, then, "They just rode off toward town."

"Much obliged," Clayton said, and climbed back in the saddle. That wasn't really much help, but maybe they weren't in a hurry to leave town. Maybe they might still be around. A saloon would be the best place to look.

Riding back toward the hotel, he saw Jim and his deputy riding hard to meet him. "Take a look at this!" the sheriff yelled as he rode up beside Clayton. "It was under my office door."

Clayton grabbed the piece of paper Popwell held out to him, and quickly read the brief warning: *The bank is fixing to get robbed this morning.* "What the hell . . . ?" Clayton started, and all three turned at once to look in the direction of the bank at the corner of the street. It seemed peaceful enough, but there were three horses at the rail out front. He didn't wait to talk about it. Turning the sorrel's head in that direction, he gave it a sharp kick. There wasn't time to puzzle over who might have left the note under the door. It could be a ruse, somebody's idea of having fun with the young deputy while the sheriff was off hunting. Whatever, it deserved immediate attention.

The three galloped up to the bank. Grady, anxious to make his reputation as a lawman, came out of the saddle before his horse was fully stopped, and before Clayton could caution him, charged through the door. He was met by a .44 slug that caught him in the shoulder, spinning him around to drop on the step beside the door. Clayton and Popwell dived for cover, the sheriff at the corner of the building and Clayton on the walk beside a front window.

"The next one in that door gets the same thing!" Clell Ballenger called out.

"Where in hell did they come from?" Yancey demanded. He turned to confront the bank manager, who was lying facedown on the floor beside his two employees. "You got some kind of signal?" He pressed the barrel of his pistol hard against the banker's skull. "How'd they know what was goin' on in here?"

"I swear," the banker pleaded, "there's no signal. I don't know how they knew."

"It don't matter a helluva lot how they found out," Clell said. "The fact is they're out there." He called back over his shoulder to Skinner, who was busy stuffing money into their saddlebags, "Hurry up in there!" To Yancey, who was covering the hostages, he said, "Keep your eye on 'em." Moving up to the front wall, he eased up close to the door. "Hey, out there!" he yelled. "You hear me?"

"Yeah, we hear you," Popwell answered while watching Clayton crawl by the window to help Grady move to safety.

"Well then, you'd better listen real good," Ballenger called back. "I've got three of your fine citizens layin' on the floor in here, and unless you want a bullet in the head of each one of 'em, you'd better clear out of there. Leave them horses right where they are, and start walkin'." When there was no immediate response from the lawmen outside, he threatened, "I mean right now. Clear that damn street or I'm gonna shoot the first one."

Popwell looked at Clayton for direction. Clayton nodded his head. "All right," the sheriff said. "We're goin'. Ain't no need for anybody else to get hurt."

Inside the bank, Ballenger watched as the sheriff and Clayton helped the wounded deputy walk. As they backed up the street, Clell got a better look at their faces. Suddenly he blurted, "It's that son of a bitch! I know that bastard. That's that damn marshal, Clayton. I owe him!" He stuck his pistol out the door and fired a couple of shots that missed all three men. They had already moved too far away for accuracy with a pistol. He cursed his luck.

"You 'bout done?" Yancey called back to Skinner.

"I'm done," Skinner replied, and entered the lobby from the manager's office with two stuffed saddlebags, one on each shoulder.

"We've got to get the hell outta here," Yancey said. "Clell, the street clear?"

"I'd like to stick around here till I shoot that bastard," Clell responded.

"Gawdammit, Clell," Yancey shot back. "To hell with that marshal. I want to live to spend some of this money. Is the street clear? Can you still see 'em?"

"No," Clell answered, "they're gone. I don't see nobody on the street now."

"All right, let's move!" Yancey roared. "They won't be gone long." He reached down and grabbed the back of the bank manager's collar. "Come on, we're goin' for a little walk." He pulled the quivering man to his feet while Ballenger stepped cautiously outside the door.

Satisfied that there was no one close enough to take a shot at them, Ballenger waved his partners on. "Bring old Mr. Moneybags out here in front of us." He waited until Yancey shoved the frightened bank manager toward him. "Now we'll see how much your fellow citizens think of you," he taunted, and held the banker in front of him. "Skinner, throw them bags on the horses and untie them other horses."

With little choice but to do as Ballenger ordered, Clayton and the sheriff hurried to reach the building at the end of the street with Grady Jacobs supported between them.

"Can you take care of him?" Clayton asked when they reached the alley between the barbershop and the undertaker. When Popwell said he could, Clayton nodded and slipped into the alley. Running as fast as he could in high-heeled boots, he sprinted behind the stores and saloons. Wishing he had his rifle instead of a pistol, he cut back up the side of the bank just in time to hear several gunshots as Skinner scattered the horses. Straining for breath, the result of not having run all-out for quite some time, he rounded the front corner of the building in time to see the three galloping away. There was time for one shot. Skinner, trailing behind the other two, was the only reasonable target. Clayton stopped running. His heart was pounding so hard from his sprint that he had to strain to hold his arm still while he aimed the pistol. The shot slammed into Skinner's back, between his shoulder blades. He stayed in the saddle, his body flopping back and forth drunkenly for what seemed a long time before he finally keeled over sideways and slid from the saddle.

Clayton cocked his pistol again, but knew it was useless to fire. He could only watch as the two outlaws disappeared between the buildings. Still breathing hard, he turned one way and then another, trying to spot his horse, but the sorrel was nowhere to be seen. The street suddenly filled with people, coming from the stores and shops now that the shooting seemed to have stopped. Popwell called out from the other end of the street that he was taking Grady to the doctor. Clayton acknowledged that; then with pistol still in hand, he walked up to the body lying in the dusty street.

He reached down and rolled the corpse over on its back. The face was unfamiliar, one of Ballenger's gang he supposed. *That only leaves three*, he thought. He stood up again and stared in the direction Ballenger had fled, fighting off a feeling of frustration over the opportunity he had missed. If he had known beforehand of the planned bank holdup, they could have set a trap to capture the three of them. They might have had time to prepare a surprise party for Ballenger if they had gone to the sheriff's office as soon as they rode into town. That thought led him to speculate on the origin of the warning note.

It was natural to assume that Clint Conner was most likely the author of the note—especially when he considered the fact that one of the four he chased had cut out the night before. It had to be Conner. He had saved the prison guard's life. There was no doubt about that. Clayton was beginning to realize that Clint had no choice in the matter of joining the escape. The thought of it bothered Zach Clayton's regimented mind. He preferred things to be cut-and-dried, black or white, criminal or law abiding, and Conner's behavior muddied up the situation. In the end, he knew he had to do his job, and that was to catch criminals. Conner might have done the best he could to help the side of the law, but he was still an escaped horse thief. And Clayton reminded himself, he sure as hell didn't turn himself in again.

"I'm wastin' time," he muttered in frustration, knowing

that Ballenger was getting away while he stood there specu-
lating. "Run and fetch the undertaker," he said to a boy who
had inched up to look at the dead man. The next order of
business was to find his horse. That didn't take more than
ten or fifteen minutes. He found the sorrel behind the hotel
where he had joined Popwell's and Grady's horses in the
shade of a cottonwood tree.

His first impulse was to jump in the saddle and gallop
after Ballenger, but with the start they already had, he knew
it was back to tracking the two outlaws. In view of that, he
decided to take the sheriff's and deputy's horses back to
Popwell's office. And while he was at it, he figured he might
as well stop by the telegraph office and wire Laramie to keep
the warden informed on the progress of his hunt.

The sheriff stepped out of the doctor's door when he saw
Clayton leading the horses back toward his office. "How's
the boy?" Zach asked when Popwell walked out to meet him.

"He's gonna be all right. Caught one in the shoulder. Doc
says he'll be fine." He nodded toward the extra horse Zach
was leading. "Looks like you got one of 'em. I'd better
round up a posse to go after the other two."

"I'd rather you didn't, Jim," Clayton insisted. "I don't
have the time to wait on it, and I think I've got a better
chance of slippin' up on 'em without the bother of a posse."
Clayton had never cared to ride with a posse. It had been his
experience that a bunch of armed ordinary citizens caused
little more than confusion, and was seldom successful in
tracking down a seasoned outlaw like Clell Ballenger. They
only added to his responsibility to keep them from getting
killed.

"Suit yourself," Popwell replied, "but I'm willin' to give
you all the help I can. After all, I am the sheriff here, and
they sure as hell pulled a holdup in my town." He knew

Clayton's reputation as a loner, but he felt it was his responsibility to offer.

"I appreciate it, Jim. I know I can count on you if I need to." The issue decided as far as he was concerned, he changed the subject. "There's a saddlebag full of the bank's money on that feller's horse. At least they got part of it back."

The sheriff nodded, then broke out a grin. "You didn't draw a little expense money outta that saddlebag?"

Clayton reflected the grin. "I thought about it, but it's all there. I reckon I ain't smart enough to be crooked." He reached down to shake his friend's hand. "Well, I got to go to work. I'll be seein' you."

"Watch your ass with them two," Popwell said in parting.

"I always do," Clayton replied.


Clayton stopped at the spot where Ballenger and Yancey had entered the river, evidently heading south. The thought of the lone traveler he had met on the road north of Fort Collins sprang to his mind. If that man was who he now suspected, it meant that of the three he was bound to bring in, two were heading south while the other was heading north. It was something to think about, but did not make his decision difficult. He would head south after Ballenger.

The river was relatively calm at this point, allowing for an easy crossing. There seemed to be an obvious spot on the far bank to leave the water, so he headed for it. Upon reaching the other side, he stopped to search for tracks. His were the only ones to be found. Not really surprised, he walked the sorrel west along the bank for about a quarter of a mile without success. Turning around, he retraced his steps, noting that the sorrel's tracks were easily evident. A little farther than a quarter mile past the point where he had left the river he found two sets of tracks.

From that point, leaving the rocky riverbank, he saw

there was some effort taken to avoid leaving a trail, but to a skilled tracker like Clayton there was little challenge. Generally they had followed the river east, instead of heading straight south toward Denver. After a couple of miles where the river snaked its way through a thick forest of pine, the tracks led back into the water. *This is where they're hoping to lose me*, he thought. He guessed right, for he spent the better part of the afternoon before discovering a faint hoof-print left on a grassy bank some three-quarters of a mile upstream. Scouting in the general direction indicated, he finally found another print to verify that the trail pointed north. *Cheyenne*, he thought as he led his horse into the dense forest of pine, surprised that they had changed direction. It was almost impossible to follow a trail in the thick bed of pine needles that covered the floor of the forest, so he was forced to go primarily on instinct with an occasional bent branch or rubbed bark to reassure his guess. By the time he left the pines and struck their trail leading up into the hills, it was growing too dark to continue. When he figured he had gone as far as he reasonably could, he made his camp for the night.

# Chapter 4

Arthur Conner pulled a burning splinter from the fire and used it for a match to light his lantern. Stepping out onto the small porch, he held the light up before him and called his dog. "What's the matter with you, Ned? Come here." The dog had started barking at something fifteen minutes before and wouldn't stop. Arthur finally decided Ned must have heard something, so he went out to take a look. He had already had a couple of coyotes in the barn this past week, trying to get to the chickens. Thinking of that now, he told himself that he should have brought his shotgun, but when he walked inside the barn, there was no predator to be seen.

"Damn crazy dog," he muttered, then thought as long as he was at it, he might as well check the horses in the corral. Going out the back door of the barn, he had taken only a few steps toward the corral when he was startled by the sudden appearance of a dark figure leading a horse toward him.

"Still hard to sneak up on ol' Ned." The voice came low and soft. Arthur stopped in his tracks, stunned and confused. "Evenin', Pa. I didn't mean to scare you."

"Clint?" Arthur gasped. "Clint? Is that you, boy?" The hand holding the lantern was shaking with excitement now.

"Yessir," Clint replied. "It's me. I didn't wanna slip in

here like this, but I had to watch the house for a bit before I rode in. I wanted to make sure you were alone."

"My God in heaven," Arthur exclaimed, and strode forward to meet his son. "I can't believe it's you." He held the lantern up so he could look at him. "I swear, you don't look none the worse for three years in prison. I believe you've growed into a man." He reached out and gave his son a one-armed bear hug, then stepped back and demanded, "And why the hell wouldn't I be alone?"

"Well," Clint said, hesitating, "there might be somebody lookin' for me."

"Done come and gone," Arthur replied. "Sheriff's deputy came out from Cheyenne yesterday lookin' for you."

"You already know I broke out, then," Clint said.

"Yeah, I know. Come on, put your horse in the barn, and we'll go in the house and fix you somethin' to eat. You hungry? I ain't never known you when you wasn't."

"Pa, I didn't have no intention of breaking out of prison. I was bound to serve my time, but I got caught in a situation where I had to run with those other fellers, or be left behind with a bullet in my head."

"You don't owe me no explanation, son. You've always tried to do the right thing. And that includes when you took that Appaloosa from Judge Plover. I don't blame you none, never did. They ought'n to sent you to prison for that. That man ain't fittin' to own horses." He watched until Clint pulled the saddle off and filled a bucket with oats for his horse. "Come on and I'll find you somethin' to eat." He led the way to the house.

Before stepping inside, Clint paused to pet the dog for a few seconds. "Now after makin' all that fuss, you want your ears scratched," he said. "Maybe you remember me after all, huh, boy?" He gave Ned a couple of dismissal pats and followed his father into the house. As soon as he entered the room, he felt a shiver of emotion run through his entire body as he looked around the familiar scene after an absence of three years.

Watching his son carefully, Arthur said, "Ain't much changed since you've been gone. I finally built a new table. That's about all, I reckon."

Clint followed his father's eye to the kitchen table. He nodded, but did not comment. His father had threatened to build a new table for years to replace one that wobbled precariously from two mended legs. It was a job that no one had the time to get around to, and one that always caused his father to swear every time a cup of coffee or a pan of fresh milk was caused to slop over when someone leaned too hard on one end or the other. "She's solid now," Arthur said, and smacked the table with the palm of his hand. Feeling awkward in his attempt to make small talk, he decided to cut right to what he really wanted to know. "How come you broke out, son?"

"Like I said, I didn't really have a choice," Clint replied. He then went on to relate the details of his escape with Clell Ballenger and Bob Washburn, and his subsequent split with the outlaws.

"Did you kill anybody?"

"No, sir," Clint answered.

Arthur nodded his head thoughtfully. He was satisfied that as long as Clint hadn't taken anyone's life, he could be forgiven for anything else that might have happened. "Well, what are you plannin' to do now? Like I said, the sheriff's deputy was already out here. I expect he'll be back. It might go easier on you if you turned yourself in instead of waitin' for them to come lookin' for you again."

"I ain't goin' back, Pa. I just stopped by to see you before I head up to Montana Territory. I aim to lose myself up in the high country, maybe go on to Canada. It liked to killed me being locked up for three years. If I go back now they're bound to add time to my sentence. I ain't goin' back."

Arthur didn't know what to say. He had always been a law-abiding man, but he understood his son's feelings. Clint had always been a child of the forests and hills, more at home under the stars instead of a cabin roof. It was indeed cruel and unjust punishment to keep his son incarcerated, punished for his compassion for a mistreated horse. Knowing it unlikely that Clint's mind could be changed once he had decided upon something, he shrugged to signal the issue settled. "It ain't exactly a good time to be ridin' up to Powder River country," he warned. "I don't know how much you heard, being locked up in that prison, but there's been a lot of trouble with the Sioux and Cheyenne durin' this whole last year."

"I heard about it," Clint said. "I intend to stay clear of any Indians." He hesitated a moment before broaching a subject that had bothered his conscience. "Pa, I know you were probably countin' on me to help you here when I got out of prison, and I'm sorry I'm not gonna be here to do it."

"Don't fret about it," Arthur said. "I'm doin' all right. I've got Charley Simpson workin' for me. And to tell you the truth, Charley ain't good for nothin' but ranch work. So I don't know what ol' Charley would do if you came back and I had to let him go." Deciding the matter closed, he went to the stove and picked up the coffeepot. Handing it to Clint, he said, "Go fill this with some water while I grind up some coffee. I've got some corn bread left from supper, and I'll see if I can find somethin' else for you to eat."

"I need to swap these clothes I'm wearin' for somethin' better," Clint said. "You didn't throw out all my old clothes, did you?"

"They're in your room, right where you left 'em," Arthur replied.

"Good, 'cause I can't wait to shuck these I got on." It had disgusted him to have to wear Bob Washburn's shirt and pants, and he was anxious to discard them. He was not surprised to find that his old clothes were a trifle tight across the chest and shoulders, but he could still wear them. Feeling more at ease then, he sat down at the table again to eat.

They talked late into the evening like two old friends instead of father and son. Arthur was aware of the change in his son that prison had wrought, whether good or bad he couldn't say, but there was a sense of quiet maturity that was not in the boy when he was sent to prison. Arthur decided that Clint was doing the right thing; he had no business in prison. Arthur went to bed that night believing that justice had at last been served.

Up before sunup, Clint was in the barn saddling his horse when Arthur came from the house. "Morning," he said when his father walked in. "I thought I'd get outta here before Charley comes to work. No need to let anybody know I was here."

"Hell, Charley wouldn't tell anybody," Arthur said. "He won't be here till noon, anyway. I'da been up before this, but we stayed up a long time past my bedtime last night."

Clint smiled. His father had always considered it a matter of pride to be the first one up in the morning. And he always had an excuse for those times when he wasn't. "I wouldn't have been up so early myself, but I guess I was havin' a hard time gettin' used to a soft bed again." In truth, Clint had learned to sleep anywhere after three years on a straw tick spread over a board frame.

Arthur held his lantern up as he looked Clint's horse over, a habit brought on from years of raising horses. "Where'd you get him?" he asked while looking in the gray's mouth. "Kinda long in the tooth, ain't he?"

"He's stolen," Clint answered. "One of the prisoners I broke out with stole him from the prison corral."

"Damn, that ain't good," Arthur involuntarily uttered.

"I know, but he's all I got right now, and I'll be takin' him a long way from here." He cast a critical eye at the flea-bitten gray horse and shook his head. "At least he's better than the one I was ridin' before him."

Arthur thought about the situation for a moment more. "He might be all right for a packhorse, and you'll be needin' a packhorse."

"Well, yeah, but—"

Arthur interrupted. "I got a horse for you." With Clint about to protest, his father started toward the corral. "Come on," he said. A faint streak of morning light snaked over the hills to the east, and Arthur set the lantern down at his feet. "That buckskin dun over there next to the trough—I bought him off a fellow about a month ago. He's saddle-broke and stout—got a little bit of rascal in him, too, plumb rowdy sometimes. Day after I brought him home, he was nippin' at the other horses in the corral just to see 'em run round and round. He'll make a fine horse for you."

Even in the dim morning light, Clint couldn't help but admire the horse, but it seemed like an awful lot to expect from his father. "I appreciate it, Pa, but that horse probably cost you a pretty penny, and I can make do with the gray."

"There ain't gonna be no discussion about it," Arthur insisted. "You can't go ridin' off to Montana on that old buzzard-bait. Besides, I figure I owe you for that Appaloosa you loved so much. If I hadn't sold that damn horse, you wouldn't have gone to prison. I want to get rid of that damn buckskin, anyway, before he runs the other horses ragged."

His father's statement caused him to think. He had never blamed his father for his arrest, and it had never occurred to him that his father might feel in some part responsible.

"Hell, Pa, the reason I got sent to prison was because I did a damn fool thing. It wasn't anybody's fault but mine."

"I want you to take the horse, anyway."

The horse wasn't the only thing he gained by visiting his father. By the time he left, Arthur had loaded the packhorse with supplies and utensils, as well as insisting that he trade the old model Winchester for his dad's '73 model. He rode away from the little ranch southwest of Cheyenne well mounted, well armed, well supplied, and with a little money in his pocket. "I'll be seein' you one day," he said in parting. "Maybe I'll find me a place to raise some cattle and horses up in the high country, and you can move up there with me."

"That would suit me fine," Arthur said, knowing in his heart that he might never see his son again.

It was well past sunup when Clint said his final farewell and pointed the buckskin north. There was a feeling of sadness over leaving his father again, but at the same time a sense of relief, as if his soul was free to start on a clean slate. Intending to pass to the east of Cheyenne, he planned to head toward Fort Laramie, possibly following along the route of the old cattle trails that led from Cheyenne to Montana Territory. From there, he planned to follow whatever urge struck him at the time. Happy to be rid of Clell Ballenger and his sidekicks, he could now look forward to discovering a new country where thoughts of prison and outlaws were left far behind him.

His father had been accurate in his evaluation of the buckskin dun. The horse seemed willing and strong as the two new partners crossed the railroad tracks east of Cheyenne, and by the time they reached Lodgepole Creek, he was thinking over names for the horse. Remembering what his father had said about the spirited gelding, he decided to call him Rowdy. "Rowdy," he pronounced. "I like it." He patted the buckskin on the neck. "How do you like it?" The horse snorted and tossed his head. "I'm gonna consider that a yes."

By midafternoon he felt reasonably certain that he had struck the Shawnee Trail. There were enough signs that revealed evidence of the old cattle trail that had extended the Goodnight-Loving Trail beyond Cheyenne. He was on his way to Montana, unaware of the dark cloud that shadowed him from Colorado.

# Chapter 5

Zach Clayton stuck doggedly to the trail he had followed from Fort Collins. He had held his horse hard to a fast pace, but had not, so far, gained any ground on Ballenger and Yancey. It did not discourage him. He knew that he would eventually catch up to them, as sure as the sun rose and set every day. He had never failed to run down any man he chased. His patience and determination were well-known among lawmen and outlaws alike throughout the territory.

The outlaws had stopped to rest their horses on Owl Creek, some five or six miles south of Cheyenne. Clayton sat on his heels by a burnt-out campfire and stirred the ashes with his finger. They were not that far ahead of him now, judging by the warmth of the ashes. They had rested their horses before moving on. He found their tracks on the other side of the creek, veering toward the east, obviously intending to skirt around the town. He had made up some ground on them, but his horse was in need of rest. He decided on a short rest for his horse; then they could both walk for a couple of hours in an effort to make up a little more ground. He pulled the saddle off and let the sorrel graze while he sat with his back against a cottonwood. He had hoped the two outlaws would ride straight into Cheyenne, where there was

always a fair chance they would get slowed down by a saloon, making his job easier. At least their tracks were easily
followed. Late afternoon found him saddling his horse
again. Picking up the tracks on the east side of the creek, he
started out leading the sorrel, figuring he had a few hours of
daylight left before being forced to stop for the night.

The next morning, as soon as it was light enough to follow the tracks, he was in the saddle again. He found their
next campfire around noon about fifteen miles north of
Cheyenne. The ashes were still smoking when he stirred
them. *He was close.* He stroked the sorrel's neck and said,
"It's time to make you work a little, boy." Stepping up in the
saddle, he gave the horse a little kick with his heels, starting
out at a lope.

"I knew it, dammit!" Yancey blurted. "I had a feelin' we
weren't done with that son of a bitch. I've been in this business too damn long not to know when I'm being dogged by
a lawman."

Ballenger, kneeling by the tiny stream that meandered
down through a narrow ravine spotted with sage and berry
bushes, wiped his mouth on his sleeve and rose to his feet.
"Whaddaya lookin' at?" he asked.

"That damn marshal, Clayton," Yancey replied heatedly.
"Dammit, Clell, I told you he'd be doggin' us. I'd bet my
share of the money that Clint Conner was the son of a bitch
that tipped them off."

"Well, you've been lookin' over your shoulder ever since
we left Colorado," Ballenger said, less concerned, but interested if the rider was indeed Zach Clayton. "You probably
drawed him to us, you was lookin' so hard." He climbed up
to the top of the ravine beside Yancey and looked in the direction his partner pointed. "I expect it's him, all right," he
said, although the lone rider was little more than a tiny fig-

ure on the treeless prairie behind them. The feeling in his gut
was enough to verify it.

"It's him," Yancey stated emphatically.

"He's rode a long way to get killed," Ballenger said. He
turned to look back down the ravine where the horses were
drinking. "And this looks as good a place as any. Come on."
He started back down the side of the ravine to get his rifle.
"Better tie the horses to a bush so they don't run off when
the shootin' starts."

Back up at the rim of the ravine, the two gunmen picked
their spots to lie in wait for the unsuspecting lawman. Lying
flat on their bellies, they watched as Clayton drew near,
waiting for him to come within range. "I got ten dollars that
sez my shot is the one that hits him first," Ballenger said.

"You got a bet," Yancey replied with a confident grin.
"You ain't seen the day you could outshoot me."

Clayton eased his horse back to a slow walk after having
held the sorrel to a steady lope for some time. The trail, now
leading over a series of cuts and ravines at the base of a low
butte, was easily identified because of the tall grass on this
side of the hills. There remained two distinct trails left by
Ballenger and Yancey, fresh enough so that the grass had not
yet recovered. From prior trips through this part of the territory, Clayton knew that this was a small area of tall grass.
The tracking might not be as easy on the northern side of the
hills. But if he was in luck, he figured he might catch up to
them by sundown. He discovered in the next few minutes
that his progress had been even greater than he had figured.

He heard what sounded like *zip-thunk*, moments before
he heard the crack of a rifle. The sorrel screamed in pain,
and before Clayton had time to react, a second bullet thudded into the horse's chest. He tried to turn the frantic animal,
but the horse's instincts told it to run. It tried to gallop off to

one side, but staggered and stumbled. Clayton came out of the saddle just as the mortally wounded horse crashed to the ground.

With bullets ripping the ground all around him, he scrambled quickly to take cover behind his fallen horse while angrily cursing himself for riding blindly into an ambush. One look at the sorrel's wounds and he knew the horse was gone. He apologized earnestly for causing the faithful animal's death as he ended the sorrel's misery with his pistol.

Lying on the ground behind the carcass, he looked behind him, then to each side. He had been caught on open prairie with no apparent cover readily available. His horse would have to do. Pulling his rifle from the saddle sling, he tried to pinpoint the source of the attack. He soon figured out that his assailants were firing from the rim of a ravine about a hundred and fifty yards away. *I guess I'm just lucky they didn't wait till I got a lot closer*, he thought.

Sharing Clayton's thought, Clell Ballenger expressed his displeasure. "Dammit, Yancey, why the hell couldn't you wait till he got in decent range? Now we got no choice but to waste a helluva lot of ammunition, tryin' to get a lucky shot."

Too anxious to win his bet with Ballenger, Yancey could only offer a lame excuse. "Hell, I thought I could hit him." He shrugged. "At least we got him pinned down. He can't move from behind that horse."

"We coulda used that horse," Clell fumed.

"Even if we don't get a shot at him, at least he ain't gonna be doggin' us no more. Why don't we just ride on now?"

"I want him dead, dammit," Ballenger insisted. "I don't wanna look around a month from now and see that son of a bitch on my tail again."

"He ain't shot back once," Yancey said. "Maybe one of them shots caught him."

"I doubt it," Ballenger replied, and gave his partner a withering glance. "He's just got more sense than to waste a lot of cartridges when he ain't got a likely target."

Yancey pumped a couple more slugs into the sorrel's carcass. "I've got that horse sighted in," he said. "If that marshal shows his head, I'll get him." As if cooperating to prove Yancey's point, Clayton eased the rifle over the saddle and took aim at the rim of the ravine. Yancey immediately pulled the trigger, sending a slug to embed in the saddle inches from Clayton's head. "Hot damn!" Yancey brayed. "I told you I had him! Let him stick his head up there again!"

Clint pulled Rowdy up short, turned his head to face the wind, and listened. There it was again. This time he was sure it was a rifle shot—someone hunting, or someone in trouble. Judging from the sound, it was probably two or three miles away. A few moments passed, and then he heard more shots, too many for a hunter. *None of my affair*, he thought, and nudged Rowdy into motion again. But he found it difficult to ignore when the shooting continued sporadically. He remembered his father's warning about Indian activity in the area. *Not this close to Cheyenne*, he told himself. Finally his conscience called upon him to at least have a look to make sure some settler wasn't in trouble. He turned Rowdy's head west and prodded him into a lope.

The gunfire continued as he drew closer until he felt certain it was just beyond a gentle rise that almost formed a ridge between him and the source of the shooting. Knowing he would be silhouetted against the blue sky behind him if he rode over the top of the ridge, he dismounted and left his horses there below the rise. Making his way the remaining distance on foot, he dropped to his knees and crawled the final few feet.

The first thing he saw was a man lying behind his dead horse, obviously pinned down in the open on a flat expanse of prairie. While he watched, he heard a few more rifle shots that sent slugs pounding into the carcass, causing the trapped man to try to lie even flatter. Scanning back a hundred and fifty yards or so, he finally sighted the shooters on the edge of a ravine. After another minute, he decided there were two of them. There followed a few moments of hesitation on his part. What he had stumbled upon, he wasn't sure, but it was obvious who the victim was. Whether he deserved it or not was impossible to say. He decided the only way he might be able to tell who was in the right and who was in the wrong was to get around behind the two riflemen to get a better look. Could be they were Indians, and they had bushwhacked the man trapped behind the horse. Looking beyond the ravine, he saw that his best chance was to circle all the way around to the base of the hills behind the two shooters.

Pulling slowly away from the top of the ridge, he stayed on hands and knees until sure he could stand up without being seen. Back to his horses, he mounted and nudged Rowdy into a lope once again. It took fully half an hour to make a wide enough circle to position himself directly behind the bushwhackers in the ravine. He pulled his horses up as close as he dared before leaving them in a narrow gully fifty or sixty yards away. Pulling his rifle, he climbed up to the top of the gully and dropped to the ground to look the situation over.

There was nothing but flat open ground between his gully and the ravine, so that was as close as he dared go. He discovered, however, that he had a clear view of the two men lying at the opposite lip of the ravine. They were not Indians. He stared at them for a long moment, still uncertain as to what he should do, if anything at all. Then as he continued to stare, one of the men rolled over on his side to say something to the other, and Clint almost grunted aloud his cry of surprise—*Ballenger!*

For a moment, Clint was stunned. How could this be? It was almost too much to believe that, in this vast Wyoming prairie, he had once again crossed paths with Ballenger and Yancey. He had thought he would never see the notorious killers again, having assumed that Ballenger and his cohorts were heading down into Colorado. Recovering immediately, he took another long look. There were only two. He searched as much of the ravine as he could see, looking for Skinner, but he was nowhere to be seen.

It was a hell of a turn of events, but one thing he felt sure he could assume—the man pinned behind his horse had to be the innocent party and most likely a lawman after them for robbing the bank in Fort Collins. Without further thought, Clint raised his rifle and sighted it on Yancey. When the rifle spoke, Yancey yelped in pain and rolled over and over. Clint quickly shifted his aim and pulled the trigger again, but Ballenger moved to the side just in time to cause the bullet to miss. Without a clear target now, Clint cranked round after round into the chamber, spraying the side of the ravine with lead.

Caught in a panic of confusion, Ballenger and Yancey scrambled down off the slope amid a hailstorm of slugs zipping by them and ripping up the ground. "Let's get the hell outta here!" Ballenger yelled as he stumbled down to the bottom of the ravine. Yancey, his left arm soaked with blood from a shoulder wound, needed no encouragement. Without their knowing who, or how many their assailants were, there was no thought beyond escape in the minds of both men. "How bad are you hurt?" Ballenger shouted at his partner as they galloped along the bottom of the ravine.

"Shoulder!" Yancey called back. "I don't know how bad."

They followed the ravine to the point where it widened at its origin on a hillside, then made their way, running the horses flat out through a maze of low treeless hills. When the horses began to falter from the strain, they were forced to let up on the weary animals. Looking back over his shoulder, Ballenger said, "I don't see nobody. I don't think they saw which way we went."

Yancey, breathing almost as hard as his horse, winced in pain when he replied, "I say we just keep ridin'. I need to tend to my shoulder." He wasn't sure whether Clell was of a mind to circle back to retaliate, but if he was, it was going to be without him.

"The son of a bitch had help," Ballenger said. "I don't know how they got around us, but we were damn lucky to get outta there."

"*You* were lucky," Yancey growled as he stuffed his bandanna inside his shirt to try to stop the bleeding.

"They wouldn'ta caught up with us at all if you hadn't laid around in your blankets this mornin'," Clell grumbled.

"I didn't know we were in a by-God hurry till we spotted him this afternoon. Hell, I didn't notice you up so damn early."

Ballenger was staring back the way they had just come. "You see anybody?" he asked, forgetting the bickering for the moment.

After a pause, Yancey answered. "We lost 'em. Let's get movin' before they start searchin' these hills." With no choice but to rest the horses, he started walking, leading his horse.

Clint stood on the side of the gully, reloading his rifle while watching for any sign of the bushwhackers' return. He waited until he felt sure they had gone before going back for his horses. He was undecided at first about riding down to help the man trapped behind the horse. Chances were he was a lawman chasing Ballenger and Yancey. What if he wasn't, but an innocent victim of ambush by the two? Even while telling himself that he was a fool to do it, he decided to see whether the man was alive or dead.

His question was answered when he approached to within fifty yards of the lead-filled carcass. Clayton rose to one knee, watching him carefully before standing up to meet him. "Mister," he said, "I'm mighty glad you came along."

"You looked like you could use a little help," Clint said as he pulled up beside him and dismounted. "I don't think those two will be back. They lit out toward the west."

"I'm much obliged," Clayton said. "They left me in a fix." He studied his young Samaritan closely, thinking maybe he had seen his likeness on a poster. Growing more confident in the identification, he casually pulled his vest aside to show his badge. "I'm a U.S. deputy marshal. I was chasin' those two when they ambushed me."

"Is that a fact?" Clint replied, careful to maintain an indifferent manner.

Clayton watched Clint's facial expressions closely as he continued. "Yeah, they're a couple of bad ones. One of 'em escaped from the territorial prison a few days ago with two other prisoners. I shot one of 'em over in Fort Collins. These two took off up this way, but they musta split up with the other feller because he left the night before." The picture of a lone rider he had passed on the road into Fort Collins one moonlit night came to his mind, and he had a strong feeling that it was the same man he was now talking to. The thought caused a plethora of conflicting decisions.

Clint was not comfortable with the direction of the conversation. He cursed himself for coming to help the marshal, but he had no choice now but to maintain a calm exterior and hope to bluff his way through. "Well, looks like your manhunt has hit a snag for now," he said. "I don't like to leave a man on foot out here, so I reckon I could let you have my packhorse to get you back to Cheyenne."

"Why, that's mighty neighborly of you, Mr. . . . what was your name?"

"Smith," Clint replied too quickly to come up with something original. "I reckon you'll be headin' back to get another horse."

"Oh, no," Clayton replied. "My job is to go after those convicts." He gave Clint a knowing smile. "All of them." There was an awkward moment of silence while the two stood facing each other. "Now, if I was a bettin' man," Clayton went on, "I'd bet that you'd more'n likely answer to the name of Conner instead of Smith." The sudden tightness of Clint's jaw told him he was right. He was a little reluctant to take the next step since Clint had just gotten him out of a serious situation. There was a series of acts that indicated Clint Conner was a decent man—saving the prison guard's life, the warning note about the bank job, and now his own rescue. In view of all that, he could elect to let him go on his way. But Clayton could not turn his back on his responsibility, and Clint was an escaped convict. It was Clayton's job to bring him to justice. It was as simple as that.

Clint took a backward step toward his horse, and quicker than a lightning flash, Clayton's hand came up, his .44 leveled at him. He shook his head regretfully. "Sorry, son, but I'm gonna have to take you in."

"Why, you ungrateful son of a bitch," Clint responded. "I shoulda left you lying behind that damn horse."

"I understand how you feel, and I appreciate what you done. I'll mention it to the judge, and maybe he'll go easy on you, but I've got to do my job. It ain't up to me to decide the right and wrong of things." He motioned with his pistol. "Now take your left hand and unbuckle that gun belt. Do it real slow. I don't wanna have to shoot you, but I sure as hell will if you don't do like I tell you."

With no choice but to do as he was told, Clint let his gun belt fall to the ground. "Now you'd best unload that pack-horse and put my saddle on him," Clayton ordered. Clint said nothing, went to the packhorse, and started working on the straps his father had fashioned. When he had untied one of the large canvas packs, he backed away from the horse, holding the pack in his arms, pretending to look for a place to set it down. "Just drop it on the ground," Clayton ordered impatiently.

"It's got flour and such in it. I don't wanna spill it," Clint said.

"Jesus!" Clayton scoffed. "Whaddaya care? You ain't gonna be usin' it." He stepped forward and reached out to jerk one end of the pack out of Clint's hands. "Drop the damn thing."

In one swift move, Clint shoved the canvas sack into Clayton's chest, launching his body after it. The deputy's re-flexes caused him to pull the trigger, but the thrust of Clint's shoulder drove Clayton's arm down and the bullet went into the ground between them. In desperate combat, Clint grabbed Clayton's wrist before he could bring the pistol to bear again and drove him to the ground. As the two men wrestled for control of the weapon, Clayton learned that he had underestimated the strength of the quiet young man. With his neck in a headlock that threatened to break his spine, he was forced to release the pistol. Clint quickly grabbed it, and like a cat, rolled off the stunned lawman, and was on his feet.

With the pistol leveled at Clayton, Clint gave the orders.

"Now we're gonna sing the same song, but with a different verse," he said. "Pick up that pack and tie it on again."

"You're makin' a helluva big mistake," the deputy marshal said, rubbing the wrist that Clint had almost broken.

"I believe you're the one who made the mistake, seein' as how I'm the one holdin' the gun. Now hurry up and tie that pack on."

Clayton, believing he had judged the man accurately, continued to balk. "You ain't a killer. You're not gonna shoot me, so why don't you just hand over the gun?"

Clint stood gazing at the cocksure lawman for a long moment. "Maybe you're right," he said. And before Clayton could form the confident smile he intended, Clint struck him hard on the chin with the weapon, knocking him to the ground. "Now get up and do what I tell you. And make no mistake, I will shoot if I have to."

Clayton took a minute to clear his head before climbing to his feet a more subdued man. Clint took the opportunity to quickly buckle on his gun belt again. When the pack was secure once more, Clint picked up Clayton's rifle and stepped up in the saddle. "You're the one who chose to play the game this way," he lectured the deputy. "I've paid enough for the mistake I made three years ago, and I'm not goin' back to that prison. It's about fifteen miles back to Cheyenne, just a good stretch of the legs." He glanced around, looking for a spot. "See that low mesa over there? I'll leave your guns over near the base of it."

"You'd best shoot me," an angry Clayton spat, "if you don't wanna see me again, 'cause I'll hunt you down if it takes the rest of my life."

"Mister, I hope you've got better things to do with your life," Clint said in parting.

*   *   *

His first camp after leaving Marshal Zach Clayton on foot was beside Horse Creek. It was not lost on him that he was no more than forty miles or so from the Wyoming Territorial Prison where he had spent the last three years of his life. It was not a comfortable feeling, and he was anxious to get an early start in the morning to be on his way, seeking to leave Wyoming behind him. He thought about his confrontation with Clayton. The deputy marshal should have completed his walk back to Cheyenne by then, and no doubt sent wires to every town that had a telegraph pole. In view of that, he planned to avoid towns of any size. He would cross the Chugwater tomorrow and head northwest, planning to cut between the Laramie Mountains and Fort Laramie. Once across the Platte, he would head in a more northeasterly direction, hoping to avoid Sioux or Cheyenne war parties.

Two days of steady riding found him in camp by the north fork of the Laramie River near the base of the rugged Laramie Mountains. Riding up into hills dotted with pines and evergreens, he doubled back to check on his back trail to make sure no one was following him. It was strictly precaution, for he didn't expect to see anyone. But since he had accidentally run into Ballenger and Yancey, he thought it best not to leave anything to chance. It was only after another day and a half, when he crossed the Platte a few miles east of Fort Fetterman, that he discarded his concern over being followed. Turning Rowdy a little more toward the east while keeping a general northern course, he rode over rolling grassland with distant horizons in all directions. One man, alone in a seemingly endless prairie, he at last felt free of civilization's restraints. There was no sign of mankind, white or savage. He imagined he felt as Adam had before God sent Eve to keep him company. Maybe the only difference was a wide prairie instead of a Garden of Eden.

# Chapter 6

Joanna Becker paused to listen to a bird calling outside the back window. It was an odd call, she thought, unable to identify the species. It sounded like a meadowlark, but she had never seen a meadowlark in these hills. She swung the large iron pot away from the fire and stirred the rabbit stew with a long wooden spoon. Swinging the pot back over the fire, she paused again when she heard the bird once more, this time on the other side of the cabin.

"Want me to set the table?" her mother asked as she sat by the front window, sewing a patch on her father's shirt.

Knowing her mother wanted to finish the shirt so he could wear it the next day at the sluice box, Joanna replied, "No, it can wait. Daddy and Robert won't be back for at least an hour yet." The afternoon was fading rapidly, and soon there would be little light coming through the open window. She gave her mother a smile. "This stew isn't going to be ready before then, anyway, as slow as it's cooking." Her husband, Robert, had told her that morning that he and her father planned to move the box upstream about a hundred yards, and would probably be home a little later than usual.

The two men had been working hard for the past four

months to get the cabin ready for winter while trying to work a mining claim at the same time. When they came to the Black Hills from Omaha in the early spring, Robert had boasted about the plentiful game close to the cabin. "We'll never have to worry about havin' meat on the table," he promised. The problem was he never had time to hunt for fresh meat. Joanna and her mother had fashioned a trap that had caught the rabbit now simmering in the iron pot. She smiled when she thought about the surprised look she would see on Robert's face when he came home expecting more salt pork.

*Robert*, she thought with a concerned smile. The quest into the Black Hills to search for gold had sounded so adventurous when they started out from Omaha. It had turned out to be an unrewarding labor from dawn to dusk as the men worked to build a rough cabin while filling a sluice box with colorless dirt. The only other choice was to go to Montana Territory with her uncle and two other families in hopes of creating a farm community. The search for gold had seemed much more compelling. Joanna honestly believed that had not Robert been excited about the prospect of striking it rich, her father would most likely have chosen to go to Montana with his brother.

It made little difference now, she decided; the die had been cast. Maybe the gold they had hoped to find would be turned up any day now. Troubling her mind lately was Robert's lack of enthusiasm for almost anything. She guessed that maybe he was just tired. His interest in her seemed nonexistent except on the occasional nights when he felt the need to relieve himself of his anxieties by availing himself of the use of her body. The episode was always short and to the point as he groaned and struggled to keep the noise down in their tiny room next to her parents. *Maybe*, she thought, *if I were not so plain . . .*

"There it is again," she said.

"What?" her mother asked.

"That bird, can you hear it? There, hear it? It's on the other side now." As soon as she said it, a chilling thought came to her mind. With a worried glance at her mother still sitting by the window, she walked over beside her and peered out into the lengthening shadows. She saw nothing at first, but as she continued to stare, she suddenly caught a movement in the shadows, and her heart stopped for a beat. "Robert?" she called, hoping it was her husband by the corner of the cabin. She turned to speak to her mother, but was startled by the look of terror on the old woman's face. She turned then to see the cause of her mother's fright, the painted torso of a Sioux warrior framed in the kitchen window.

Too terrified to scream, she murmured, "Mama . . . ," and turned toward the shotgun over the mantel. Before she could take a step, the door was suddenly flung open and two warriors burst into the cabin. She started to run to the fireplace, but one of the warriors, a solid brute of a man with wide shoulders, caught her by the wrist and threw her to the floor.

"Sit!" he commanded, glaring menacingly while the warrior at the window joined them. Horrified by the specter of the three painted savages crowding into the tiny cabin, both women sat paralyzed while the Indians began plundering the room. "*Mahzah-wah-kahn*," the savage who had been at the back window said, pointing to the shotgun over the mantel. One of the others, shorter than his two friends, nodded and quickly took it from the pegs and examined it, turning it over several times before grunting his approval. He grinned at Wide Shoulders, revealing a gap where a tooth had once been.

When Wide Shoulders spotted the pot bubbling over the fire, he picked up the wooden spoon Joanna had dropped.

Dipping into the pot, he sampled the stew. *"Le ta < ku hwo?"* he demanded. "What is this?" he repeated in English.

"Rabbit," Joanna managed to force out of her throat.

The warrior took another spoonful and grunted, *"Wa<'ste,* good." He motioned for his friends to help themselves.

Thinking that maybe they might leave them in peace if shown some kindness, Joanna's mother got up from her chair. "If you and your friends are hungry, we could . . ." That was as far as she managed before being struck hard by the warrior standing closest to her. Joanna screamed and scrambled to her feet, only to be forced down roughly by the English-speaking Indian. "Sit!" he demanded, and gestured with the stone-headed war club he held.

She jerked her hand free of his grasp. "How dare you strike a defenseless old woman!" she exclaimed, and rose to go to her mother's aid.

Gap Tooth drew back to strike her, but hesitated when Wide Shoulders said, "Wait!" He stood watching her as she helped her mother back in the chair. "Mother?" he asked calmly, but without compassion for the older woman now trembling and confused. His friends, no longer interested, returned their attention to the stew, dipping in with their hands and making short work of the supper.

"Yes," Joanna answered while blotting the blood from her mother's face. The old woman simply stared straight ahead in shocked confusion, obviously stunned by the viciousness of the blow to the side of her face.

An interested observer, Broad Shoulders watched Joanna's efforts to get a response from her mother. When she got up to go to the water bucket to dampen the apron she had been using to clean the blood from her mother's face, he repeated the command, "Sit!"

"No!" she replied, her face taut with anger, and started toward the bucket on the table.

He slapped her hard across the cheek, and hissed, "I say sit!"

Staggered, but still on her feet, her face stinging from the blow, she gritted her teeth and thrust her chin out defiantly. "I'll tend to my mother. Now, you take your savage friends and get out of my house!"

Broad Shoulders' face flushed with fury for a split second before relaxing to form an amused smirk. "I fix mother," he said softly. Then before Joanna could react, he whirled and struck the unsuspecting woman with his war club, smashing her skull.

Struck helpless by the horrifying sight of her mother's head recoiling from the blow, Joanna felt her throat choking with a soundless scream that paralyzed her lungs and blocked her breath. She felt herself gasping for air, but could not stop the darkness that seemed to be filling her brain. The last image she could remember before losing consciousness was that of her mother's head lolling drunkenly to one side as her body crumbled from the chair. When awareness next entered her brain, she found her hands were tied around the neck of the one horse in her father's corral, and Broad Shoulders in the process of tying a rope to her ankles beneath the horse's belly. Seeing that his captive was regaining consciousness, Broad Shoulders pointed his war club at her, gesturing. "You not good," he warned, "I fix like mother."

Karl Steiner urged his horse up the slope, following his son-in-law through the pines that covered the ridge above their claim. It had been a long day with nothing to show for their efforts, but he was hopeful that the new location upstream would soon show some color. As the horses made their way around the rocky ledges that crowned the top of the ridge, Karl thought about his daughter's husband, whose image was now softened by the growing darkness. Robert seemed to be a nice enough young man, but it seemed to Karl that he had taken to complaining about the work and the lack of instant wealth from the mountain stream. It might have been a mistake to undertake this joint venture with Robert and Joanna. Maybe it would have been better if he and Sarah had stayed in Omaha and let the young folks seek fortunes in the Black Hills. *Hell, I still outwork him every day,* Karl thought. *He just doesn't have the patience to wait until we strike some solid color.* Sarah would scold him for criticizing Robert. As long as he makes Joanna happy, she always said.

As far as Karl could tell, Joanna didn't look particularly happy. *But I guess I can't really blame Robert for that,* he thought. It had been nothing but long, hard hours ever since they first raised tents on French Creek, only to be escorted out by the soldiers trying to enforce the treaties with the Indians. Like all the other prospectors, they simply moved to another location, playing hide-and-seek with the army in the forbidden hills. He was still optimistic about the little stream they had settled on near the western edge of the Black Hills. His thoughts were interrupted when he realized that Robert had stopped.

Pulling even with his son-in-law, he inquired, "Something wrong?"

Robert was peering down through the trees, trying to see through the gloom of the evening. "Just seems kinda strange," he replied. "Usually smell smoke, even see a little from the chimney on top of this ridge."

"Maybe the wind's just changed," Karl offered, not really concerned. He nudged his horse and started down the ridge in the lead. Although they often saw smoke from the ridgetop, the cabin itself was not visible through the trees until about halfway down. The first clue that something was amiss was when Karl came upon an empty corral. Still, it was not enough to cause him to worry. "Sarah," he called out, "Joanna." It struck him as rather odd that no one came to the door to greet them.

"What?" Robert asked when he pulled his horse up in the yard.

Karl dismounted. "I said I wonder where the women are." Becoming more concerned by the moment, he hurried toward the front door, hesitating only briefly to pick up a couple of pieces of calico that lay on the ground, as if someone had dropped them.

Robert, now sensing something wrong, pulled his rifle from the saddle sling, and stayed back while his father-in-law stepped inside the cabin. Within seconds, he heard Karl's cry of anguish. He ran inside the cabin then and found the grieving man with his wife's body cradled in his arms, rocking back and forth while he sobbed. "Joanna!" Robert cried when he looked frantically around the ransacked cabin, but his wife was not there. Hoping with all his might that he would not find a second corpse, he lit a lantern with trembling hands, and searched the cabin again, looking under overturned benches and tables. The quilts that partitioned off the two bedroom areas were missing, and there was no one in the beds.

There was no doubt in either man's mind that the cabin had been visited by Indians, and Robert tried not to think about what fate his wife might have suffered. With Karl still lost in his grief, Robert went outside and searched all around the cabin and the corral. There was no sign of Joanna. The Indians had taken her.

When he went back inside, he found that Karl had managed to pull himself together. He laid Sarah's body gently back on the floor. When he saw Robert, he asked, "Joanna?"

Robert shook his head slowly. "We've got to find Joanna," Karl said, getting to his feet. "We've got to find my daughter before they kill her, too."

"We can't go after 'em now," Robert said. "We can't track 'em in the dark. Can't even see which way they started."

After a sleepless night, morning finally came to the little clearing by the stream. Preparing to make coffee, Robert hesitated when Karl insisted they not wait to have breakfast. "I've heard what those Indians do to white women," he said. "We need to find Joanna before they have time to harm her."

"All right," Robert said, and put the coffeepot down. He did not voice the thought in both of their minds that she might already be dead.

Neither man was skilled at tracking, but the trail the Sioux left from the cabin was obvious even to a novice. It led down into the floor of the valley where it turned to the west. They were encouraged to find no evidence that the party had stopped soon after leaving the cabin, giving them hope that Joanna was still alive. In the late afternoon, they lost the trail at a fork in the Beaver River. Searching in a circle that encompassed the two forks, they failed to find any tracks other than their own. By the time darkness descended upon them, they were forced to admit they had no idea where the warriors had taken Joanna.

Grief-stricken, they went through the motions of making camp, neither man with much to say to the other, knowing they had failed, and helpless to do anything to alleviate their despair. Despondent and defeated, they started back to the cabin to bury Sarah Steiner.

# Chapter 7

After leaving the Platte three and a half days behind him, Clint Conner lay flat on his belly at the top of a long, low ridge. His horses waited behind him farther down the slope where they would not be seen by the small party of Indians passing to the west some seventy-five yards from where he lay. They were not the first he had seen; some were in large parties, and all seemed to be heading in the same general direction, toward the Powder River. It was the reason he had decided to ride farther to the east as he made his way north.

He had managed to steer clear of the other Indians who had crossed his path, but he had almost blundered into the group he now watched from the hilltop. Three men and a woman, he could now tell as they reached a point closer to him. The woman appeared to be sick, he thought, for she rode slumped forward. As they came even closer, he realized that the woman's horse was being led by one of the warriors. While Clint watched, the warrior gave the lead rope a sharp yank, causing the woman to grab on to the horse's mane, for there was no saddle under her. As she raised her head, Clint recoiled, startled. Her hair was raven black, but her face was white. *A white woman! A captive?* Maybe she was with them by choice. Then he noticed that her wrists were tied, as well as her ankles beneath the horse's belly. There was no decision to be made. She was a captive. He would have to try to free her. How to do it was the problem to be worked out. He was accurate enough with a rifle to get one of them, maybe two, at this distance, but then he ran the chance that the other would escape with the woman. Also there was the risk that if they were fired upon, they might kill the woman and then run. They had guns, but he could not tell from that distance whether they were repeating rifles, single shot, or shotguns. At any rate, they were armed and they outnumbered him. He felt pretty sure his best chance to get all three of the warriors was to wait until they made camp, and then go in under the cover of darkness. He slid back away from the top of the hill, and went to get his horses.

Because of the open terrain, he was obliged to stay well behind the party as he followed them, often losing sight of them and relying on his ability to find their tracks. It was not always easy, owing to the numerous old tracks that intermingled. It led him to believe that the Sioux, and probably the Cheyenne, were gathering for some reason, and that equated to more trouble for every white man. He squinted up at the sun, trying to determine how many hours remained before nightfall. With no notion of where the big congregation of Indians was to take place, he just hoped the three he followed would make camp before joining the rest of their brothers. If they didn't, there was little chance he would be able to help the woman. He couldn't fight the whole Sioux nation.

The last hours of sunlight had faded away before the Indians came to a river where they made their camp. Clint wasn't sure, but he guessed that the river was probably the Belle Fourche. When certain they were stopping for the night, he settled for a dry camp in a shallow ravine where he could wait for darkness to cover the prairie between the two camps.

It was not a long wait, but it seemed long. Most of the time was spent at the head of the ravine, watching the glow of their campfire. Finally the glow softened as the flames died out. Still he waited until he felt reasonably certain they had retired to their blankets for the night. Checking his rifle once more, he decided it was time.

A rough guess told him the camp was approximately three or four hundred yards distant. Leaving his horses, he started walking across the open plain toward the tiny glow in the cottonwood trees along the riverbank. As he came closer, he brought his rifle up before him, ready to shoot at the first sign of alarm. There was no cry of discovery, or discernible motion of any kind. The camp was still. He hesitated when the horses tied in the trees began to whinny and shuffle around nervously, but their nervousness went unnoticed by the three Indians. Shifting his gaze from the horses back to the sleeping forms around the embers of the dying campfire, he searched for that of the woman. At first he could see only three bodies. Then he spotted the woman, bound hand and foot and tied to a tree near the horses.

Satisfied that she was out of the line of fire, he walked into the camp, his rifle ready before him. The short, gap-toothed warrior was the first to discover the sinister visitor. He sat up, childlike in his attempt to brush the sleep from his eyes. The peaceful night was shattered by the crack of Clint's rifle as a .44 slug smacked into the warrior's chest.

In rapid succession, he leveled the Winchester to pump a fatal shot into each of the other two as they sprang from their blankets. It was all over in a matter of seconds, and the peaceful night was quiet again except for the frightened sounds from the horses.

Joanna Becker lay still, terrified by the abrupt explosion of gunfire, her mind a maelstrom of conflicting thoughts. The suddenness of the grim executions by the dark figure, now methodically prodding each body with the toe of his boot, caused her to fear that more trouble was to come her way. Evidently satisfied that all three were dead, he turned in her direction. She could not help but cringe against the trunk of the cottonwood as he started toward her.

"Are you all right, ma'am?" Clint asked as he stood over her.

The tone of his voice, soft with compassion, calmed her fears at once. She relaxed and replied, "I think so." In truth, she was not certain how bad the many cuts and bruises on her face and body were. Her captors had not been gentle with her. Some of her abuse she vowed never to speak of to anyone. All that mattered at the moment was that she had been saved. As he knelt down to untie her, she could not hold back the tears of relief. "Thank you," she uttered softly. "Thank you for saving my life."

"I'm glad I happened on you," he replied.

"They killed my mother," she sobbed. "My husband and my father," she asked anxiously, "are they looking for me?"

"I don't know, ma'am. Like I said, I just happened along." He removed the last of the ropes from around her ankles, and looked her over as best he could in the darkness. It appeared that she had several cuts on her arms and shoulders, and her face was badly bruised and swollen beside her left eye. His heart went out to her when he speculated on what she must have endured at the hands of her captors. "Can you walk all right?" he asked. When she nodded, he continued. "I expect it might be a good idea to leave this place. We can go downstream a ways till we find a better place. Then we'll see about takin' care of some of these cuts." The site the warriors had chosen to make their camp seemed to be a common crossing of the river. And considering the number of Indians he had seen during the last several days, he thought it best not to take the chance of being caught with three dead warriors.

He helped her to her feet and watched her to make sure she was all right. She seemed unsure of her balance at first, but soon recovered her composure. "I prayed to God to either send me help or take my life," she said, her words halting and barely audible, tears streaming down her face again.

He really didn't know what to say to her. He had compassion for her, but words of consolation did not come easily to him. "Well, you're all right now. We'll get outta this place and get you somethin' to eat—fix up your cuts." That was all he could come up with to ease her distress. "I'll see what we can use as far as guns or cartridges go, and I'll take a look at their horses."

"One of those horses is my father's," Joanna said.

"Yes, ma'am," he replied, and left her standing there while he took an inventory of the Indians' weapons. After a moment, she followed him as he examined an old Henry rifle. She stood gazing down at the cold features of the broad-shouldered Sioux warrior after Clint moved on to pick up the shotgun beside one of the other bodies. After a couple of moments, she looked around her and found a large rock the size of a loaf of bread. With tears gushing forward again, this time in unbridled fury, she held the rock up as high as she could, then slammed it down with all her strength in the warrior's face.

Hearing the solid thud of the stone as it crushed the face of the corpse, he turned to see the woman glaring down at it, her fists clenched, her face drawn in anger. Realizing that he was staring at her, she turned to him and simply said, "That shotgun belongs to my father."

"Right," he replied, again at a loss for response. He paused briefly by the third body, and seeing nothing of value beyond an early model Remington single-shot rifle, moved on to get the horses.

He thought about keeping all four of the horses, but decided that he didn't want to herd the three extra. He did decide to take the opportunity to trade the prison horse for one of the Indian ponies, a paint, deeming it a definite upgrade. Taking one of the Indian saddles, he put it on Joanna's horse. "It might not be the most comfortable saddle," he told her, "but it'll beat ridin' bareback." After witnessing her final farewell to the broad-shouldered warrior, he was a little reluctant to touch her, but she willingly accepted his hand in helping her up in the saddle. Then he led her horse back to retrieve Rowdy and upgrade his packhorse.

Following the dark riverbank downstream, they rode for over an hour until Clint selected a deep gully leading down from the bluff. In a short time, he had a fire going and coffee was not long after. There was little he could do to fix her wounds, but she insisted that all she needed was to clean them and wash herself in the river. Once she had finished her bath and dried with a blanket Clint had taken from one of the warriors, she seemed content to warm herself by the fire.

Clint handed her a cup of coffee. "Get you a little somethin' to eat, and then we'll catch a couple hours' sleep before sunup." She merely nodded in return. "What's your name?" he asked.

"Joanna Becker," she said.

"All right, Joanna. My name's Clint Conner. Where's home? Where did those Indians grab you?"

"I don't know exactly," she confessed. "We have a cabin on a stream back there in the hills. My husband and my father were working a claim, but I don't know how to get back there from here." She tried to be calm, but she could not hide her dismay. "They killed my mother." She tried to continue, but could not keep from sobbing. He waited until she gathered herself once more and went on. "I know my husband's looking for me, but I don't know how to get back."

"Never mind," he assured her. "We'll get you back home," knowing as he said it that it would not be such an easy task. He sliced two generous slabs of bacon from what was left of the side he had taken form Clell Ballenger's supplies and dropped them in his frying pan. As he tended the sizzling meat, he glanced up at Joanna. With the firelight flickering upon her swollen face, he decided he might have been wrong about her. When he first found her, he thought she was a little older. But on closer inspection, he decided she was not much older than he. It was just the battered face that misled him. "Don't worry," he assured her. "I'll get you back to your husband safe and sound." He hoped he wasn't making a boast he couldn't keep.

By the time they had finished the coffee and bacon, there were not many hours of darkness left. Clint gave Joanna a blanket to wrap around herself and made her a bed with his saddle blanket and an oilskin slicker. Although it was still summer, the night was chilly enough to call for a blanket. She lay awake, watching him until the soft steady sounds of his breathing told her he was asleep. Only then could she relax and permit sleep to overtake her. He seemed an honest enough young man, but her recent ordeal at the hands of the Sioux warriors caused her to be wary of any strange man. When sleep finally came, it captured her completely, fueled by her total exhaustion.

She was awakened by the gentle touch of sunlight upon her cheek. Opening her sleep-swollen eyes, she was at once alarmed. *He was gone!* Immediately a bevy of worrisome thoughts filled her head, causing her heart to beat with alarm as she stared at the empty space where he had made his bed.

Concerned when going to sleep about the possible attempt for the stranger to seek relief of his lust, she had thought that he might simply choose to sneak off and leave her. He had told her that he was on his way to Montana. Evidently he didn't care to have the bother of a woman.

Almost in a panic at this point, she flung the blanket from her, frantic to see whether he had left her a horse to ride. In her haste, she tripped over a fold in her blanket, fell to her knees, and scrambled to her feet again only to discover the horses gone from the willows where they had been tied. She almost cried out in anguish, but stifled the cry in her throat when she saw Clint beyond the willows, leading the horses up from the river. Feeling awkward and foolish, she returned to fold her blanket, hoping he had not witnessed her panic.

"Mornin'," Clint called out when he saw that she was up.

"Good morning," she returned sheepishly. If he had seen her little show of fear, he did not let on.

"You were sleepin' so soundly, I didn't have the heart to wake you," he said. "You feelin' strong enough to ride?" When she answered yes, he went on. "If you're needin' some privacy to do whatever you gotta do, there's a pretty thick stand of fir trees beyond those willows. I'll be makin' us some coffee while you're gone." She nodded and immediately took her leave.

When she returned, he could see that she had freshened her face and tried to comb her hair with her fingers. He stopped what he was doing to examine her face in the early-morning sunlight. "Worked you over pretty good, didn't they? I believe a little bit of the swellin's gone down, though." He gave her a warm smile then. "You're gonna have a black eye for a day or two."

She smiled, almost blushing in her embarrassment, knowing how she had mistrusted his motive for rescuing her, and then thinking he had deserted her. She knew then, looking into his rugged and honest face, that she could trust him with her life as well as her honor—an honor that she now deemed worthless. She felt compelled to apologize. "I owe you an apology, Clint."

"For what?" he asked.

"For being so much trouble," she lied, "and I want to thank you again, sincerely, for what you did."

"No trouble a'tall," he replied cheerfully. "I'm on my way to Montana, and I ain't on any time schedule to get there." He gave her a reassuring smile, relieved to see that she had gained control of her crying fits. "If we're gonna get you home again, I need to know how long you've been gone, and from what direction you came. When I first spotted you, you were headin' straight west. Did they bring you most of the time in that direction?" She nodded. "How many days did you travel?"

She almost had to stop to think about it. It had seemed an eternity. "Three nights before the night you came," she said, shuddering inwardly when she recalled.

"Can you tell me anythin' more about it, flatland, hills, mountains, rivers?"

"Our house is in the mountains. When they took me, we left the mountains, but we rode through some smaller mountains before we reached the prairie where you found us." She remembered one thing more then. "We crossed a river before we got into the smaller mountains."

That told Clint that it was going to be one hell of a challenge to find the stream she described, or even the area of the mountains her home was in. He had never been in the Black Hills, but he had heard tales about them from his father—tall, rugged mountains, covered with evergreen trees, meadowlike valleys of grass leading to rocky gulches. The Sioux called them Paha Sapa and considered them to be the center of the world. According to the treaties, white men weren't even supposed to go there. "Tell me about the river," he said.

Details began to return to her mind as she tried to look back in her memory. "I remember that we crossed a river where it looked like it forked with another river. My hands and feet were tied to the horse, and I was afraid I was going to drown if the water got too deep." She shook her head as if trying to rid it of the memory. "It wasn't very deep, though," she added softly.

With no more information than that, he figured the only plan left to him was to head southeast to pick up the Indians' trail where he had first encountered them. Anxious to re-unite her with her husband and father as quickly as possible, he said, "We'll start out to the east as soon as you eat some-thin'. I know your family is worried about you."

After a ride of five or six miles, Clint recognized the low line of hills from which he had watched the raiding party, but it was the middle of the day before he found their tracks. Kneeling beside the trail, he looked back toward the east and the blue-black silhouette of the hills in the distance. Glancing at Joanna then, he said, "I reckon home's that way." He stepped up in the saddle and started backtracking. "We'll be lucky to reach those hills before dark."

Forced to circle back when he lost the trail at the head of a wide ravine, he had to slow down to make sure he didn't repeat the mistake. Knowing the horses would have to rest soon, he looked ahead, hoping to see a line of trees or shrubs that would indicate the presence of a stream. Seeing no sign, he pushed the horses on. It was then he heard Joanna call his name.

"Clint," she uttered almost in a whisper.

When he turned toward her, he saw her looking off to her right. Following the line of sight, he spotted half a dozen In-dians on a mesa some seven or eight hundred yards distant, their ponies in a single line, motionless as they watched the white man and woman passing toward the mountains. *Oh, shit*, he thought. It was at least three miles to the foothills they had been riding toward, and it appeared the warriors had the angle and could easily cut them off before they reached those hills. To make matters worse, the horses were tired and in no shape for an extended gallop. "Just keep ridin'," he said to Joanna. "We'll get as far as we can before they decide to jump us."

"Maybe they haven't seen us," Joanna said fearfully, her face drawn in a concerned frown.

"Maybe," Clint answered, knowing they'd have to be blind not to. He held Rowdy to a slow, leisurely pace, hoping the Indians would hold off long enough for him to find some form of cover. He saw very little, as he scanned the treeless terrain before them. The line of warriors on the ridge turned and, keeping pace with him, paralleled his path. Like him, they were still deciding where best to engage the enemy. *You just keep riding*, he thought. The longer they waited, the more time he had to find a place to make his stand. Holding steady to the trail he had been backtracking all morning, he finally decided that he wasn't going to find any better place to defend than the shallow ravine he was approaching. He figured the six warriors weren't going to let him reach the foothills now less than two and a half miles away, so he decided to take his stand in the ravine.

"This is as good a place as any," he said to Joanna. "We'll lead the horses down to the bottom, and I can get up behind those rocks on the rim with my rifle."

"Shouldn't we try to reach the hills?" she replied, worried.

"They're not gonna let us reach those hills, and this is the best place between here and the hills."

"Maybe they're friendly," she said, unconvincingly. "They haven't done anything but follow us."

"If they were friendly," he answered patiently, "they would most likely have rode on down to meet us." He guided Rowdy down into the ravine. It seemed to be a signal for the Sioux, for they stopped and appeared to be discussing a plan of attack. After a few minutes, they turned their ponies down the slope, and spread out in a fanlike formation, gradually picking up speed as they descended the ridge. *I'd hoped they'd stay more bunched up*, he thought.

Dismounting, he led the horses to the bottom of the ravine. "There ain't nothin' to tie the horses to," he said. "We don't want 'em to get scared by the shootin' and run off. Can you hold 'em?" She nodded, but did not show a great deal of confidence. "You can do it," he assured her. "Just sit down here on the ground and hold on to the buckskin and the paint's reins. I'm gonna be busy up on the side, but I'll keep an eye on you." When he saw the worried look in her eyes, he said, "I'm gonna get you home safe."

Figuring he had five or ten minutes before they were in rifle range, he used the time to fill his pockets with extra cartridges and load the Henry as well as his Winchester. Taking another look at Joanna, he felt reasonably sure that she was out of harm's way, provided he could hold the warriors at bay. As an extra precaution, however, he pulled her father's shotgun from the pack and loaded it. Handing it to her, along with his pistol, he said, "If somethin' happens to me, use the shotgun first, then the pistol, but I don't plan on you havin' to use 'em a'tall." With time running short, he scrambled up the side of the ravine to take his place behind a waist-high rock.

Satisfied that he had a field of fire covering a hundred and eighty degrees, he laid the Henry on top of the rock where it would be handy if he got caught with not enough time to re-load his Winchester. Ready for the assault, he waited.

After glancing briefly at the woman sitting at the bottom of the ravine to make sure she was all right, he shifted his gaze quickly back to the warriors bearing down on him. He was confident in his accuracy with his rifle, but he waited for the Sioux warriors to advance to within one hundred yards, knowing that he could not miss at that distance, even with a moving target. The warriors were not as patient and opened fire when still a good way beyond that distance.

At the bottom of the ravine, Joanna flinched when she heard the zip of a rifle slug pass overhead, and the cracks of the rifles. Frightened, she looked up above her at the man who had promised to take her home. Only moments before, he had been scurrying around, hastily loading his weapons, securing the horses, then scrambling up the slope. Now he seemed almost serene, patiently watching the approaching danger as rifle slugs teased the air around him. She could not help but find reassurance in the calm confidence of the man, and she somehow knew that, six or six hundred savages, he would find a way to protect her. With a new sense of confidence, she banished her feelings of fear and concerned herself with holding the horses.

Still holding his fire, Clint watched the progress of the charging warriors, anticipating their plan of assault. It was obvious to him that the four near the center of their arc were intent upon laying down a blistering rain of fire to keep him pinned down—while the two at each end hoped to flank him, or even circle behind him. With that in mind, the first targets he selected were the flanking riders. He would be in serious trouble if they got behind him. While bullets ricocheted off the rock and ripped up the dirt around it, he continued to hold his fire.

When the Indians reached a spot on the prairie he had

mentally selected, he rose slightly and unhurriedly took careful aim. The Winchester spoke with solid certainty, and the warrior on the left flank tumbled from the saddle. Without hesitation, but with no haste, he turned and sighted on the rider on the opposite flank with the same results. The sudden deadly response stopped the warriors' charge, causing the four remaining to scatter for safety. Acting quickly now, Clint knocked two more of the raiders out of their saddles before they were able to retreat. The last two galloped away to safety.

He figured the Sioux warriors would not try that again, but he knew you could never be sure about Indians. So while there was time, he hurried down the slope to Joanna. "Get mounted," he said. "We've got some time now to reach those hills." As soon as he secured the extra weapons, he led her out of the ravine and headed toward the hills to the east at a gentle lope. The horses still needed rest, but he figured he would take care of that as soon as they reached the security of the foothills.

Having been unable to see what was taking place above her, Joanna was startled to see the bodies scattered about in the sage and short grass prairie. She had only heard four shots from his rifle, and she counted four bodies. Two of the riderless horses stood watching them while the other two galloped off in the general direction the retreating Sioux had taken. When Clint led them out again, the two Indian ponies that had remained followed along behind them for a few hundred yards before stopping to watch the two riders. Clint pulled up and turned back to look at the Indian ponies. Though he hadn't wished to be burdened with extra horses before, it now occurred to him that it would be worth the trouble for a start in Montana.

"Wait here," he told Joanna, and rode back to the standing horses. He had a hunch that if he led one of them, a mare, that the other would follow, so using the reins as a rope, he slipped them around the mare's neck and tied the other end to his packhorse. The mare went along obediently, and after hesitating to make up its mind, the other horse followed the mare. When he caught up with Joanna again, he said, "Might as well start buildin' a herd."

Ahead of her, sitting tall in the saddle, his lean body riding easy with the motion of the buckskin gelding, the miracle she had prayed for while a captive led his horses toward a line of wooded ridges. She thought of her husband and couldn't help but compare. She could not imagine Robert under similar circumstances. She promptly reproached herself for comparing them. It wasn't fair to Robert. Her thoughts went then to her father and her husband, her father grieving over the loss of her mother. *They must both be sick with worry about me*, she thought. *What if we find our way back to the cabin? They may be off looking for me.*

Karl Steiner stood beside the grave of his beloved wife, Sarah. He was still unable to look at the grave without seeing images of her crushed skull, but he needed to talk to someone about the feelings that were troubling his mind. "I miss you so much, darlin'," he blurted between the tears that started. "I don't know if I can make it without you." He turned to look back at the cabin to make sure Robert couldn't hear him. "I'm goin' to go look for Joanna if I have to search every Sioux camp in the territory." He paused to think about what he had just vowed. Robert was not set on venturing out to Powder River country. Maybe he was right; maybe it was suicide, but Karl could not sit there and do nothing when his daughter was a captive in some Indian village—if in fact she was still alive. It was hard to know what to do. Robert was right about one thing, there were so many Indian camps and villages in the Powder River valley alone that odds were astronomical they would happen upon the one where Joanna was held. His daughter had always been a spunky girl, even as a child, and he had a small glimmer of hope that she might escape her captors and return home. This slim possibility was the only reason Karl was still delaying his search for her.

Robert Becker sat at the table and contemplated the circumstances in which he now found himself. The entire plan to pan for gold had been an unlucky and disappointing venture for him. The Indians didn't want them there. Even the army wanted them to leave, and yet he had let Joanna talk him into continuing the ill-fated venture after leaving French Creek. His enthusiasm for the prospect of striking it rich had been dulled considerably by the hard work it required. And now the threat of Indian attacks caused him to fear for his life.

He sipped his coffee, now lukewarm in the metal cup, thinking about the last time he had seen his wife. He missed Joanna, but it amounted to certain death if he and Karl tried to find her. It irritated him that he could not make the old man understand that. Karl even thought that she still might escape and return to them. That thought troubled Robert. How many Sioux bucks had already had their way with her? The idea of it turned Robert cold inside, and he was not sure he would ever be able to overcome that disgusting truth. How could he ever take her into his bed again after she had been ruined by the savages? The mental picture of it seared his brain, and he admitted to himself that he did not want her back. He made his decision then. He was going back to Omaha, this quest for gold be damned.

There was no use trying to explain his feelings to his father-in-law. Karl was too set in his ways to understand that it served no good purpose to sacrifice another young life after the loss of Joanna. He would say nothing about his decision to Karl tonight, but would pack up his things and leave in the morning.

Morning brought a chilly breeze sweeping across the eastern slopes of the mountains. Robert was up early and packing his saddlebags when Karl came out to find him. "Mornin'," he said. "You're up early." When Robert nodded without speaking, the old man asked, "You thinking it's time we went looking for Joanna?" He guessed that Robert wasn't thinking about working the sluice box. They hadn't worked since Joanna's abduction.

His pack ready, Robert finally spoke. "I'm thinkin' it's time I went back to Omaha."

Karl didn't understand. "What are you talking about?"

"I'm goin' back home," Robert said. "We've both lost our wives, and there ain't no sense in stayin' out in these god-forsaken mountains any longer waitin' to get scalped. You're welcome to go with me, but I'm aiming to leave this mornin'."

"But Joanna's still out there somewhere," Karl insisted, astonished by his son-in-law's decision. "We'll find her."

"Karl," Robert responded impatiently, "we don't know she's even alive, and chances are she ain't."

"But we have to look for her," Karl pleaded.

"Even if we found her, she ain't the same woman that left here. You know that."

"I don't know any such thing!" Karl blurted angrily as Robert stepped up in the saddle.

With eyes cold and unfeeling, Robert stared down at his father-in-law. "You comin' or not?"

"Hell no, I ain't coming with you, you sorry dog. Go on! Get the hell away from here," Karl raged. "I always knew Joanna was too good for the likes of you."

"I'm sorry, Karl, but there ain't nothin' here for me no more. No hard feelin's, though."

"Get the hell gone before I get my gun and shoot your sorry ass," Karl replied. He stepped back and watched his son-in-law ride out of the clearing, feeling like the last man left on the face of the earth.

# Chapter 8

The uniformed guard tapped lightly on the office door before opening it far enough to stick his head through. "Clayton's here, Warden," he said.

Warden Nathaniel K. Boswell looked up from his desk. "Well, tell him to come on in," he said, and leaned back in his chair in amused anticipation of the deputy marshal's report.

Deputy Marshal Zach Clayton strode into the office. The trace of chagrin he wore on his face bore proof that he knew full well the reception awaiting him. Boswell did not disappoint.

"Howdy, Zach. I hear tell you've taken to riding the train lately," the warden said. "Have a seat. I heard you've been doing a little walking, too." He could not suppress all of the grin that threatened to spread across his face. He could well imagine the embarrassment for Clayton following his encounter with the escaped felons, resulting in his having to walk to Cheyenne, then take the train back to Laramie. Zach Clayton was a proud man, although he would never admit it.

Clayton and Boswell had known each other for a number of years, from the time when Boswell was a sheriff. He knew before he walked in that his old friend was going to ride him hard for this one. "Yeah, Nat, I reckon you can crow a little about this one, but it ain't over yet."

"According to your telegram, you had one of 'em, but you let him get away and leave you on foot," Boswell said, enjoying the interview. "How'd that happen?"

Clayton smirked and rubbed the healing cut on his chin. "He was very persuasive," he replied, "so I told him to go along and I'd just walk back to Cheyenne. Hell, it wasn't but fifteen miles." He went on to tell Boswell how he had happened to ride into the ambush with Ballenger and Yancey. "As for young Conner, that's a hard one to figure out. If he hadn't jumped those two from behind and run 'em off, I might still be pinned down behind my horse. It's hard to arrest a man after he's just saved your bacon." He paused, thinking about it. "But I took the oath, so I arrested him"—he shook his head as if finding it hard to believe—"and then let him get the jump on me."

"Got any ideas about Ballenger and the other fellow?" Boswell asked. "Where they might be headed?"

"None at all," Clayton replied. "They could be heading anywhere, but I'd bet on Montana Territory, Bozeman or Helena most likely. They'll show up before long, rob a bank or hold up a stage, and then I'll be right behind 'em."

"Zach, we could turn this over to another marshal in Montana," Boswell suggested.

"Hell no," Clayton responded at once. "I'll run those bastards down if I have to go to Canada to catch 'em. I ain't ever quit on a job." His dark eyebrows lowered to form a heavy frown. "I'll catch young Conner, too." His frown deepened. "He might be a little harder to run down, 'cause he ain't likely to rob no banks or nothin'. He just wants to lose himself somewhere, but one of these days he'll turn around and I'll be standin' there."

Expecting nothing less from the reliable deputy, Boswell

said, "All right, it that's what you're of a mind to do. But, Zach, that country's dangerous right now. You watch yourself."

Joanna Becker knelt beside the gently flowing creek, trying to see her reflection in the water. It was not dark enough to reflect a clear image, giving her a distorted picture of her battered face. Much of the tenderness had gone from the bruises left by the brutal wide-shouldered savage, but she feared the cut on one side of her face would leave a scar. *What will Robert think?* she asked herself. "He'll understand," she said softly in reply.

She continued to stare into the water, touching her bruised face lightly with her fingertips. The touch caused her to shiver when she remembered the abuse that had brought about her wounds. She vowed that she would never tell her husband the full extent of her abuse. It might break his heart. She looked up from the creek to glance at the stranger who had rescued her and protected her as he led the horses up from the creek and prepared to saddle them. She thanked God for Clint Conner, marveling that he would interrupt his life to see her safely home. She also thanked God for the man's decency. Out in these mountains, removed from all civilization, he could easily have used her and then abandoned her, and no one would ever have known. But she had learned that Clint was a man of integrity and honor, a man she could put all her trust in.

Reminding herself that she should help him break camp, she quickly splashed water on her face and smoothed her hair back. She couldn't block the thought that crept in as she patted her face dry. *He's seeing me at my very worst,* she thought. She was well aware that she was not really a pretty woman, but she knew that she was not truly homely, either.

*Just plain*, she thought, and then scolded herself for even wondering whether it mattered how she looked to Clint.

"I expect we'd best get goin'," he said when Joanna walked back from the creek, "if you're ready."

"I'm ready," she replied as cheerfully as she could manage. "I'll just rinse out the coffeepot and put out the fire."

Looking over the saddle as he tightened Rowdy's cinch, he watched her as she hurried about the campfire. He couldn't help but admire her spirit after what she had suffered. She had tried not to be a burden to him. Last night she had insisted that she should prepare their supper. "I should do something to carry my weight," she had proclaimed, and mixed up some pan biscuits with the flour he had brought from his father's house. *They were pretty good, too*, he thought. *Her husband's a lucky man.*

In the saddle again, they started out, following the creek through a series of foothills, Clint first, leading his pack-horse, and Joanna coming on behind. The prior two days had been spent tracing various springs and streams through the mountains in hopes that they would lead to some place Joanna recognized. None had, but the creek they were now on was only a few hundred yards from its confluence with a river that Joanna guessed might be the Beaver. Upon reaching the river, there was a question as to the proper direction to turn, north or south, in hopes of finding the forks that she remembered crossing when abducted. "I'm sorry," she said, "I don't honestly know."

He nodded patiently, and stood up in the stirrups to look around them. "Judging from the direction of their trail before we lost it back there, I'd say we need to go south." Then without waiting for further discussion, he turned Rowdy in that direction. Riding with the dark outline of the Black Hills on their left, they had progressed no more than two or three miles when Joanna spurred her horse up beside him.

"There!" she exclaimed, pointing ahead. "There's the fork with this river. I remember that!"

There were more than a few game trails leading down from the mountains to the river. They all looked the same to Joanna. She could not say which trail was the one her abductors had taken down to the river. Clint examined each likely prospect for sign, but could find none. Finally, he decided to follow the one that looked to be the most used, and they started up through the pines. It was late in the afternoon when the trail turned and led them back toward the river. The second trail they picked seemed more promising when it led up over a small ridge and then took them down into a long narrow gulch that cut deep into the mountains. "We came this way!" Joanna exclaimed as the gray rocky walls closed in to form a narrow passageway, and memories of that dark horrible night returned to her. Her throat tightened as she recalled those terrifying moments.

Seeing the terror registering in her face, he tried to reassure her. "Well, that's good," he said softly. "We'll have you home soon, and you'll be back with your husband and your father."

She nodded and the moment of anxiety passed. Pointing up the trail, she said, "It's not far now, just on the other side of that ridge." The worry of seconds before was replaced by anticipation of her reunion with her husband and father, and she pushed ahead of Clint, anxious to go home.

Karl Steiner looked over the supplies he had gathered to take with him. They seemed meager to set out with on a trip that could last for a long, long time. Seeing the small quantity of flour and coffee beans, he said, "I shoulda opened those packs that son of a bitch had on his horse," thinking of his son-in-law's sudden departure. "He damn sure took a generous share."

He paused to listen when his horse whinnied in the corral, but made no effort to investigate until he suddenly heard a horse lope into the clearing. He dropped the sack of coffee beans and grabbed the rifle propped against the table. Running to slam the open door, he was stopped in his tracks, hardly believing his eyes.

"Papa!" Joanna cried breathlessly when she saw him. Sliding from her horse, she almost stumbled in her excitement to reach her father.

Stunned almost to the point of collapsing, the old man had to grab the doorjamb for support until he realized that it really was Joanna returned from the dead. "Oh, baby girl," he repeated over and over as he looked at his daughter's bruised and swollen face. Pulling her close in his arms, he whispered, "You're home, you're home." Still holding his daughter tightly, he glanced up to discover a man slowly walking his horse into the clearing. Astonished, he asked, "Who's that?"

Without relaxing her embrace, she said, "Clint Conner, he's the reason I'm back home safe." Releasing him then, she asked, "Where's Robert—at the claim?" The moment of joy for Karl was suddenly lost, replaced by one of reluctance. Seeing the baleful look in her father's eyes, she exclaimed, "Is Robert all right?"

Knowing of no way to tell her that would not devastate her, he came out with it. "Robert's not here. He packed up and went back east."

"What?" she gasped, unable to understand. "Why?"

"Why? I don't know," he said, not wishing to tell her that her husband didn't want her after she had been with the Indians. "Because he ain't fit to wear men's clothes, I reckon. It's good riddance I say." He motioned toward the supplies covering the table. "I was fixing to go search for you again, but he wouldn't even do that." He held her by her shoulders and looked into her eyes. "It's better you found out what he was made of now, instead of later on," he said.

Joanna was staggered, her brain reeling as much as it did from the physical blows she suffered from the broad-shouldered warrior. *Robert gone!* She felt all the blood drain from her head, and had to sink to the floor to keep from fainting. With the unspeakable abuse she had endured, she expected to need some time for herself to recover. But if she never spoke of these things, she had hoped Robert would understand, never question her or press for details. There had never been any thought that he might abandon her. It was not her fault she had been abducted. How could Robert blame her, and look upon her as soiled? He didn't even wait around to find out for sure.

A silent observer to the tragic homecoming, Clint found himself furious for Joanna. In the few days they had traveled together, he had known her to be a fine and decent woman, and deserving of an understanding husband. As his fury subsided, he felt a wave of compassion for the jilted woman, but there was nothing he could think of to alleviate her pain. So he turned Joanna's horse out in the small corral and left the grieving father and daughter to their sorrow without the intrusion of his presence.

He was checking the buckskin's front hooves when he heard Karl Steiner coming up behind him. He stood up to face him. "Mr. Conner," Karl greeted him, and extended his hand.

"Clint," Clint corrected him, shaking his hand.

"Clint," Karl repeated, talking with a thick German accent. "I apologize for my lack of hospitality, but it was a bad time for my daughter. I had to tell her some bad things."

"Yessir," Clint responded. "I couldn't help but overhear. I'm real sorry for Joanna. She deserves better. I'm sorry about your wife, too. I expect I'd best get along and let you folks have your privacy."

"No, sir," Karl replied emphatically. "I wouldn't hear of it. Joanna told me what you did for her—and for me. I have you to thank for giving me back my daughter. No, sir, I insist you stay with us. Joanna's strong. She's in the house now, starting supper, and she would never forgive you if you didn't stay."

"I don't wanna be in the way with her feelin' so bad right now," Clint said.

"Clint, she wants you to stay. She feels she owes you for her life. Hell, man, I owe you for bringing my daughter back. Anything you want that I can give, I owe you."

Clint nodded his surrender. "A cup of coffee'll do, I reckon."

"Well, I can certainly manage that," Karl said with a wide grin. "Put your horses in the corral with mine and come on in the house."

As soon as her father left to go talk to Clint, Joanna went to her room and changed out of the dirty torn dress she had been wearing since she was taken. She told herself to be strong, that she could live with the stigma of being discarded, and she was determined to show a strong resolve for Clint's sake. She was burning the dirty dress in the fireplace when the men came in. It could have been washed and mended, but she would never wear that dress again, and she didn't want it around to remind her.

"I hope that wasn't supper," Karl said, not really having seen what was going up in flames.

Clint got a glimpse of the material he had been seeing every day, and knew at once the significance of the cremation. Joanna glanced in his direction, but would not meet his gaze lest he saw the redness from crying. "Sit down, Clint," she said. "I'll get you some coffee." There were so many things troubling her mind, her mother's death, her captivity, her husband's desertion, but she was determined to remain strong at this moment. There would be time later, when alone in her bed, when she could succumb to her grief.

Clint watched her closely as she went about preparing a meal for them. It seemed there was a sadness in her face that was not there while the two of them were searching the mountains for the cabin. He felt that it was not entirely due to the shock of finding her husband gone, but also because she was faced with the reality of her mother's death. During the time when the two of them were concerned with the possibility of being found by another war party, there was little time to dwell on other things. His concern now was the sense of security she and her father might feel just because they were home. In his mind, there was no safety for the two of them in this remote cabin. It was just a matter of time before the next war party found them. Further thought on the matter was interrupted when Joanna set a plate of beans and biscuits before him.

"Sorry, but this is about all I could scare up on short notice," she said. "It's not much for grown men, but maybe it'll keep your stomach warm."

"I'm afraid I haven't been thinking much about fresh meat for a while," Karl apologized.

"I reckon that's understandable," Clint said. "That's one thing I can do for you. I'll go huntin' in the mornin'. Lord knows I saw plenty of sign on the way in."

When supper was finished, Clint and Joanna's father remained seated at the table drinking coffee while Joanna cleaned up the dishes. After listening to Joanna's account of the days following her rescue, until they showed up here at the cabin, Karl began to tell Clint about his journey from Germany when Joanna was a baby. And before he wound down, he had taken Clint through every phase of his and his family's life, from New York to Missouri, to Omaha, and finally to this cabin in the Black Hills. Halfway through, Clint caught Joanna's gaze, and she rolled her eyes heavenward as a sign of boredom. Clint smiled at her, understanding the old man's need to talk about the past.

Finished at last, Karl paused to light his pipe, puffing out great clouds of gray smoke. "I guess I've been doing all the talking," he confessed. "I must apologize."

"Quite all right," Clint replied.

"What about you, Clint?" Karl asked, settling back in his chair. "Joanna said you were on your way to Montana."

"That's a fact," Clint said.

Hoping for more of a response than that, Karl continued to probe. "Where in Montana?"

"Can't say for sure. I reckon I'll know when I find it."

"You got family?" Karl asked in an effort to get his guest to open up a little. Unnoticed by both men, the question prompted Joanna to pause and listen.

"Nope, just my pa back in Cheyenne," Clint answered, reluctant to delve any deeper.

"What are you planning on doing when you get to Montana?" Karl pressed.

As interested as her father in the young man's plans, Joanna, however, perceived the reluctance on Clint's part. "Papa, for goodness' sake, let the poor man drink his coffee. You'll wear him out with your questions."

Her father jerked his head back with a mock expression of surprise. "I'm sorry. I didn't mean to be nosey." He chuckled and winked at Clint. Then to Joanna he explained, "I had already been thinking about pulling out of here myself, even before those savages ran off with you. I hadn't said anything to Robert about it, but I was thinking about going on up to the Yellowstone with your uncle Frederick. That's why I was interested in what part of Montana Clint was heading for. We weren't scraping enough gold out of that stream to buy salt and flour. And Frederick has always tried to get me to join him up there." He glanced over at Clint then. "My younger brother went out to Montana with two other families a year ago. They're farming a strip of land on the lower side of the Yellowstone River where the Tongue River connects with it. I thought if you're going up Montana way, it might be a good time for us to pull up stakes and go with you—as far as the Yellowstone, anyway. There ain't a helluva lot of summer left, so I was thinking I'd better get going if we're going to do it. I think it would be better for Joanna, too, to be around other folks instead of wasting away up here with an old man. Of course, you might not want any company." He looked at Clint and waited for his response.

"It's fine with me," Clint replied at once. "I think you're asking for more trouble if you stay here in these mountains by yourself." He was actually relieved to know that Joanna would not be at the mercy of any roving Sioux raiding parties that happened upon the isolated cabin. Equally relieved, Joanna smiled her approval.

The next few days were spent in preparation for the journey north. It could have been done more quickly, but for the need for fresh meat. So Clint spent one day hunting in the mountain ridges for deer. As he had noticed before, there was plenty of deer sign close to the cabin, and they were not hard to find. He came upon a small herd drinking from a spring at the bottom of a ravine. Since he planned to smoke the meat to preserve it, he passed up a shot at a ten-point buck in favor of a medium-sized one. He wanted a deer that was in good condition without much fat; the less fat, the better and quicker the meat would dry.

Back at the cabin, he and Karl cut four forked stakes to support the drying frame they fashioned; then the venison

was cut in strips to hang from racks made from tree limbs
over a fire pit dug in the yard. One whole day was required
to properly dry the jerky, but there was enough to last them
for the journey to Montana. When all was ready to depart,
Karl closed the door to the cabin that had been his family's
home for only eight months. He and Joanna made one last
visit to the grave of his late wife before stepping up in the
saddle. There were no happy memories left there by him or
his daughter as they followed Clint up the side of the ridge,
each rider leading a packhorse, loaded with the earthly pos-
sessions of all three.

With no real knowledge of the country they had set out to
cross, they went back in the general direction Clint and
Joanna had come from when he brought her home. Reaching the Belle Fourche, they decided to follow the course that
Clint had originally picked before his encounter with
Joanna's abductors. "I figured on holding to a north and
slightly west trail, figured I had to hit the Yellowstone somewhere," Clint said. "Once we strike the Yellowstone, I
reckon then we'll have to figure out which way to go to find
your brother's place."

Less than a day's ride found them approaching the banks
of another river. Recollecting the planned route that his
brother had told him about back in Omaha, Karl speculated
that it might be the Powder, and he knew that the place his
brother described was at the confluence of the Tongue and
the Yellowstone. "If we keep bearing to the west, we'll
reach the Tongue River," he said. "Then we can follow it
north to the Yellowstone."

"That suits me just fine," Clint responded. "I ain't ever
seen any of this country before."

They camped by the river that night and started out on a
more westerly course the next morning. A little before the
sun was directly overhead they came upon a trail apparently

left by an entire village of Indians on the move. The trail led directly from the west, causing Clint and Karl to decide it best to turn a little more north so as not to chance overtaking them. Stopping only long enough to rest the horses, they pushed on until almost nightfall, crossing several other trails of smaller Indian parties heading west. As the sun settled lower in the prairie to the west, they spotted another river by the line of trees in the distance. "I was hoping we'd come up on a stream or river or something before dark," Karl said.

"Maybe I'd better ride on ahead and take a look around before we go ridin' into those trees," Clint decided. "As much Indian sign as we've seen today, I wouldn't be surprised if there was someone else camping there already."

"Might not be a bad idea," Karl concurred. "Joanna and I will stay back here below this ridge till you call us in."

With his rifle cradled across his arms, Clint held Rowdy to a comfortable lope until he reached the edge of a line of cottonwoods that bordered a river. Walking the buckskin slowly through the brush and trees, he looked the bank over for the best place to camp. He had just about settled upon a spot when he noticed that Rowdy's ears, seldom still, were now pricked up as if he heard something. *Could be he senses something*, Clint thought, *animal or man. I'd best take a look.*

He dismounted, looped Rowdy's reins over a berry bush, and with his rifle ready, walked farther along the bank. By then the approaching evening dusk had descended upon the riverbank and the daylight faded away, affording him the cover of darkness. He had walked no more than a few dozen yards when he discovered the cause of Rowdy's concern. Through the trees that skirted the water, he saw the faint flicker of a flame. *That's what I was afraid of*, he thought, and cautiously edged his way to get a better look.

Before moving any closer, he paused to check the wind,

concerned that a horse might announce his presence. He determined that he was downwind, so he kept moving forward until he reached a large cottonwood that afforded ample cover while giving him a better look at the camp. He was immediately relieved to see only two horses and apparently one man sleeping on the other side of a small campfire. From the look of things, he wasn't sure whether he was an Indian or not.

He considered whether he should hail the camp or go back and get his horse and then ride in. Even if he was a white man, Clint had no way of knowing what manner of man would be traveling through Indian country alone. Maybe, he thought, it might be wiser to go back for Karl and Joanna, then move downriver a mile or so, and let this traveler be. *Probably the smartest*, he decided, and turned to retrace his steps.

Making his way through the darkened trees, he returned to his horse to find Rowdy still fidgeting nervously. "It's just me, boy," Clint said in an effort to calm the horse. "Looks like a peaceful traveler. We'll just let him be."

"I'm right glad to hear that, friend." Clint whirled at once, his rifle before him, searching for the source of the words. "Take her easy, there," the voice came again, "you ain't got nothin' to fear from me."

Although he still couldn't tell which tree the man was behind, Clint relaxed his defensive stance. He figured if whoever it was intended to shoot him, he would already have done so. As soon as he did, a gnarled little knot of a man stepped out from behind a tree, dressed head to foot in buckskins. He carried a Remington Rolling Block rifle, and when he rested the butt on the ground, the muzzle of the long heavy barrel was even with his shoulder. As speechless as if a gnome or a forest spirit had suddenly materialized from the darkness, Clint stood gaping at the little man.

"I seen you when you was ridin' across that ridge back yonder," the man said. "These days, it's a good idea to check on who's checkin' on you, so I circled back around here while you were takin' a look at my camp."

Clint couldn't help but chuckle, even though he'd been outfoxed by the harmless-looking little man. "I reckon that's fair enough," he allowed.

"What in tarnation are you doin' out here? Ain't you heard about Little Big Horn?"

"No. What about it?"

The elfish little man explained that there had been a terrible battle on the Little Big Horn, and that Colonel George Custer had suffered a massacre. Though mildly shocked by the news, Clint figured there was nothing he could do about it now. "My name's Clint Conner," he said. "I've got a couple of friends back yonder behind that last ridge, a man and his daughter. We were fixin' to make camp, on our way to Yellowstone country."

"Billy Turnipseed," the little man replied, stepping forward to shake Clint's hand. "Go on back and get your friends, and you're welcome at my campfire. I done et, but I'd be proud to boil you some coffee—if I had some coffee beans. You ain't got some by any chance, have you?"

Clint laughed again. "Yeah, we've got some coffee. I'll go fetch my friends." He slipped his rifle back in the saddle sling and stepped up on Rowdy.

Billy backed away to give him room to turn the horse. "I'm thinkin' you might be the feller that shot them Injuns over near the Belle Fourche. I heard that Red Hand said that man rode a buckskin horse like this one, and had a woman with him." Clint checked the big horse momentarily, wondering whether that might change things. Billy grinned and said, "They said he had a *Spirit Gun* that didn't miss." He turned to go to his camp. "Go get your folks, and we'll drink some coffee. I ain't had no coffee in a long time."

When Clint led Karl and Joanna into the little clearing by the riverbank, Billy Turnipseed had recharged his fire and moved his saddle back away from it. After the introductions were made, Clint and Karl took care of the horses while Joanna ground some coffee beans, and soon the coffeepot was boiling away. Although Billy had already eaten, he reconsidered and accepted Joanna's offer to share their supper. She made a thick soup by boiling some of the deer jerky with dried beans, thickened with a small amount of flour. It was good eatin', Billy testified.

While they sat around the fire, finishing the coffee, Billy told them how he happened to be a lone trapper and hunter in the midst of several Indian tribes that were growing more and more hostile. "I've rode the Powder River valley, up and down, back and forth, for over fifteen years by my calculations—at least as nigh as I remember. I've trapped over as far as Three Forks, up the Milk and the Musselshell, and the Missouri as far as Fort Benton. But mostly, I've been after buffalo for the last few years."

"How is it you don't have any trouble with the Indians?" Karl asked.

"I get along fine with the Injuns," Billy said as he wiped the remains of his soup from his whiskers and licked his fingers. "Lived with 'em for a few years—old Angry Bear's Lakotas. They even give me a name, *Sung ma< he tu.*"

"What's it mean?" Karl asked.

Billy giggled. "Coyote," he said. "Old Angry Bear said I weren't much bigger than a coyote, but I could take a buffalo down just the same."

Clint found the spry little man entertaining, with his shaggy beard draped across his wrinkled face from ear to ear like a tablecloth spread over a knotty oak table. "Don't the Sioux resent you killin' buffalo?" he asked.

"Nah, not me. They know I just kill what I need to get by. I ain't doin' it to sell the hides." He winked at Joanna and said, "Ever' once in a while, though, I take a couple of extra hides to swap for coffee and tobacco."

"Which way are you headin'?" Clint asked when there was a lull in the conversation.

"South," Billy answered, "goin' to Fort Laramie. Maybe trade them hides you seen under my blanket."

Clint laughed. He explained to Karl and Joanna that Billy had placed his blanket over a bundle of hides to make it look like a man sleeping while he circled around to Clint's horse. "Well, I didn't know how friendly you folks were," Billy confessed.

"Maybe you can give us a little help," Clint said. "None of us know the country we're ridin' through. We camped last night on a river, took us all day to get here. Is this the Powder?"

"You really don't know where in the bejesus you are, do you?" Billy replied patiently. "No, son, this ain't the Powder. This is the Little Powder. That river you camped on last night I expect is the Little Missouri. You say you're tryin' to get to the Yellowstone?"

Clint nodded and said, "Where it meets the Tongue."

"Whaddaya wanna go there for?"

"My brother and some other families are farming some land near there," Karl said.

Billy grimaced at the mention of farmers, but offered his advice. "You'd best follow this river north. It'll take you about two days before you come to the fork where this meets up with the Powder. You can cut across northwest from there, 'cause you wanna strike the Tongue and follow that on in. I oughta tell you, though, after you leave the fork at the

Powder, you'll strike a fair-sized creek in about half a day. You might wanna follow that creek for another half a day or so before you go west again to strike the Tongue. There's a lot of Injun goin's-on in that country right now. There's whole villages of Injuns scatterin' in all directions since the fight at the Little Horn. You folks best keep a sharp eye where you're goin' 'cause they ain't too friendly to white folks." He cocked an eye in Clint's direction. "Especially one that's killed four of Red Hand's warriors. I expect Red Hand's already lookin' for you. I noticed the lady rode in settin' an Injun saddle, and I'd guess three of them horses is Injun ponies. They ain't wearin' no shoes." He turned his head to talk directly to Clint then. "So you keep your eyes open, son, and keep that Winchester you're totin' ready to use."

With the dawning of a new day, they bid farewell to Billy "Coyote" Turnipseed and followed the Little Powder north. The strange little man left, happily carrying a small sack of coffee beans given him by Joanna after warning Clint once again to be careful. Heeding Billy's advice, Clint kept an observant eye out as they made their way north. They rode close by the river, since it was the quickest cover available in case of an encounter with hostiles, but they saw no sign of Indian activity all day long. At the end of the day they rode into the trees to make camp.

Joanna walked along the riverbank until she was certain she was out of sight of the camp. Once she was sure of her privacy, she removed her shoes and stockings, removed her cotton underpants, and waded out into the cool water. With her skirt tied up around her waist, she walked out until the water was well over her knees. Looking around her again, fearful of being seen by one of the men, she then examined the large bruises on the insides of her thighs. Blue and just beginning to turn yellow, they no longer ached as before, but the sickening feeling the sight of them provoked would live with her a long time. She thought then of Robert, and pictured him riding away from the cabin, unable to bear the thought of living with a wife who had been ravaged by savages. *Maybe I shouldn't blame him*, she thought. *Robert was not a strong or capable man.* She surprised herself with the thought, realizing that she had never labeled her husband that way before. She was not ready to admit that it was probably brought about by a comparison with Clint. She resolved to think less of Robert Becker. That part of her life was over.

Clint came to an abrupt halt when he was suddenly surprised by the sight of the young woman standing in the river in water over her knees. With her skirt tied up around her waist, there was a generous portion of her slender thighs exposed. He could not help but pause a moment to stare, grateful that her back was turned toward him. But a moment was all he would allow himself before quietly turning around and withdrawing to search for firewood on the other side of the camp. The incident set his mind to thinking, however, and he wondered what manner of man Robert Becker was. *He couldn't have been much*, Clint thought, *to go off and leave his wife like that.* He considered for a moment the possibility that he might take a wife someday. *I can't see it*, he decided. *I'll probably be a loner all my life—end up like Billy Turnipseed.*

# Chapter 9

Just as Billy Turnipseed had said, they came to the fork of the Little Powder and the Powder in the afternoon of the second day. There were plenty of signs that a fairly large village of Indians had recently camped there. They were obviously moving fast because there were no signs of tipi rings, but many cook fires.

"It wasn't too long ago," Clint commented after examining the ashes in one of the cook fires. "I expect if we'd gotten here day before yesterday, we mighta been invited for supper."

"We mighta *been* supper," Karl retorted. "I'm just as glad we're late."

Clint glanced at Joanna. Her tight frown told him that she was not ready to joke about anything to do with the Sioux. He quickly changed the subject, thinking that she would be a lot more comfortable away from the abandoned Sioux camp. "There's still a lot of daylight left. Maybe we could keep moving, and hope to strike that creek he told us about before dark." Joanna quickly agreed, and Karl was willing to ride on.

*   *   *

Lying flat on his belly on the grass-covered crest of a long mesa, Clint watched the procession of Lakota men, women, and children on the opposite bank of the creek. At a distance of approximately three hundred yards, he could count twenty-two horses with eight male riders, and maybe five female. Walking along with the rest of the pony herd were a number of women and children.

"Are they still heading off to the northeast?" Karl asked as he crawled up beside Clint. That was the general direction of most of the Indian trails they had crossed during the past two days.

"Nope," Clint answered. "They started followin' the creek." He looked up at the fading afternoon light. "I expect they're gettin' ready to make camp." He turned back to Karl. "We'd best cut around this mesa and strike the creek a mile or two north of their camp."

They continued north, following the creek until darkness threatened to overtake them. Finally selecting a spot where a stand of willows and berry bushes provided a suitable screen from any chance riders that happened by, Clint said, "This'll have to do, I reckon. I'll build a fire in that gully after I see to the horses."

"I can build the fire," Joanna said. "You and Papa take care of the horses."

"All right," Clint said. He couldn't help but notice that her "take charge" attitude seemed to have surfaced again since leaving the spot where the Sioux camp had been.

Supper was the same as every night before since leaving the cabin, beans boiled with some of the deer jerky. Clint would have killed fresh meat but for the presence of so much Indian sign. In fact, they continued to come upon so many recent trails of Indians on the move that Joanna approached Clint with a request before they went to sleep that night. "I want you to let me have that pistol you left with me when the savages attacked us in the ravine," she said.

"Why, sure," he replied. "I'da given it to you before if I knew you wanted to tote a gun." He went at once to get it from his saddlebag. Upon returning with the weapon, he checked the cylinder. "It's loaded with five cartridges. It's settin' on an empty cylinder. Just cock it and she's ready."

He gazed into her eyes as she took the revolver, reading the deep determination registered there, and immediately felt the hurt in her heart. She did not request the weapon for the sole purpose of helping to ward off an Indian attack. He wished that he could promise her that he would let nothing happen to her, but he knew that she wanted the pistol to ensure that she would never be taken alive by hostiles again. "I'll get you to your folks," he said softly.

She nodded, then withdrew to her blanket. If any man would defend her, she was confident that Clint would be the one man who could. But even Clint could not prevail against an attack by a group as large as the camp they had seen that afternoon. *I will never be taken by savages again*, she vowed as she tucked the revolver up under her blanket.

The night passed without incident, and respecting Billy Turnipseed's advice, they continued north along the creek for another day before striking due west to find the Tongue River. Once it was found, they followed the winding river through seemingly endless stretches of open prairie for two days before sighting what could be nothing but the Yellowstone in the distance. They discovered a rough shack on the south bank just before dusk, providing an immense sense of relief to see some sign of white men, even though a hand-painted sign nailed over the door proclaimed the building to be a saloon. The next order of business was to find Karl's brother.

"I can go in and ask," Clint suggested to Karl. "A saloon

ain't a fit place for a lady, so you and Joanna can wait out here."

"All right," Karl said, "but don't go in there and start drinking unless you bring me a bottle, too."

"I'm goin' in for directions, only. We'll drink after we get where we're goin'."

"Frederick Steiner?" the bartender, a short, heavyset man, echoed. He scratched his bald head while he tried to recollect. "I can't say I know the man."

"He's supposed to have a place near here," Clint said. "I think there's a few families that claimed land to farm."

"Well, if they're farmin', it would have to be on this side of the river. The land on the other side ain't much fit for farmin'."

There were a couple of men drinking at the rough plank bar when Clint walked in, and they paused to listen to the conversation. One of them, a coarse-looking man with a face full of whiskers, wearing two six-guns with the handles facing forward, spoke up then. "You might be lookin' for that group of German folks that moved onto some land east of Wolf Creek."

"That sounds like the folks I'm lookin' for," Clint said.

"I can tell you how to get there. Just follow the river east," the stranger said, "past the tradin' post, I'd say a good four or five miles. The first house is just the other side of Wolf Creek. I think there're three houses all told, if I remember correctly. I ain't been over that way in about six months."

"I'm obliged," Clint replied.

"If you're drivin' a wagon, it might be rough goin'. You're gonna have a slew of deep gullies to get around. Might be a little chancy in the dark."

"No wagon," Clint replied as he turned to leave. "Much

obliged." The stranger and his companion strolled casually over to the door behind him.

Outside, Clint repeated the directions to Karl and Karl nodded slowly. "Sounds like the place," he said. "Frederick said there were three families that started out from Omaha."

"Accordin' to what that fellow said," Clint recalled, "it's four or five miles to the first house, and we don't have any idea which house is your brother's. You wanna try to find him tonight, or wait till daylight?"

Karl paused to give it consideration. "It is getting pretty late. Might be best to make camp one more night and look for Frederick in the morning." He turned to his daughter then. "How about it, Joanna, think you can stand one more night on the trail?"

"I think it would be a lot better than rousting everybody out in the middle of the night, since Uncle Frederick doesn't even know we're coming. Besides, we don't even know how to find his house. It could be any one of the three."

"All right," Clint said, eyeing the two men lolling against the saloon doorjambs, "but I think we oughta ride on down the river a piece before we make camp."

Leading the way, and picking his path carefully in the moonless night, Clint guided the buckskin downstream, holding close to the banks of the Yellowstone. After a mile or so, he came upon a clump of cottonwood trees that formed a screen around a grassy knoll. "This looks like as good a place as any," he announced.

They dismounted, and while the men took care of the horses, Joanna built a fire. Soon venison strips were sizzling over the fire and coffee was boiling in the pot. The conversation was light on this last night on the trail. The dangerous passage through the Powder River country was behind them and spirits were high. "What are your plans now that we're almost there, Clint?" It was Joanna who asked the question.

Clint shrugged his shoulders. "I'm not really sure. Like I've said from the beginning, I wanna see the territory, maybe ride on to the mountains west of here." He preferred not to mention that he felt it necessary to locate a place where he didn't have to worry about being found by a lawman.

"You oughta stay on here with us," Karl said. He had taken a liking to the young man during the past week.

"Oh, I don't know," Clint replied, "I ain't much of a farmer."

"I expect it wouldn't take a lot to show you how," Karl said, then chuckled when he added, "I found out I'm a better farmer than a gold miner."

Watching Clint's reaction closely, Joanna commented. "I think Clint still hears the call of the wild hawk. He wants to raise his horses and live the free life with no crops to look after or hold him in one spot." Even though she believed it to be true, she wished it were not so. She felt safe when Clint was around.

"Maybe," Clint replied. "I've got a long way to go before I can be thinkin' about raising horses. All I've got is Rowdy and those three Indian ponies, and Rowdy can't do much to make a herd. He's a geldin', so he don't even glance at that little mare. I think I've got a lot of work ahead of me before I can call myself a wrangler."

The conversation changed to speculation about the morning when they would find Frederick's place, and after a while, Karl announced that he was turning in. "Tomorrow's a big day," he said, and moved a little away from the fire to make his bed. Joanna and Clint remained to talk for a short while before deciding they should follow Karl's lead.

Moving off to the opposite side of the fire from the

woman and her father, Clint rolled up in his blanket. Soon the camp was quiet except for the steady rhythm of Karl's snoring, but Clint could not fall asleep. His senses told him all was not right, and he kept thinking about the two men at the saloon, especially the one who did all the talking. He had the look of a predator about him, and although he had been friendly enough, Clint didn't trust him. After a while, when the sense of alertness would not leave him, he crawled out of his blanket, pulled his rifle from his saddle sling, and walked back in the trees to check on the horses.

Rowdy lowered his head and rubbed his muzzle against Clint's chest, and received a scratching behind his ears in return. While Clint was stroking his horse's neck, Rowdy's ears suddenly pricked up and the Indian horses whinnied softly. Always alert to the horses' warning signals, Clint quickly looked around him in the darkened grove of trees. He saw nothing at first glance. Then a slight motion off to his left, like a fleeting shadow, caught his attention and he dropped to one knee. Peering into the dark shadows, he could not detect any movement, but he was sure that his eyes had not been playing tricks on him. Continuing to stare into the inky void, he began to inch toward the spot where he thought he had detected movement. He quickly dropped to one knee again when suddenly two shadows separated from the black tree trunks and moved toward the camp. He didn't have to guess who the visitors were.

Moving as quickly as he could through the brush while making as little noise as possible, he hurried to overtake them, but they had already reached the sleeping figures by the fire before he cleared the trees.

The sudden report of a pistol split the still night air, bringing Karl and Joanna bolting up from their slumber. "Time to get up!" the man with the shaggy beard shouted. He fired another shot into the ground beside Karl. "Let's have a look in them packs. You might as well save us the trouble of goin' through 'em. Tell us where the money is and maybe you'll live a little longer."

His partner, a tall thin man, had set eyes upon Joanna. His lips parted in an evil grin and he said, "You might live a little longer at that, sweetheart." Joanna cringed and pulled her blanket up close to her neck. Then it occurred to him. "Where's the other one?"

He was answered by the sound of a Winchester rifle cocking. "I'm right here, asshole."

The thin man made a fatal miscalculation when he attempted to raise his pistol to beat a rifle slug already on the way. He took a couple of steps backward before dropping to the ground, shot through the heart. His partner, quicker of wit, immediately grabbed Joanna, pulled her to her feet, and held her before him with the barrel of his pistol pressed against her throat. "Now, damn you," he spat, "me and the little missy here is gonna back outta here real slow. This here .44 has got a hair trigger, so I wouldn't advise you to try nothin' fancy."

Clint said nothing, but put the rifle butt against his shoulder and took dead aim. He walked slowly forward, following his prey while the bearded one dragged Joanna away from the fire. The rifle never wavered as Clint stalked the man, who held Joanna tightly before him, keeping the gun pressed against her neck while trying to keep his head almost hidden behind hers. Clint continued to stalk, waiting, his rifle aimed, until the man looked quickly behind him to see where he was going. It was only for an instant, but when he jerked his head back to watch Clint, he was met with a bullet that put a neat hole in the middle of his forehead.

Joanna screamed when the rifle suddenly barked and the bullet thudded against her abductor's brow. She felt the pistol drop from her throat, and the man sagged to the ground, killed instantly. Her nerves shattered, she screamed out in relief, but also in anger. As Clint walked up to make sure the second outlaw was dead, Joanna ran to him and threw her arms around him, screaming, "Damn you! You could have killed me!" Still trying to control her emotions, she pressed her face against his chest, not sure whether to thank him or curse him for risking her life.

"I knew I wouldn't miss," he calmly explained.

Karl, still in a mild state of shock over the sudden chaos that interrupted his sleep, could do little more than gape at his daughter clinging to Clint so desperately. When he finally found his voice, it was only to utter, "What . . . ? Where did they . . . ?"

"That's the two fellers back at the saloon," Clint explained while totally aware of the young woman still pressing tightly against his body.

Suddenly aware as well, Joanna released him and quickly backed away. "I'm sorry," she said, embarrassed to have surrendered to her emotions. "I thought I was shot. I felt the bullet right next to my face."

His composure regained, Karl shook his head in wonder. "That was a helluva shot," he said, "a dangerous shot."

"I knew I wouldn't miss," Clint repeated earnestly. "I couldn't let him back outta here with Joanna. They weren't plannin' on leavin' any of us alive. They didn't wear masks or anythin' to keep us from seein' their faces."

"He's right, Papa," Joanna said. "They planned to kill us all." *And something worse for me before they killed me*, she thought. Only then did she remember the loaded revolver tucked under the edge of her blanket, and chided herself for lacking the presence of mind to have used it.

With Karl's help, Clint dragged the bodies away from their camp and deposited them in a deep gully near the river. Then Clint walked back along the river until he found their horses tied in a clump of berry bushes. *Well, it ain't the way I planned to build a herd*, he thought, *but there ain't no use in leaving them.*

In spite of the fact that there was no more danger, there was not much chance of deep sleep for the rest of the night. The morning sun was greeted with a general sense of relief as Joanna rustled up some breakfast while Clint and Karl loaded packs and saddled horses. Clint checked on the bodies again, ridding them of weapons and ammunition before breaking camp and leaving the tragic scene behind them. A clear day before them, and the anticipation of reuniting with brother and uncle, served to lighten the atmosphere for the travelers, but Karl would never forget the machinelike reactions of his young friend in the execution of the two men. He would also remember his daughter's clinging to Clint instead of running to her father. That could signal trouble ahead.

"So, you're Frederick Steiner's brother," Peter Weber exclaimed, amazed by the visitors at his door. "I should have known without you telling me. You favor him." He turned to call back in the house, "Martha, come out here and say hello to Frederick's brother and his daughter."

Clint stood by the horses and watched the introductions. Martha Weber made a big fuss over Joanna, and in a few minutes the Webers' two teenage sons joined the meeting. Then Clint was drawn into the mix, and Karl tried to explain that he was not Joanna's husband, Robert. The Webers tried to persuade them to come inside so Martha could fix a meal, but understood when Karl insisted that he was anxious to find his brother.

"Well, you can't miss Frederick's place," Weber said. "Just follow that wagon track along the river. His is the next house you'll come to." The whole Weber family stood in the yard and waved them good-bye.

"Nice folks," Karl commented as he rode alongside Joanna.

They rode about three-quarters of a mile before they spotted a sturdy log house where a creek emptied into the river. There was a large garden in front of the house with a man and a boy cleaning out a couple of rows of dead vines. Karl started chuckling as he kicked his horse into a fast lope and headed toward the two. Frederick looked up, startled by the sudden appearance of a man on horseback. He stood up then, seeing two more riders, leading horses, coming along behind. "Hey-yo! Freddy!" Karl sang out as he drove the horse into the corner of the garden.

"Karl!" Frederick exclaimed, hardly able to believe his eyes. He turned quickly to his son. "As I live and breathe, it's your uncle Karl!" Dropping his hoe, he ran to meet his brother. Karl jumped out of the saddle and the two brothers embraced with an abundance of back-slapping and bear hugs. "I swear, I never thought you'd come out here. What happened to the gold mining?" Before Karl could answer, he exclaimed, "And you brought Joanna and Robert with you! Where's Sarah?"

Karl paused but a moment to shake hands with his nephew, John, before replying, "Well, truth is, I brought Joanna. Robert went back east." He paused and swallowed hard before going further. "Sarah's dead, killed by Sioux Indians."

Frederick was shocked. "Oh my Lord," he moaned. "I can't believe Sarah's gone. I'm so sorry, Karl." He paused and shook his head sadly. "And Robert, too?"

"Like I said, Robert took off after the Indians hit us. Left Joanna to her fate."

"Well, who is that fellow with her?"

Karl explained as quickly as he could before Clint and Joanna rode up to join them. In summary he said, "His name's Clint Conner, but the truth be told, he's an angel sent down to bring Joanna and me safely here." There was no time to offer explanation in answer to Frederick's look of astonishment.

"Uncle Freddy!" Joanna gushed, and ran to give her uncle a hug.

As he had at the Webers' place, Clint held back and watched the reunion, smiling for the obvious happy occasion while he tried to keep his little herd of horses out of Frederick's garden. Within minutes, the party was joined by Frederick's wife when she realized what was taking place in the garden, and the round of hugs was started again. After Frederick told Bertha about the death of her sister-in-law, Karl beckoned for Clint to come forward to be introduced.

"Welcome to my home, Mr. Conner," Frederick said, extending his hand. "Karl told me he was owing to you for seeing him and Joanna here safely."

"It's Clint," he answered awkwardly. "I was comin' to Montana, anyway."

"Well, let's don't stand out here in the garden," Bertha Steiner interrupted. "Come on up to the house and we'll find you folks something to eat."

"I'd be obliged if I could turn these horses out in your corral," Clint said.

"Sure," Frederick replied. "John can help you with those saddles and packs." His son stepped forward to shake hands with Clint.

While Clint and John took care of the horses, Karl explained Clint's presence and the absence of Robert. He told them about the futile attempts to pan gold in the Black Hills, the subsequent attacks by Indians, and the latest attempt upon their lives by outlaws. "But thanks to Clint's help, we finally made it here."

"I hope you've come to stay," Frederick said. "We've got a fine little farming community started here."

"That's what we had in mind," Karl said. "I hoped that I could find some good land and go back to farming."

"I'd take it as a godsend if you'd think about staying here with us," Frederick said. "To tell you the truth, I took on a bigger piece of land than I can handle. With just John and me, it's more than I can keep up with. I could sure use some help. Whaddaya say, Karl? We can build onto the back of the house so you and Joanna could have your own space, and we'll run this place together."

"Sounds good to me," Karl quickly agreed, and they shook on it while Bertha and Joanna beamed their approval.

"You couldn't have come at a better time," Frederick said. "I've got a field full of oats that are just about ready to harvest. John and I were gonna ask Weber next door if he could give us a hand. Now we won't have to."

Feeling a strong need to clean up before sitting down at the supper table, Clint borrowed a bar of soap from Bertha, picked up his saddlebags from the barn, and walked up the creek until he was out of sight of the house. After stripping down to his underwear and applying the soap liberally to his body, he rinsed in the cool water and returned to the bank to dry off. Thinking it had been too long between shaves, he rummaged through his belongings until he found the razor he had brought from his father's house. With no strap to sharpen the instrument, it produced a pretty rough shave, necessitating a second pass across his face. Although it left his face feeling raw and sensitive, he felt clean for the first time in a while. Changing into his cleanest dirty shirt, he pronounced himself fit to dine in genteel company.

Conversation in the kitchen stopped when he walked in, and he immediately felt a sudden flush of embarrassment as he witnessed the startled expressions on the faces of the women. "I thought I'd best clean up a little bit," he explained apologetically.

Bertha glanced at Joanna and grinned before turning back to behold the minor transformation of their guest. Joanna's look of astonishment slowly turned to a pleased smile. "Sit yourself down at the table—we're about ready to eat."

When he was told of the plans for the two brothers to go into partnership on the land, Clint felt that his obligation to Karl and Joanna was completed. His main concern was for Joanna, and now he felt she was safe and with people who cared for her. "I reckon I'll be movin' on in the mornin'," he told them as they sat around the supper table.

Joanna tried to hide the look of distress that suddenly registered upon her face. No one noticed it except Bertha, who smiled her understanding. Flushing slightly, Joanna quickly looked away before asking, "What are you going to do?"

Clint shrugged. "I guess I'm just goin' to see what I can see," he said.

"Which way you heading?" Frederick asked.

"I expect I'll look around this part of the country for a little bit, and then head west. I've got a strong notion to see the Rocky Mountains, maybe find me a spot on top of a mountain someplace where there's plenty of game for food and hides."

"And just live like a wild man?" Joanna blurted, unable to hide her disappointment.

"I reckon," was all he replied. He could not tell her that he felt he had no choice. The image of Zach Clayton entered his mind when the deputy marshal vowed to come after him. Then it suddenly hit him, like a punch in the solar plexus.

For the first time since his escape from prison he wished with all his heart that he had served his sentence, that he was free to do whatever he wanted without fear of running into a lawman. He looked up then to discover Joanna's gaze fixed upon him. "Maybe it ain't the way I want it," he offered in lame defense.

"Don't feel like you have to go right away," Frederick said. "You're welcome to stay on awhile until you get rested up and maybe get a few good meals in you. Bertha's a pretty good cook." He didn't express it, but from what Karl had told him about the young man's skill with a rifle, he might be handy to have around for a while. Ever since the news of the Custer massacre on the Little Big Horn, there had been reports of stray bands of Indians moving through the Yellowstone Valley.

"I wouldn't wanna be a bother," Clint replied.

"It's no bother," Bertha said. "Seems to me we owe you more than that."

Joanna said nothing, but watched Clint's reactions closely, waiting for his response. When he allowed that he might stay on for a couple of days if Bertha was sure he wouldn't be a burden, she quickly turned and busied herself with the supper dishes, afraid they might read the relief in her face.

When it was time for bed, Bertha suggested that Clint could sleep in the kitchen by the stove since the cabin was lacking in enough rooms for everyone. Clint graciously declined, saying he would be fine in the barn with his horses. Being an astute woman, as well as an observant one, Bertha said, "Joanna, why don't you take a lantern and go out with Clint so he can see to spread his bedroll?"

"John can do that," Frederick suggested.

"I want John to help me set up some beds for you," Bertha insisted. "Joanna can do it."

"You don't need to bother with that," Clint said. "I reckon I can—"

"Come on," Joanna interrupted. Taking the lantern Bertha offered, she started for the door. "You don't wanna spread your bedroll over something one of the horses left on the floor."

She held the lantern for him while he untied his bedroll from his saddle and spread it on some hay in a corner of the last stall. "Well, I reckon that'll do just fine," he said. "I appreciate the help."

"You're welcome," she said. "I haven't really had a chance to tell you how much I owe you—we owe you, Papa and I—for coming with us." When he started to protest that it wasn't necessary, she stopped him. "Clint, I owe you my life. I will always be grateful. I'll never forget what you did for me."

Embarrassed, he stared down at his feet and mumbled, "I'm just glad I came along when I did."

"So am I," she said. He looked up to meet her gaze. She whispered, "Thank you," and quickly reached up and kissed him lightly on the lips, then spun around and left him standing confused in the dark.

He went to bed, but he did not sleep for some time, his mind laboring now with thoughts new to him, the memory still lingering of her lips on his. He could not deny that he had come to look upon the woman fondly, but he had attributed his feelings to compassion for her misfortunes. He tried to recreate the incident in his mind. Her kiss had been quick, and maybe really only on the corner of his lips. She might have intended to kiss him on the cheek, as a sister would kiss her brother, and accidentally came too close to his lips. Perplexed, he told himself to forget about it. She was just grateful to him for saving her life.

# Chapter 10

Three days out of Fort Laramie, Zach Clayton followed an old trail that the army often used when heading north through the Powder River country. He didn't particularly like the idea that the three fugitives he was after had a sizable head start, but it didn't cause him excessive worry, either. A man confident in his ability to do his job, he knew he would strike their trail somewhere, and that he would prevail in the end. He didn't have to continue his pursuit of the three escapees into Montana. The job could have been passed off to the marshal in that territory, but he had volunteered to go after them to finish the job he should already have completed. He had never failed to bring in a fugitive he had been sent after, and he didn't want these three to be on his record. Aside from that, he felt a strong desire to rid the world of Clell Ballenger and Pete Yancey. The other one, the young man, he almost wished he could let go, but he knew that he couldn't.

He quickly put those thoughts aside when he spotted a single rider crossing a low mesa directly ahead of him. At that distance, it was impossible to determine it to be Indian or white, but it paid to be cautious until finding out which.

There was a narrow ravine to his right, so he decided to take advantage of it until he could identify the rider.

Leading his horse down into the ravine far enough to get it out of sight, he dismounted, drew his rifle, and knelt at the rim. Seeming to be in no particular hurry, the rider came down from the mesa to intercept the trail Clayton was following. Instead of crossing it, he turned onto it, now heading straight for the deputy marshal. Resting his rifle across his knee, Clayton watched the rider carefully. As he came closer, he at first thought it to be an Indian. But when the rider approached within a hundred yards, a grin crept slowly across his face. "Billy Turnipseed," he murmured.

He returned to his horse and mounted. Then he waited until Billy was just about even with the mouth of the ravine before suddenly riding up out of it to startle the unsuspecting little man. Billy pulled his horse to a stop while fumbling with his rifle in an attempt to pull it from his saddle sling. He had it barely halfway out when he recognized the laughing deputy riding toward him. "If I was a Sioux warrior," Clayton said, "you'd already be buzzard bait."

"Damn you, Zach Clayton," Billy fumed. "You're lucky I didn't shoot you." Trying to quickly regain his composure, he said, "I ain't worried about no Sioux warriors, anyway. I ain't got no trouble with Injuns." With his nerves settled once more, he grinned smugly. "I knew there was somebody hidin' in that ravine from way back yonder."

"Yeah, I could tell," Clayton chided him, "by the way you damn near fell offa that crow bait you're ridin'."

A bit embarrassed, and eager to change the subject, Billy asked, "What are you doin' up this way? Chasin' after some poor soul, I reckon."

"That's a fact," Clayton replied. "I'm lookin' for two lowlifes all right. One of 'em broke outta prison, name of

Clell Ballenger, and his sidekick, Pete Yancey. You ain't run into 'em, have you?"

"Nah. I ain't seen 'em. I ain't seen no white men for a spell. I been livin' with Angry Bear's folks on the Horn up until he moved his village to join up with ol' Sittin' Bull. Just come from the Big Horns. The only folks I've seen was three folks headin' to some settlement on the Yellowstone." He paused to chuckle over the thought of the encounter. "A young couple and an old man—I think the old man was the woman's pappy. Anyway, I wouldn't bet on them makin' it. They didn't know where they were or which way they were headin'. I had to tell 'em which way to go. They'll be damn lucky if they don't meet up with a Lakota war party."

"Is that so?" Clayton asked, only mildly interested. "It's a helluva time for three white people to be travelin' this territory alone. Did you catch their names?"

"Nah," Billy replied, then tried to recall. "The pappy's name was Claude or somethin' like that." He scratched his chin for a moment before remembering. "The other'n, the young one, his name was Clint." He shook his head confirming his memory. "Yep, Clint somethin'."

Clayton's interest was immediately triggered. "Clint Conner?"

"Mighta been," Billy said. "That sounds right."

"Ridin' a buckskin?"

"Matter of fact," Billy replied.

The deputy's mind was racing. The young fugitive just kept crossing his path. Billy might not have remembered the last name correctly, even though the old fellow seemed pretty sure. But who were his companions, the man and woman? "Where'd you meet these folks? How long ago?"

"Two or three days ago," Billy replied. "Have you got any tobacco? I swear I ain't had nothin' decent to smoke for five months."

Clayton smiled. He had never met Billy Turnipseed when the odd little man didn't ask for something. "Yeah, I've got a little bit of tobacco." He stepped down from his saddle and dug into his saddlebags. "Now, tell me exactly where you met up with these folks, and which way you sent 'em."

While Billy lit up his pipe, he told Clayton all he remembered about his overnight visit with the three travelers he met on the Little Powder. When he had finished, there was no doubt in Zach's mind that the young man Billy had camped with was Clint Conner. Still, it left him in a bit of a quandary. He was much more concerned with capturing Ballenger and Yancey than he was with Conner. He was convinced that Clint was not likely to cause anyone any trouble, while the other two were apt to murder and steal. To be considered, however, was the fact that he could only guess where Ballenger and Yancey were, and he knew now where Conner was, or thereabouts. He was sworn to bring all three in, so the sensible thing was to go after Conner before he took off somewhere else. He wasn't happy about it, but he decided to go after the bird in hand.

"I'm much obliged, Billy," Clayton said. "I reckon I'd best get goin' if I'm gonna catch up with Conner. You got your pouch? I can let you have a little more of this tobacco to hold you till you get to Fort Laramie."

"Yes, sir, I shore do," Billy replied at once. He pulled out his tobacco pouch and loosened the string. Peering down into the pouch, he expressed surprise. "Well, my stars, I didn't know . . . Why, there *is* a little bit of tobacco in there after all." He handed the pouch to Clayton.

Zach just shook his head and chuckled as he accepted the bag. Shaking a generous pinch of tobacco into it, he then handed it back to the grinning little man. "You take care of yourself, Billy."

\*      \*      \*

It was a pleasant time for Clint Conner, the first such time in several years. At Frederick and Bertha's insistence, as well as because of his personal desire, he stayed on for longer than the couple of days he first proposed. The Steiner brothers were happy to have his help harvesting the oats, and he gained a constant admirer in the person of thirteen-year-old John.

Nothing beyond polite conversation took place between Joanna and him as far as vocal communication was concerned. But for those who more closely observed, Bertha in particular, the silent signals of deeper thoughts were blatantly evident. It was inevitable that these thoughts and questions would come to surface between the two young people.

When the harvesting was finished, Clint spent more time with his horses, figuring that Rowdy and the other horses were getting fat and lazy while he had been working in the fields. Joanna walked out to the corral one afternoon when she saw him saddling the buckskin. "Where are you off to?" she asked.

"Nowhere in particular," he replied, "just thought I'd ride a little of the rust offa Rowdy." He smiled and shrugged. "I reckon all of 'em need a little exercise."

"If you'll saddle that little mare, I'll ride with you," she said. "I'm not ready to start supper yet, and I'd enjoy a ride." She paused, smiling. "Unless you don't care for any company."

"No, ma'am," he replied, "I'd be glad to have your company."

"Good . . . I'll just go tell Aunt Bertha I'm going." She turned and went to the house while he went into the barn to get her saddle.

"You take your time, honey," her aunt said, a satisfied smile traced along her closed lips. She took a step toward the bedroom door to sneak a peak at her niece as Joanna fretted over her appearance in the mirror.

*Why were you born so damn plain?* Joanna asked herself as she pinched her cheeks and smoothed her hair. *Would it have been asking too much for a little less forehead and a little more chin?* She traced her fingertip along the one scar that remained after her abduction by the three Sioux warriors. Aunt Bertha had told her that it was hardly noticeable, but to Joanna it stood out like a brand. Seeing it always reminded her of the circumstances under which it was received. *It's the best I can do*, she decided, turning her head first one way and then another in an effort to check her hair.

"You young folks enjoy your ride," Bertha said as Joanna started for the door. "Take your time. I don't need any help fixing supper." Joanna responded with an embarrassed smile, almost colliding with her uncle coming in from the barn.

"Where are they going?" Frederick asked Bertha after Joanna went out.

"Just going for a ride."

Aware of the smug look of mischief upon his wife's face, he took a long look after his niece before closing the door. "I don't know about this," Frederick fretted. "Joanna's a married woman."

"Bull feathers," Bertha replied. "If she's married, where's her husband? I never thought Robert Becker was good enough for Joanna, anyway. I'm not surprised he ran away at the first sign of trouble." Thinking of Clint then, she said, "Besides, I like that boy. I think they make a good pair."

They started out, following the wagon track that led to the third house in the line of families that came out together from Omaha. Leaving the road at the corner of Frederick's property, they continued on, following the river. As he looked across the Yellowstone, it was apparent to Clint why all the settlement was on this side of the river, for high rolling hills began at the very bluffs on the far side and extended as far as the eye could see. It was in his nature to want to explore the endless stretch of prairie and badlands on the other side. *Maybe at a later time*, he thought. After about an hour, they came upon a little island at a bend in the river. With several large willow trees and separated from the riverbank by only a dozen yards of shallow water, it looked to be a pleasant place to rest while the horses drank. He cast a questioning glance in Joanna's direction, and she, understanding, nodded.

"Probably oughta let the horses drink," he said, and guided Rowdy down into the water. She followed him across to the island and they dismounted.

"What a lovely little island," she said, walking among the willows. "I should have brought along a picnic basket." She found a grass-covered hummock and sat down to enjoy the late-August sun, knowing there would not be many warm days left to enjoy before the winds began to chill. She watched Clint as he led the horses up from the water and dropped their reins, standing by them while they began to graze on the lush grass. She felt safe and comfortable, remembering the days when they were always looking over their shoulders wondering if Sioux warriors were in pursuit. After a few moments, he walked over to stand by her.

"I expect we'd best turn back, before your aunt starts to worry about you," he said.

"She knows I'm all right as long as I'm with you," Joanna answered. "It's so nice here. Let's stay for a little while longer." There were thoughts running through her mind that she told herself she should not be thinking, thoughts that he might even be appalled to know. In truth, he had never exhibited particular interest in her as a woman, a fact she couldn't help but attribute to her plain features and her soiled past. He might have the same feelings that Robert had about women who had been with Indians.

"This is a right peaceful spot," he said, and sat down in the grass beside her.

They talked for a while about the land, and her father's plans to farm it with her uncle. He talked about the possibility of raising cattle and horses on the endless grasslands and the talks with her uncle of rumors that the railroad would soon come this far. After a lull in the conversation occurred, she asked the question to which she was most interested in gaining an answer.

"Are you thinking about staying here to raise your horses?"

He hesitated before answering. "Well, to tell you the truth, I hadn't planned to when we first got here."

"But now?" she pressed, sensing a change in his attitude.

"Well, now I ain't so sure," he allowed awkwardly. "This is nice country, as good a place as any, I reckon." He found his words getting all tangled up in his mouth before he could spit them out. "I mean if there was some way to know if I should stay or not . . ." He couldn't express the uncertainty he felt.

She decided to take a chance. "You mean whether or not I want you to stay?"

His face registered the helplessness he felt, reluctant to admit that she had exposed his hidden thoughts. "I've got no right to—" he started, but she interrupted.

"Because I do," she said softly. "I want you to stay." The look on his face told her that he was not repelled by her, but quite the opposite. Smiling as she looked into his eyes, she took his hand in hers, held it for a moment, then guided it around her waist. Leaning into him, she kissed him. This time it was no light kiss, and it left him with no doubt of the intent behind the caress.

He took her in his arms, passionately returning her kiss, shutting out all feelings of guilt, overcome by the moment, and hardly believing it was happening. With both parties knowing where it would lead, and anxious to arrive, he laid her back on the warm bed of grass, where she eagerly answered his urgent needs.

When they had reached passion's promise, they lay back together, she in his arms, content to stay there forever with her head resting upon his shoulder. The thought struck her at that moment that this was the first time she had really felt such passion, realizing that Robert had never taken her to such heights. For a brief moment, she allowed thoughts of guilt to creep into her mind, but immediately rejected them, hoping to banish them forever. She had honored her marriage vows. Robert had discarded her and left her to her shame. Now, like a candle suddenly lit in a dark cave, she saw new promise where before there was none, and she realized the honesty of it. Clint knew of her shame, and accepted her without baggage from the past. It occurred to her then that she was in love, and maybe for the first time.

They remained there, she with her head on his shoulder, for some time until Rowdy became impatient and strolled over to rub his muzzle on Clint's stomach. "I guess he's tellin' me it's time to get goin' back," Clint said. He sat up and watched for a moment while Joanna, slightly embarrassed now, recovered her clothing. He realized then that there was something he must tell her, reluctant though he might be.

Sensing a seriousness come over him, she paused to look him in the eye. "If you're about to tell me this was all a big mistake, I don't wanna hear it," she scolded.

"Joanna, I've gotta tell you somethin' I shoulda told you from the first."

Not waiting to let him finish, she reproached him. "Now

that we've had our roll in the grass, you remember there was an Indian there before you."

"No," he quickly replied. "That ain't it at all. I don't fault you for that. Hell, it wasn't your doin'."

"Then what?" she demanded. "You just remember you've got a little wife waiting for you back in Wyoming? Well, guess what, I've got a husband somewhere, too. You're not the only one with a guilty conscience."

"No, dammit," he exclaimed, getting more than a little annoyed with her accusations. "Just shut up a minute and let me finish."

She realized then that her insecurities had again taken control of her emotions because of a dread of rejection and fear that she had been used to simply give him physical relief. When she indicated that she was calmly awaiting what he felt he had to say, he revealed that which he had been reluctant to tell. "I'm an escaped convict from the Wyoming Territorial Prison," he started out bluntly. Almost staggered by his statement, she nevertheless showed no alarm and heard him out as he told her his story and how he happened to be on his way to Montana when he came upon her.

Although still astonished by his confession, she was not horrified by the time he had explained everything. "You mean you were sent to prison, really, because of compassion for a horse?" she asked.

"Well, it wasn't just any horse," he quickly responded. "It was an Appaloosa gelding that trusted me, and I couldn't let that horse take the abuse he was gettin' from the judge's foreman."

"And that's the only crime you've committed? They sent you to prison for that?"

"It was until a few weeks ago when I stole the horse I escaped prison on," he said.

"But six years," she wondered. "Isn't that a long time for just setting one horse free?"

"I reckon not, if it's a judge's horse."

It was a dilemma, and one that had taken her completely by surprise. She wasn't quite sure what to think about it. She trusted her instincts that told her he was a decent man who had been dealt a cruel hand by fate. She thought of the man who had come to her rescue, risking his life repeatedly to save her and her father. She remembered the firm but gentle hand that had seen her safely home to find her mother dead and her husband gone—the vigilant guide that saw her and her father safely to this country. This was not the work of a common horse thief. These were traits found in decent, honest men. She decided that she accepted his story completely, and knowing he anxiously awaited her verdict, she told him as much.

"What happened here today was supposed to happen," Joanna told a relieved young man. "It will be our secret until we have time to think about what should happen next." She gazed at the imprint in the soft grass where they had lain, then looked around her at the fragile willows. "This place will always be our special place," she whispered. She was certain then of what she wanted to happen, but decided to be careful about mentioning marriage and family until she really knew the seriousness of his intentions. As for him, he was still in somewhat of a mystified daze, still finding it hard to believe it had happened.

"Where's Clint?" Bertha asked when Joanna hurried into the kitchen.

"Putting the horses away," Joanna answered. "I thought I'd better help you with supper."

"Did you have a nice ride?" Bertha asked, taking note of

the flush in her niece's cheeks while rolling out biscuits on the table.

"Yes, it was quite pleasant."

Bertha's tiny, tight-lipped smile appeared and she said, "Looks like it put a little rosy in your cheeks."

"Really?" Joanna responded. "The wind, I guess."

"Probably," Bertha said as she continued rolling out her dough. "Maybe you might wanna change your skirt, though, and tomorrow when I do the wash, we'll see if we can get some of those grass stains off of the back of it."

Joanna flushed scarlet and twisted around trying to see the back of her skirt. "I don't know how that happened," she said, trying to convince a grinning Aunt Bertha. "I think I did that this morning when I gathered the eggs."

"Most likely," her aunt agreed, thoroughly enjoying her niece's discomfort. "Hurry and change and you can set the table."

At supper that night, no one observed the frequent glances between Joanna and Clint, with the exception of Bertha, who very seldom missed anything. As for Clint, he felt a huge weight had been lifted from his shoulders, having confessed his dark secret to Joanna and knowing she believed in his innocence. Supper was especially enjoyable on this occasion.

# Chapter 11

"What'll it be, mister?" Malcolm Gordy asked the wiry stranger with the drooping mustache. The owner of Gordy's Saloon made a symbolic gesture of wiping the rough bar with his dirty rag.

Zach Clayton took a moment to look around the empty room before walking over to the bar. "What have you got that won't kill a man?" he asked.

"I don't serve nothin' but the best whiskey I can get," Gordy replied defensively.

"Well, I'll take a chance on one shot of it."

Gordy looked his customer over while he poured Clayton's drink. When he set the bottle down on the bar, Clayton eyed the shot glass carefully. "I figure if I'm payin' for a shot," he said, "I'd expect to get a full shot. How about fillin' that glass the rest of the way?"

"That is a full shot around here," Gordy grumbled while filling the glass.

"Much obliged," Clayton said, and tossed the whiskey down his throat. The fiery liquid scalded his throat, leaving him with tears in his eyes and speechless for a few seconds. When he could talk again, he rasped, "If that's the best you can get, I won't complain about a half-full glass next time . . . Damn!"

Gordy grinned, satisfied with a small measure of revenge. "I ain't seen you in these parts before," he said.

"Last time I was up this way there was nothin' but a few tents here," Zach said. He opened his coat to display his badge. "I'm a deputy marshal, and I'm looking for a man that mighta come through here a week or so ago. He was travelin' with another man and a woman." When Gordy failed to respond, he added, "Young feller."

Gordy knew exactly whom he was referring to, but he was not in the habit of helping the law. Many of his customers were men on the other side of the law. He gave this some extra thought, however, because of the recent demise of two of his regulars. Johnny and Red had been friends of his, and their deaths cost him money. He wouldn't mind seeing the man who killed them pay for the deed. "I seen him," Gordy said after a lengthy pause. "He was in here for a drink, but I don't know where he come from or where he went."

Clayton had a feeling the bartender knew more than he was telling, but he thanked him and went on his way. He rode comfortably, not asking for more than a leisurely walk from the chestnut roan he rode. There had been changes since last he was in this part of the territory with a cluster of tents and shacks that was almost enough to be called a town. When he came upon a trading post that he remembered, close by the bank of the river, he decided to stop.

Hitching his horse at the rail out front, he took a look around before going inside. When he had been there two years before, there had been stacks of hides—buffalo, beaver, deer—piled high at the side of the building. Now there were only a few skins in a stack no more than waist high. The thing that surprised him most was the sight of a couple of plows resting against the building.

Inside, the trading post looked more like a dry goods store with tools, harnesses, and bolts of calico in addition to the regular stock of cartridges, skinning knives, and traps—all evidence of civilization approaching. Before asking about Clint Conner, he made conversation with the clerk, a young man who, it turned out, was the son-in-law of the proprietor Clayton had remembered.

"Yes, sir," the clerk responded to Clayton's remark about the changes. "The business in hides is way down from what it used to be, but we've got more settlers moving in every month, so we're selling more dry goods. The army had some surveyors in here just a month ago. They're thinking about establishing a fort here. We might have us a town before you know it."

"You might be right," Clayton replied. He then identified himself as a deputy marshal and described Clint Conner. "I've got a real important message for him," he said in case the clerk might be hesitant to inform on him. "I'm just hopin' he's still around here somewhere. You see him lately?"

"Matter of fact, I have," the clerk replied. "He came in yesterday with Frederick Steiner's boy, John, to buy some sugar and flour. I knew I hadn't seen him before. He said he was just visiting for a spell."

"Well, ol' Clint will be tickled to see me," Clayton said. "Maybe you can tell me how to get out to . . . Steiner did you say?"

"Yes, sir, Frederick Steiner—just stay on the road by the river about three miles. It'll be the second house after you cross Wolf Creek."

"These folks, the Steiners, you know them pretty well?" Clayton asked.

"Yes, sir. They're fine people, said they were German. They're farming a few hundred acres by the river. There was three families that came out here together, and they've been trading with me right regular."

"Appreciate it," Clayton said, and bid the clerk good day.

He pulled the roan to a stop at the head of a wagon track that led from the road up to the second house after crossing the creek. Reaching up to the wide brim of his hat, he pulled it down snug on his head, a habit he performed unconsciously when he was about to accost a fugitive. Nudging the roan then, he rode up to the plain frame house and dismounted. He was met at the edge of the porch by Frederick Steiner.

"How do?" Steiner greeted him, and waited for Clayton to state his business.

"Howdy," the deputy returned. "Is Clint around?"

"Clint?" Frederick responded, surprised. "You know Clint?"

"Sure do," Clayton answered. "Is he around?"

"Why, I think he's in the barn," Frederick said, not really sure where Clint was. His son, hearing his dad talking to someone, came out on the porch. Frederick turned to him and said, "John, go out to the barn and fetch Clint." John nodded and jumped off the porch. Back to Clayton, Frederick asked, "You ride out from the settlement?"

"Yes, sir, I did."

"Why don't you come on in the house and sit down while John fetches Clint? Maybe we've got some coffee still in the pot."

"Why, that would be real nice," Clayton said with a warm grin. It was the first time he had ever used this approach in making an arrest, but he was confident that he knew his man. Conner was not a killer. He was convinced that he was a decent man who had just taken a step in the wrong direction. It was fairly obvious that these folks had no inkling of Clint's past. As for confronting Clint, Clayton felt the best place to keep the arrest from getting nasty was in the midst of the family who had evidently taken him in. He figured Clint would not want to involve the family in any violent action.

Following Frederick inside, he nodded to Karl and the two women, all with puzzled expressions to greet him. Totally confident in his assessment of the man he was there to arrest, he graciously accepted the cup of coffee offered by Joanna and answered yes when asked if he wanted sugar. When she brought the sugar, he reached for it, causing his coat to gap slightly, enough so that she glimpsed the shiny metal object pinned to his shirt. She froze, spilling some of the sugar on the table. Guessing that she had seen his badge, and by her reaction, maybe knowing Clint was in trouble, he quickly smiled and took the sugar bowl from her hand. "No need to bother," he said, "I'll just brush it off with my hand."

"Clint ain't there," John said as he returned from the barn. "I don't know where he is."

"He was there a minute ago," Karl said. Like Frederick and Bertha, he was curious about the purpose of the stranger's visit to see Clint. Their curiosity was transformed into alarm in the next few seconds.

"Damn!" Clayton uttered, and sprang up from his chair, suddenly realizing he had been recognized. He rushed to the door and ran toward the corral. The puzzled family followed him out to the porch, astonished by his actions, and stood watching as he charged toward the barn.

"That's far enough," Clint warned when Clayton appeared in the barn door. Rowdy, already saddled, stood between him and the deputy marshal, Clint's Winchester resting across the saddle and aimed at Clayton.

Clayton stopped at once. "Hello, Clint," he said, a friendly smile upon his face. "Here you are, pointin' a rifle in my face again." He took a couple of steps more, but stopped when Clint cocked the rifle. "The last time I saw you, you helped me out of a jam, and then made me take a helluva long walk. My feet were sore for a week."

"You shouldn't have come after me," Clint said. "Why the hell couldn't you just leave me alone?" Glancing behind the lawman, he was disappointed to see Joanna and the others come in behind him. The expressions of alarm and dismay in their faces brought a feeling of great regret to his troubled mind.

Reading Clint's expression, Clayton took a quick glance to confirm what he suspected. They didn't know, with the possible exception of the young woman, of Clint's past. Knowing their presence here now was to his advantage, he made an attempt to reason with the fugitive. "I don't know how much you've told these nice folks here, so I'll spell it out for 'em. You're an escaped prisoner from the Wyoming Territorial Prison." There was a distinct gasp from Bertha and a grunt of surprise from both men beside her. Clayton continued. "That's the reason I had to come track you down. But I'm ready to tell these folks that I know you're a good man. You made a mistake when you weren't much more than a boy, stole a horse, but you only served half your sentence. If you come back with me peaceable, I'll do whatever I can to help you. I figure I owe you that, seein' as how you saved my neck back there north of Cheyenne. I'll testify about that to the judge, that and that little stunt you pulled to save the guard's life." He gestured toward the stunned gathering behind him. "Your friends here probably don't know you had no choice about escapin' with Ballenger. I'll remind the judge of that, too."

Clint was not ready to surrender. "I've served enough

time for freein' one horse from the treatment Judge Plover gave it. I ain't goin' back."

"You know I'm bound to take you back," Clayton said, his voice still calm. "What are you gonna do? Shoot me?" He shook his head slowly. "You ain't no murderer, Clint. And you don't wanna be on the run for the rest of your life. You've already served half your time, and I'm thinkin' the judge will shorten the rest of your sentence when I testify for you. The best thing for you to do is to wipe the slate clean with the law, come out in a short time a free man." Although the Winchester was still pointed at him, he thought he detected a hint of indecision in Clint's eyes. "Let's talk about it. I don't want this to come to bloodshed, but I've got no choice in what I have to do. I just hate to see you make a mess outta your life."

Clint was torn with anguish; he wished that he had more time to think about it. There were other factors that entered into his decisions now, the most important of which was Joanna. He had seen a glimmer of what might have been, and at this moment, he knew that it could never be if he was constantly on the run. He took his eyes off Clayton long enough to cast an inquiring glance in her direction. Her face, filled with distress, answered his unspoken question with a nod of her head, and she mouthed the silent words *I'll wait for you.* Still uncertain, he pulled the rifle down from his saddle. They were all startled by what happened next.

"You don't have to go anywhere with him!" John Steiner stated forcefully as he stepped up behind Clayton with a shotgun leveled at the deputy's waist. "We'll ride up in the badlands where nobody can find us."

There followed a few minutes of chaos as Frederick exclaimed, "John!" and started toward his son. John waved him and his mother back while keeping the shotgun trained on Zach Clayton.

Realizing the consequences that were sure to follow John's actions, and the certain ruination of the young boy's life, Clint knew what he had to do. "John," he said, "the deputy's right. Put the gun down. It's best I go back and clear this mark against my name."

"But we can make it, Clint," John pleaded. "I'll help you."

"I know you would, and I appreciate it, but it ain't the right thing to do. You heard what Clayton said. I won't be gone long, and your pa needs you here." He waited until the boy lowered the shotgun, then turned to Clayton. "I reckon you win." There was a sigh of relief from everyone.

"I expect it would be best to go ahead and get started," Clayton said. He could see little sense in lingering there where there might be too many things to cause Clint to have a change of heart. He held out his hand for Clint's rifle.

"Whatever you say," Clint replied, surrendering the weapon. "I'm ready."

"If we run into any Injuns, I'll give it back," Clayton said. "Might as well let me hold that pistol, too." Then he extended his hand again, this time to shake Clint's. "I'll give you my word that I'll do everything I can for you in court, and I'd appreciate it if you'd give me yours that you won't cause me any trouble on the way back." Clint nodded and shook on it.

It was a strange turn of events, a parting unlike any the deputy marshal had ever experienced before while in the process of making an arrest. Bertha quickly gathered some food for them to take and Karl filled a sack with oats for the horses. Clayton did not tie Clint's hands or feet. It was more like two friends starting out for home after a visit. He stood by his horse while Clint spoke his final farewells.

After Clint thanked Frederick and Bertha for their hospitality, he shook hands with Karl, who told him he was doing the right thing. Next he shook young John's hand, and charged him with the responsibility of taking care of his horses and the guns and ammunition he had acquired after the confrontations with the Sioux and the two bushwhackers from the saloon. "When I get back," he said, "we'll go up in the hills across the river and get us an elk."

Joanna held back while he said good-bye to the others. When he turned to find her, she stepped forward and much to the astonishment of the males in her family, threw her arms around Clint's neck. Pulling his head down to her, she kissed him with all the ardor she held in her heart. Astounded, Karl and Frederick could only look at each other and gape. When Joanna finally released him, she whispered, "I'll be right here when you get back."

"I'll surely be back," he promised, then turned and led Rowdy out of the barn. Taking one last look at Joanna, he turned the buckskin toward the road and left at a fast walk. Clayton tipped his hat politely to the two women, nodded to the men, and urged his horse to lope until he caught up with his prisoner. Side by side, they settled into a comfortable walk and headed to Cheyenne.

# Chapter 12

Covering thirty to forty miles a day, they drove a steady pace down through the Powder River valley, riding until they exhausted daylight, in an effort to pass through the still dangerous territory. The great village of Sioux and Cheyenne that had annihilated Custer on the Little Big Horn had long since splintered off in many different directions. But there was always the good possibility that many were still in the area, causing both men to watch constantly for any sign of hostile groups. At night the campfire was kept low, out of sight in a gully or other defile where possible so as not to attract any curious Lakota hunter. Since the trip would take better than a week and a half, there was plenty of opportunity for the two men to get to know each other a little better.

The first night out, Clayton had tried to sleep with one eye open. He trusted Clint at his word, but there was the nagging thought that he might change his mind after being away from that little lady back in Montana. There was no sense in taking a chance on losing him again. He finally threw precaution to the wind after the fourth day when he developed stomach cramps from eating the last of the meat Bertha had given them, the meat having spoiled after that length of time. They lost half a day's travel when Clayton was too sick to get out of his blankets. Clint had the opportunity to do pretty much whatever he wanted, but he chose to help the stricken man as best he could, never giving any thought to escape. After that, Clayton gave Clint's rifle and pistol back, saying, "Hell, if you didn't run off when I was laid up pukin' like a dog, I reckon your word's as good as gold."

Trying to make up for lost time, they pushed the horses hard the following day, never stopping until it was almost too dark to see. "Let's head for those hills over yonder," Clayton said, pointing toward a pair of buttes with a line of trees between them, indicating the presence of a stream. Guiding the horses down a rocky path cut by the narrow spring, they selected the best spot they could find in the growing darkness, and made their camp. After they'd taken care of the horses, there was little time spent sitting by the fire before turning in for the night. Clint roasted a little jerky for his supper. Clayton, his stomach still a bit tender after his bout with the tainted meat, settled for coffee alone.

The notch between the two buttes ran east to west, so the first rays of the morning sun shone directly down it, lighting tiny sparkles that danced upon the water. It was a peaceful place. Clayton opened his eyes to find himself looking into the muzzle of a pistol, pointed directly at his head. He froze, helpless to react fast enough and knowing he was a dead man.

"Don't move," Clint warned softly.

Clayton heard the ominous sound of the hammer cocking seconds before the revolver roared. Stunned, unable to believe Clint had missed at point-blank range, he rolled out of his blanket, trying to scramble to his feet, his mind a whirlwind of chaotic thoughts. When he managed to get his gun out, he stopped, puzzled by Clint's calm, smiling face as he pointed toward Clayton's bedroll and the five-foot rattlesnake lying dead beside it. "Maybe we oughta be a little more careful where we make our beds," Clint said, and holstered his pistol.

Clayton was stricken dumb for a few seconds, gaping wide-eyed, first at the snake and then at Clint. Then he finally found his voice. "Goddamn!" he exhaled. "Goddamn!" He shook his head over and over as if trying to rid it of his alarm. "I came mighty damn close to shittin' the rest of that meat in my britches. Why couldn't you just wake me up and tell me?"

Clint shrugged. "Tell you the truth, that snake musta crawled up between you and the fire to get warm, but I was afraid if you moved, it mighta struck. Besides, it wasn't that close. He musta been six or seven inches from your head."

"Oh," was all Clayton replied, but he knew for sure that he had not misjudged the character of the man he was taking back for trial.

They made the trip in eleven days with half a day lost because of Clayton's sick spell, and two delays when Sioux hunting parties were spotted. Bypassing Fort Laramie, they retraced the trail Clint had taken on his way to Montana weeks before.

"Where are you taking me?" Clint asked one evening by the fire. "Laramie?"

"No," Clayton replied. "I'm supposed to take you to Cheyenne. You'll have to go to trial there since that's where you were sentenced. Then I expect you'll be sent back to Laramie as soon as the trial is over." He watched Clint's face closely, wondering whether, now that they were within a couple of days' ride, he might be getting cold feet about returning to prison. "Maybe they'll give you your old cell back," he said in an effort to lighten his spirits. "It'll be like comin' home." He chuckled. "But I don't expect you'll be put on stable duty again."

Clint laughed. "I don't reckon." Stable detail was for men

who were not at risk of attempting escape. "It's the broom factory for me."

"Judge Wingate is a reasonable man," Clayton said. "I think when he hears all the facts in your case, you'll be outta there before that little gal of yours has a good chance to miss you."

"What'll happen to my horse and the rest of my stuff?" Clint asked.

"Well, your guns and saddle will most likely go to the sheriff's office till they decide somethin' else to do with 'em. They'll put your horse in the stable—for a while, anyway. Then they may ship him to Laramie. I ain't really sure."

"These guns and the saddle belong to my pa, the horse, too. Any way he can claim them?"

"I don't know," Clayton said. "I'll find out."

Clint had not spent a great deal of time thinking about the problem. Now he wished that he had ridden one of the Indian ponies he had captured, and left Rowdy in Montana. He didn't like the thought of the buckskin being turned out with a bunch of prison horses.

Sheriff Quinton Bridges took delivery of Clayton's prisoner and locked him in a cell to await trial. Clayton informed the sheriff that Clint was a good man, and warned him that he'd better damn sure treat him proper. He came back to check on Clint that same day.

"I've notified Judge Wingate's office, and wired the prison over at Laramie that you're in custody," Clayton said. "They promised me that Judge Wingate would try the case within a couple of days, so you shouldn't be here too long." He paused to look hard at Clint. "You all right?"

"Yep," Clint responded, "I'm all right. I've been in jail before."

Clayton nodded. "Okay then." He got up from the stool

he had pulled over next to the bars. "I'll be back to see how you're doin'." On his way out, he spoke to the sheriff. "I'll see you later, Quinton. Take care of my boy in there."

"I will," Bridges replied. He walked back to the cell and spoke to Clint. "Son, you must have somethin' on ol' Zach. I ain't ever seen him worry about a prisoner like this before. More times than not, they're pretty bloody when he brings 'em in."

The trial date was set, and on the scheduled day, Sheriff Bridges handcuffed the prisoner and escorted him across the street to the courtroom. As Bridges led him to his seat, Clint nodded to Zach Clayton on the other side of the room. Seated in the noisy room of curious spectators, they awaited the arrival of the judge. After a delay of nearly half an hour, the court clerk called out, "All rise."

Sitting stoically to that point, Clint suddenly felt a jolt throughout his whole body when the judge entered the room. *It was Judge Wyman Plover!* He started to surge forward, causing the sheriff to grab him and pull him back. "Whoa, boy, where're you goin'?"

"That's that son of a bitch, Plover," Clint blurted. "It's supposed to be Judge Wingate!"

"Plover's fillin' in for Wingate," Bridges said, unaware that it made any difference to the prisoner. "Judge Wingate came down ill yesterday and Judge Plover rode in this mornin' to try the case for him."

Judge Wyman Plover called for the courtroom to be seated, then glared at the sheriff and Clint over the top of his spectacles. "Settle your prisoner down over there."

It would be one of the shortest trials Sheriff Bridges could remember. The entire proceedings were finished in less than an hour. When Deputy Marshal Clayton was called to the stand, he asked to speak to the court on behalf of the prisoner. Judge Plover instructed him to respond to his questions with answers of yes or no. When he tried to testify on the cooperation of the prisoner and his willingness to risk his life to save that of the deputy, Clayton was told that his testimony was irrelevant to the charges against Clint. "We're here to decide whether the defendant escaped from the Territorial Penitentiary or not, and you've already testified that he did. Added to those charges is assault with intent to kill prison guard Otis Williams." When Clayton protested, the judge threatened him with contempt and ordered him to step down.

"The defendant saved that guard's life!" Clayton insisted.

Banging his gavel forcefully, Plover ordered Clayton out of the courtroom. The deputy marshal had no choice but to do as he was ordered. "Now then," Plover said after Clayton was gone, "we'll get on with this trial." He ordered the defendant to stand for sentencing. Addressing Clint, he proceeded. "Clint Allen Conner, it is the ruling of this court that you shall be returned to the Wyoming Territorial Prison, where you will serve the remaining three years and one month of your original sentence. In addition, you will serve two years in punishment for your escape and five years for the attempted assault on the guard." He banged his gavel down. "This case is closed," he announced, then after a smirk in Clint's direction, he walked out the side door.

Unable to believe what had just happened, Clint sat down heavily in his chair, staring at the door that Plover had just exited. Just as stunned, the sheriff looked down at him, wide-eyed with shock. "Damn, boy, he threw everythin' but the kitchen stove at you. He sure had it in for you."

Clint didn't speak for a few moments, still trying to right his tumbled mind. Then he looked up at Bridges and said woefully, "It was his horse I stole."

The rest of that day was a tornado of conflicting thoughts

that left Clint in a state of despair. Feeling betrayed, by Clayton as well as the vengeful judge, he cursed himself for allowing the marshal to bring him back to Cheyenne. Thinking he had been sentenced unfairly the first time, he had permitted himself to be persuaded to seek restitution from the court, aided by his deeds of compassion for the officers of the law. Looking back, now that it was too late, he thought himself a fool for swallowing Clayton's promises of redemption.

Sheriff Bridges was quite contrite about the heavy sentence Plover had laid down for his young prisoner, and tried to make up for it somewhat by arranging for a special supper from the hotel kitchen. With no interest in food, Clint ate but a small portion of it. Clayton came to visit him just before supper. Even though he explained to Clint that he had been trying to gain an audience with Judge Wingate all afternoon, he could see the complete reversal of Clint's attitude toward him. "I won't forget you," he said in parting. "As soon as I can see him, I'll get the facts to Judge Wingate." Growing more bitter by the minute, Clint didn't respond, sitting glassy-eyed on his cot as Clayton closed the cell room door behind him.

Later that evening, the sheriff came in to see him. With him, Clint saw a big rawboned man wearing a deputy's badge. "This here's Roy Spade, one of my deputies," Bridges said. "He'll be escortin' you on the noon train to Laramie tomorrow mornin'."

In contrast to the sheriff, Spade eyeballed Clint with a curled-lip look of contempt. He stepped up close to the bars of Clint's cell. "Just so you know, jailbird, I don't tolerate no trouble from jaspers like you. So it's up to you. We can have us a peaceable little ride up to Laramie if you behave. If you don't, I'll break a gun barrel across your skull and deliver you in a box. You got that?" He waited for Clint's response.

When several minutes passed without one, save the unwavering glare of the prisoner's eyes, Spade turned and left the cell room, saying, "You just remember what I told you."

The next day, it was Zach Clayton who brought Clint his breakfast, and sat talking to him while he ate. Overnight, Clint had thought about what had happened and realized that he had probably been wrong in thinking Clayton betrayed him. Still, he had abandoned all hope of having Plover's decision reversed, and the prospect of ten more years in prison loomed before him as the end of all the dreams he had allowed himself during the past few weeks.

About a half hour before noon, Roy Spade came in. "Where the hell have you been?" Bridges demanded. "I told you to be here thirty minutes ago."

"Hell, it's still half an hour before the train gets here, if it's on time, and it don't take but ten minutes to walk to the station." He took the cell key off a peg and went to Clint's cell. "Let's go, jailbird." He grinned at Bridges as he walked by.

"Have you been drinkin'?" the sheriff asked accusingly, detecting a whiff of alcohol.

"Hell no," Spade responded. "I stopped in the Silver Dollar for one little shooter this mornin', and that's all."

Bridges was still suspicious, but it was too late to do anything about it if Spade had been drinking. His other deputy had gone out to check on a report of cattle thieves operating near the Rocking-M Ranch. He watched Spade pull Clint's hands behind his back and cuff him. He seemed steady enough, so the sheriff decided Spade was probably telling him the truth.

"Come on, jailbird," Spade goaded, grabbing Clint by the arm and giving him a forceful shove toward the door.

It was only a short walk to the end of the street and the train depot. There were a handful of people on the street, and they all stopped to gawk at the deputy and his handcuffed prisoner as they passed. A couple of small boys ran along beside them all the way to the depot. Posturing for their benefit, Spade frequently gave Clint a shove in the back, usually accompanied by a mischievous grin. Clint took it in silence, even when he almost stumbled once when Spade was especially rough. All the while Clint cursed himself for willfully putting himself in this position.

The train for Laramie pulled in at about twenty-five after twelve, which the stationmaster maintained was pretty much on time for the noon train. Spade complained, anyway. He would be staying overnight in Laramie and catching a train back the next day. And the sooner he got to Laramie, the sooner he could get rid of his prisoner and hit the saloons.

He led Clint down the track to the last car. The first step was knee high, and with his hands behind his back, Clint couldn't step up on it. Spade cursed him as if it were his fault. "I can't sit down in a seat with my hands behind my back, anyway," Clint complained. "If you handcuff me with my hands in front, I can grab the handrail and get on the train, and I can sit down after we get on."

"Did I ask you anything?" Spade shot back. "You think you're the first son of a bitch I've had to take to Laramie? Turn around!" He spun Clint around roughly, grabbed his wrists, and unlocked the cuffs. Spinning him back around to face him, he said, "Stick your damn hands up here." It happened faster than Spade's alcohol-addled brain could react. Clint brought his hands up as he had been ordered, but to Spade's surprise, his own revolver was in one of them, the barrel looking him in the face. "What tha . . . ?" Spade blurted, and slapped his hand on his empty holster.

Stunned by the suddenness of Clint's move, Spade stared wide-eyed at the ominous pistol muzzle aimed at his eye. He made no move to resist when Clint took the key from his fingers. Finding his voice at last, he said, "You ain't gettin' away with this, you damn fool."

"Shut up," Clint ordered. "Put your hand in there. Make no mistake about it, I'll blow a hole in your head before I'll go back to that prison." The resolve in his eye convinced Spade that he meant what he said. The deputy stuck his hand out and winced as Clint closed the cuff around his wrist. He then pulled the other cuff through the handrail and ordered Spade to put his other wrist up.

"You can't do that!" Spade complained. "I ain't gonna be handcuffed to no damn train."

"You rather be shot down beside it? All the same to me." He pressed the pistol against Spade's forehead.

"Wait! Wait, dammit!" Spade exclaimed, and held up his wrist. Clint locked the cuff and stepped back as he heard the conductor's call to board. "We'll hunt you down for this," Spade threatened. "You're as good as dead."

Clint shoved the deputy's pistol in his belt. "You're a pretty big asshole, but I don't know if you're man enough to hold back a train. I'd say you'd best hop up on that step unless you wanna be dragged to Laramie." After a couple of loud blasts from the engineer's whistle, the engine roared into life, and the passenger cars started slowly rolling, leaving Spade no choice but to leap aboard. Clint stood beside the tracks and watched as the train picked up speed, and Spade yelled wildly at every person standing on the platform.

"What was he hollerin' about?" an elderly man who had just gotten off in Cheyenne asked Clint when he walked by.

"I don't know," Clint replied, and kept walking. "I reckon it's his first train ride."

Taking care to walk unhurriedly back from the depot, he went around behind the jail, and proceeded to the end of the street and the stables. Entering the rear of the stable, he pulled

Spade's pistol from his belt and stopped just inside the door, scanning the interior of the building. The owner, who had seen Clint and Clayton when they had left Rowdy to be boarded, was nowhere in sight. Instead, the stable was left in the care of a boy of sixteen or seventeen. Clint stuck the pistol back in his belt.

Walking nonchalantly between the stalls, he approached the boy. "I've come to pick up a horse," Clint said, "that buckskin yonder in the corral." When the boy appeared uncertain about the request, Clint went on. "Sheriff Bridges sent me to get the horse—belonged to a prisoner that just left on the noon train. There oughta be a saddle in the tack room. I'll get it." He walked on past the hesitant boy on his way to the tack room. "Well, hop to it, boy, the sheriff said right away."

"Mr. Bailey's gone to dinner," the boy said. "He oughta be back pretty soon." He was obviously uncomfortable about someone riding off on one of the horses.

"Don't have time to wait for Bailey," Clint replied. "He knows about it, anyway. Sheriff Bridges will be by to make it right." He smiled at the cautious youngster. "Now, how 'bout helpin' me out and cut that buckskin outta there? I'm kinda in a hurry."

Deciding that it must be all right if the sheriff sent the stranger over, the boy dropped the pitchfork he had been employing and hopped over the rails. He watched as Clint saddled Rowdy. "That Winchester and the gun belt was supposed to be took over to the sheriff's office," the boy pointed out. "I was fixin' to do it today," he lied.

"Don't worry about it," Clint assured him. "I'll see that it gets where it's supposed to." He stepped up in the saddle and wheeled Rowdy around.

"You say Sheriff Bridges is comin' by to settle with Mr. Bailey?" the boy asked, seeking confirmation.

"You can count on it," Clint said. "Bridges will be by." Past ready to leave, Rowdy leaped forward as soon as he felt the slight pressure of Clint's heels. Happy to be reunited, the two partners left the dust of Cheyenne behind them.

Riding free again over the rolling grass prairie, Clint felt a strong temptation to visit his father one last time, but there was the need to gain as much distance as he could from those who were certain to chase him. The sheriff and a posse, possibly Zach Clayton again, they would be on his trail soon. And his father's place was not far enough from Cheyenne to hazard a stop there now. It was too bad, he told himself, for he could have gotten some supplies from his father. He wouldn't suffer for food, anyway, since he had his rifle back.

The thing he must now decide was where he would run to. Clayton knew his heart yearned to return to Montana and the woman waiting there for him. Clayton was bound to show up at Frederick Steiner's farm sometime. Consequently, that's the last place Clint should go. But the need to see Joanna seemed to have intensified tenfold since his second escape, and he felt he owed it to her to somehow get word to her. Ever since he had left her, he felt an aching deep inside to see her again. Never having felt that way for anyone before, he was pressed to admit that he was in love. *In love.* Even the words seemed strange to him. Whatever the affliction, he knew that he wanted to be with her more than anything else. Still, he could not in good conscience bring his troubles to roost on the Steiner brothers. *I'll make up my mind later on,* he told himself. For now, he would just continue to ride north.

Riding horseback from Cheyenne to Laramie, Zach Clayton arrived at the Wyoming Territorial Prison a couple of hours past dinnertime. He went straight to the warden's office with the intention of persuading Boswell to do what he could to make Clint Conner's life easier—hopefully, even convince the warden to help with an appeal for a new trial. He was not prepared for the news awaiting him.

Warden Boswell greeted him cordially as usual, but interrupted when Clayton began his plea on behalf of the returned prisoner, Conner. "I'm sure Conner is one helluva deserving inmate," he said. "But the fact of the matter is that I don't have a prisoner by that name at the present time. I do have a fugitive by that name who's still very much at large."

Confused, Clayton responded, "Whaddaya mean, Warden? Clint Conner was tried and sentenced day before yesterday. One of Quinton Bridges' deputies brought him here yesterday afternoon."

"Well, now, one of his deputies—name of Spade—brought in a railroad car he had evidently arrested. At least he was handcuffed to the handrail." He sat observing a stunned deputy marshal for a few moments. "So from where I'm settin', nothin's changed in the status of my two escaped convicts. Ballenger and Conner are still runnin' loose. The proper thing to do is to turn it over to the chief justice in Montana Territory to put one of his marshals on their trail. They've already wired about a couple of bank holdups. Last week two men in Helena held a pistol to the cashier's head and got away with forty-seven hundred dollars in cash. They escaped on horseback." He studied Clayton's reactions to the news before continuing. "Maybe one of their men might have better luck in running Ballenger to ground."

It was a stinging rebuke from a man from whom he had always enjoyed respect and friendship. Clayton got his hackles up a bit. "Dammit, Warden, I brought Conner in. It's not my fault Spade lost him. But if you think another marshal can do a better job, then go ahead and ask for one."

A hint of a smile appeared on Boswell's face. "Why don't

you just go ahead and track him down again, but next time, bring him on back here? I don't see why there needed to be a trial, anyway. A convict escapes from here, we just catch him and throw him back in a cell again."

Leaving Boswell's office, Clayton wasn't sure he wanted to go after Clint again. The young man didn't deserve to be incarcerated. He wasn't an outlaw. He might have told Boswell to go ahead and get another marshal to do the job, but if the law demanded that Clint had to be apprehended, Clayton preferred to be the one to do it. He felt that he owed Clint. Another lawman might be inclined to shoot first and ask questions later.

As far as Ballenger was concerned, that was a different story. Clayton wanted him badly, if for no other reason than the fact the son of a bitch shot his horse. Ballenger was a menace to the civilized world, a plague upon honest men and women. So Clayton would go again. He would pack up his war bag and his bedroll and start out for Yellowstone country once more. Ballenger and the piece of dung he rode with would show up sooner or later. And he wanted to be there when he did. His gut feeling told him that Ballenger and Yancey would be intent upon putting some distance between themselves and Helena if they were the two who pulled that bank job. Where would they go? Butte, maybe, but with plenty of cash, more likely some of the smaller towns back east. There were dozens of little settlements along the Yellowstone where a couple of outlaws could work their trade.

It was settled then. He would concentrate on finding Ballenger and Yancey, since they were a menace to society. Clint would have to wait. If he disappeared into Canada or somewhere, that was the chance Clayton would have to take. The other two were more important.

# Chapter 13

Clell Ballenger braced himself in the stirrups against his horse's steep descent down a rocky slide to the bottom of the canyon. Small pebbles and loose shale cascaded around the horse's hooves, kicked up by Yancey's horse behind him. Reaching the floor of the canyon, he urged the horse onward, following the narrow canyon, reluctant to stop to rest the animal. It was not a sound idea for a couple of bank robbers to hang around Helena. The town had proper law now, but it wasn't that far removed from its vigilante days, and vigilantes were prone to hang any outlaws they caught.

"Clell!" Yancey called out from behind. "Let up, my horse is give out."

Ballenger pulled back on the reins to let Yancey catch up. "All right," he said, "I reckon we'd better rest 'em before we find ourselves walkin' outta these mountains." He looked back over the way they had come. "I think we got away clean. If anybody's on our tail, they're a helluva long way back." Both horses walked along slowly now, their heads drooping from the long, hard ride with no stops for rest. "That looks like some sorta spring or somethin' up ahead. We'll water the horses there."

"We'd better," Yancey said. "I wasn't far from havin' to

tote mine on my back." He was ready for a rest himself. The wound in his shoulder, though healing well enough, still caused him some pain.

A small spring worked its way down through a notch in the canyon wall to form a small pool big enough for both horses to drink at the same time. While the weary mounts eagerly quenched their thirst, Ballenger and Yancey sat down with their backs propped against a large rock. Ballenger pulled a pouch from his coat pocket, reached in to extract a generous pinch of tobacco, and stuffed it in his mouth. He tossed the pouch to Yancey while he worked up his chew. Yancey stuffed his jaw with a chew as well, then leaned back against the rock. After a few moments while both men took turns spitting at the same rock on the edge of the spring, Yancey spoke.

"We been on the run for two days now," he said, "and ain't nobody come after us. I think it's time we count that money and split it."

"What's the matter, Pete?" Ballenger replied, joking. "You 'fraid I'm gonna run off with all of it?"

"I been ridin' with you too long to trust you," Yancey said, halfway serious, although there was a smile on his face. "Hell, that's a lotta money in that sack. I'm wantin' to know just how rich I am." It was a big score, maybe the biggest they had ever made, and this time there was only a two-way split, unlike the days when there were as many as half a dozen riding with Ballenger. That was before Clell was caught and sent to prison. Yancey was now anxious to hold his share of the money.

"All right," Ballenger declared. "We gotta rest the horses, anyway, so we might as well see how much we got."

He took the bag from his saddle and dumped the money out on the ground. "Gawdamn," he hooted. "Look at that. Ain't that a sight to rest the eyes?" He raked the banded notes into a stack, and played with them like a child playing with blocks. "Hell, this is twice as much as we took from that bank in Fort Collins."

"Let's count it," Yancey said.

It took a while, but Ballenger counted the bundles and arrived at a total of forty-seven hundred dollars. Both men were amazed, never dreaming it would amount to that much. At Yancey's incessant prodding, Ballenger divided up the money. Since his arithmetic was not to be trusted, he did it by a simple "one for you, and one for me" method until he got down to one last odd bundle, which he divided the same way, one bill at a time.

Both men sat there awhile, chewing tobacco, spitting, and contemplating their newly acquired wealth. It *was* a lot of money, and both men afforded themselves the pleasure of thinking of the many things that much money could buy. The two outlaws had ridden together for a good many years, but forty-seven hundred dollars was enough to send the larcenous mind of Clell Ballenger to thoughts of luxuries the money could buy if it were not split down the middle. The idea caused him to glance over at Yancey and smile, wondering whether his partner was thinking the same thing. It was a tempting thought—to put a bullet in ol' Pete's head, and ride off with a stake big enough to set him up on easy street. *Maybe go to San Francisco or someplace like that*, he thought. "I reckon now it was a pretty good thing when that young feller run off with half our supplies," he said, thinking of the two-way split.

"There's plenty more little banks like that one to knock over for two good men like me and you," Yancey said. "Two's the right number. We don't need no more men like we had in the old days." The bigger share of money wasn't the only reason Yancey was glad Clint ran out on them. He no longer had to worry about that haunting dream about the .44 bullet heading straight for his eye.

Ballenger responded with a smile and a nod. He was still thinking about places he could go with all of the bank money. Putting those thoughts aside for the moment, he became restless to get moving again. "Damn, I need a drink of whiskey. Let's get the hell outta these mountains."

"We probably ain't rested the horses enough yet," Yancey replied.

"We can take it easy on 'em for a spell," Ballenger insisted. "They ain't ready to lay down and die yet, and we're almost outta the hills. Hell, they'll make it."

They mounted the tired horses and pushed on, following the canyon until finally the hills were behind them and open prairie grass before them. With the Crazy Mountains to the east of them, they continued in a southerly direction hoping to strike the Yellowstone somewhere around Big Timber. Late in the afternoon, Yancey, who was leading, pulled up short. "Lookee yonder," he said, pointing toward a small herd of cattle grazing near a tree-lined stream ahead. Ballenger pulled up beside him, and they sat there for a few minutes looking the scene over.

"I don't see but one man," Clell said after a moment more, "unless there's somebody in the trees by the water. There's a chuck wagon under them trees. Might be nobody there but the cook."

Yancey was looking at the remuda with twenty or more horses grazing off to one side. "I don't know about you," he said, "but I'd like to pick up a fresh horse."

"That ain't a bad idea. Let's ride on in and see if there's any more men around."

Percy Johnson opened his eyes when he heard the horses whinny a greeting to the two horses approaching from the north. Squinting his eyes in an effort to identify the riders, he determined the two to be strangers. "Now, who the hell . . . ?" he mumbled, and got on his feet. Reaching under the seat of the wagon, he pulled his rifle out just in case. It was mostly renegade Indians he was leery of, but two white men called for the same caution.

Seeing the old man pull the rifle, Ballenger called out, "Hello the camp. All right we come in? We mean no harm." He commented low to Yancey, "He's by hisself. Ain't nobody else around."

"Well, come on in, then," Percy called back. Holding his rifle ready in case of mischief, he watched his visitors approach. The rest of the boys were out bringing in strays, so he wasn't pleased to be alone to receive visitors, especially two as rough looking as these. "Where you fellers headin'?" he asked when they were close enough for conversation.

"We're on our way back toward Big Timber," Ballenger answered, "just two cowpokes lookin' to make an honest livin'."

"Is that a fact?" Percy said, at once skeptical. Neither man was dressed like a drover.

"Where's the rest of your crew?" Yancey asked, and started to dismount.

Percy brought his rifle up before his chest. "I've not asked you to step down," he stated evenly. "The rest of the boys is close by. I expect 'em any minute."

Yancey settled back in the saddle. Ballenger smiled and said, "There's no call to get cross with us, old man. We're just travelers on our way to Big Timber. We wasn't fixin' to ask you for nothin' except maybe a cup of coffee and a word or two of friendly conversation. Hell, we can pay you for the coffee."

Percy was left in a quandary, not sure whether he was being overly cautious or just plain unfriendly. "Well," he said, still unsure, "you're welcome to a cup of coffee, I reckon. You don't have to pay for it." He motioned with his rifle. "Pot's on the fire there, cups on the tailboard, help yourself."

"'Preciate it, neighbor," Ballenger said, still wearing a broad smile. "I don't blame you for bein' careful. There's some mean jaspers ridin' this territory. It pays for a man to be cautious." He and Yancey helped themselves to the coffee. "This sure hits the spot," he commented after a sip of the hot liquid. "It's been a hard day's ride."

Feeling a slight bit guilty for his quick appraisal of the two strangers, Percy said, "I'm fixin' to start supper for the boys. There's plenty if you two wanna stay around for somethin' to eat."

"Why, that's mighty neighborly of you," Ballenger replied. "Me and my partner here might take you up on that." He walked over to stand before Percy. "It's good coffee," he said, taking another sip. "You know, we might be interested in doin' a little tradin' with you. Our horses is pretty much wore out."

"I can see that," Percy responded, "but you'll have to talk to the boss about that."

"That's too bad, 'cause we could really make it worth your while." He glanced at Yancey, who was standing behind them now. "How's our horses, fifty dollars, and a bump sound?"

Percy's eyes widened a bit. "Fifty dollars and a bump? Whaddaya mean, a bump?"

"A bump on the head," Ballenger said with a grin as Yancey brought the barrel of his pistol down hard on the back of Percy's skull. Percy slumped to the ground, fighting to retain his senses. "Get that rope yonder," Ballenger told Yancey, pointing to the wagon. While the injured man struggled helplessly, Yancey quickly tied him hand and foot. "Let's pick us a couple of good ones and get them saddles on." Walking past the trussed-up cook, Ballenger bent low and whispered, "I was just joshin' about the fifty bucks and our horses." There was no possibility he would leave the chestnut Morgan he prized.

In a short amount of time, they were finished. Riding fresh horses, and leading the Morgan and Yancey's palomino, they set out for the Yellowstone with at least three good hours of daylight left. After riding about three miles, they spotted a rider driving a few head of cattle back toward the way they had come. Too far to hail, Ballenger took off his hat and waved a salutation. The drover waved back, causing Ballenger to chuckle delightedly. "He ain't gonna be too happy when he gets back to camp and supper ain't ready."

Two more days' ride found them at the Yellowstone River where the Boulder River joined it, and the little settlement called Big Timber for the tall cottonwoods there. They decided Big Timber offered everything they needed for the time being: a saloon, a trading post and general store, stables, and a blacksmith. "Looks to me like the very place we're lookin' for," Ballenger commented upon looking the town over. They took their newly confiscated horses to the stable and paid in advance for a double ration of oats. Lem Turner, the owner of the stable, directed them to Maggie Pitts' rooming house when they informed him that they were desirous of a real bed to sleep on, and they had the money to afford it.

Clint Conner, fugitive, made his way through Powder River country, following virtually the same path he had taken once before. With little to eat except some strips of dried jerky he found in his saddlebags, he traveled all day and half the night for the better part of a week until he had crossed the Platte River. Feeling the threat of starvation, he took the time to hunt when he came upon a herd of antelope working their way across the grassy prairie. Knowing it wouldn't be easy, he attempted to stalk the animals anyway. But to his exasperation, they would not let him approach without taking flight. Then, farther away, they would linger and graze until he drew near again. It seemed to him that they knew the range of his Winchester and managed to stay just outside it. Finally in frustration, he decided to give up chasing the beasts, and try an old trick the trappers used to employ, one his father had told him about.

Leaving his horse at the bottom of a ridge, he crawled to the top where he could see the antelope grazing five or six hundred yards distant. Knowing their eyesight to be keen, he tied his spare shirt to the end of his rifle barrel. Still lying flat on his stomach in the tall grass, he held the rifle in the air and began waving it slowly back and forth. After maybe a quarter of an hour with no response from the nonchalant herd, he was ready to declare the idea nothing more than folklore. But then he realized that a couple of the animals had stopped grazing and now stood alert, their heads turned directly toward him. He hesitated a moment before beginning his circling motion again. Their curiosity aroused, two of the animals began to slowly approach the ridge, and one or two more paused to stare at the strange object waving in the grass.

"Come on," he whispered as they cautiously crept closer and closer. "Come on." Fearing that the skittish animals might suddenly run away, he had all he could do to restrain himself from taking a risky shot. But he forced himself to have patience, waving his rifle even though it seemed to have tripled in weight. The two antelope advanced to the foot of the ridge, some two hundred yards from him, but then stopped and began to prance playfully back and forth. Afraid they might turn and suddenly bolt, he let the rifle fall slowly to his shoulder, sighted on the foremost antelope, and squeezed the trigger. The animal dropped at once while the rest of the herd sped away.

Getting to his feet, he watched for a moment to make sure the animal was down for sure. Satisfied, he hurried back down to his horse, not wishing to waste any time collecting the carcass. As he rode Rowdy across the ridge to the other side, he could feel his empty belly twisting in anticipation of the fresh meat, but his first concern was to load the antelope on his horse and find a better protected place to skin and butcher it. He didn't fancy the idea of being caught out in the open by a Sioux hunting party attracted by his rifle shot.

He rode for more than two miles before finding a place suitable to do his butchering. With water from a narrow stream that found its meandering way down the middle of a ravine, and rambling berry bushes for a screen, it offered the best choice for his camp. He didn't know if there was already someone on his trail, but he decided that he was going to have to take the chance. He needed to take a day to rest Rowdy and prepare some food for himself. There were enough dead branches from the bushes to keep a reasonable fire going, so as soon as he unsaddled Rowdy, he started the fire and then went to work skinning the antelope. Before quartering the carcass, he sliced strips from the haunch and set them over the fire to eat while he finished the butchering. The first strips were eaten half raw, such was his hunger, for he couldn't wait for them to cook. Tossing the sizzling meat back and forth from one hand to the other to cool it, he stuffed his belly full. When his appetite was sated, he felt the urge to sleep, but there was still work to do to dry some of the meat to take with him. Several times he interrupted his work to climb up to the brim of the ravine where he would sit for a period watching the prairie around him for signs of anyone approaching. He kept the periodic lookouts until darkness fell upon his ravine.

When finally he lay down for the night, he pulled his blanket over his tired body, and lay listening to the whispered sounds of the prairie night. Like the mountains at night, the prairie had its distinctive quiet. Anyone who has lain out under the stars to sleep can tell you the difference. When morning came, he ate more antelope, and packed the portion of the animal he intended to carry. With Rowdy rested, he set out again, hoping to strike the Lightning River before dark.

Pushing on across the prairie, he struck the Belle Fourche two days later, continuing along the same trail he had taken before when he had come upon Joanna. He told himself that it was the only trail he knew through that country, reluctant to admit that it was also a trail that led him closer to her. Common logic told him that he should not return to Frederick Steiner's farm, that it would be the first place Zach Clayton would expect to find him. Knowing that, he still continued on the same path, rationalizing his decision by deeming the country around the Powder and the Big Horn too dangerous for a white man alone. "I'll make up my mind when I reach the Yellowstone," he announced aloud.

Four days of hard riding brought him to the banks of the Yellowstone River, a few hundred yards upriver from the saloon where he had encountered the two men he had killed. With no desire to see the saloon owner again, he rode farther upriver to find a spot to make camp and think about what he should do.

He was not entirely comfortable with the longing he felt to see Joanna Becker again. It was a new feeling for him, one that was hard to explain. The closest thing he could relate to the annoying sensation was feelings he had experienced in the past to see the rugged Rocky Mountain country, or the longing he had experienced in prison for the sense of freedom on the outside. This new emptiness he felt was different, and far more compelling. All said and done, he had to conclude that he might be in love with the woman. *A hell of a thing*, he thought, reacting as if he had caught a disease.

"She said she would wait for me," he told a disinterested Rowdy, remembering her embrace when he had left her. "She must feel the same way about me." Insecure, even though she had promised, he wondered whether now she might have had second thoughts. After all, he was a convict. *What if her husband comes back? Who would she choose then?* "Dammit to hell!" he exclaimed in frustration. "Bein' in love is too damn hard on a man." He stood up and drained the last of the coffee in his cup. *I'll go tell her what's happened*, he decided. *I owe her that. Then I'll head west.*

No more than two days behind him, Deputy Marshal Zach Clayton sat beside a campfire on the Tongue River. He had been moving fast, not attempting to track Clint Conner. He was intent upon gaining the Yellowstone as quickly as possible, knowing where he was going. The boomtowns on the river were the most likely places to find Ballenger and Yancey. By his own admission, it was a hell of a long way to make an arrest, but he had too much personal pride invested to consider limits of jurisdiction.

Joanna Becker brushed a stray wisp of hair from her face and got up from the milking stool. She had taken over the morning milking from John, since he had the added responsibility of helping build onto the cabin for her father and her. It was not a chore she particularly enjoyed, and her young cousin was laughingly patient when teaching her how. But she had gotten to the point where the cow accepted her clumsy touch and no longer tried to swat her with her tail. She put the stool out of the way, picked up her bucket, and went back to the house to help her aunt Bertha with break-fast.

As usual, there were thoughts of Clint darting through her head, but on this chilly morning in late August the thoughts seemed constant, and she tried to picture him on the day she last saw him. She never pictured him languishing in a prison cell, because that image upset her. How long, she wondered, would she have to wait? Three years seemed an eternity now, but the marshal had said that it might be less. She would pray for that. "What . . . ?" she asked, aware then that her aunt had said something to her.

"I said, check those biscuits in the oven," Bertha said. "I think they might be getting a little too brown." She paused in her turning of the bacon in the big iron skillet to take a closer look at her niece. "Are you awake yet this morning? You look like your mind is still in bed."

"I'm fine," Joanna answered, laughing. "Just still a little sleepy, I guess." She glanced up at her aunt's typical closed-lip smile that seemed to say she understood everything you were thinking. "You know," she decided, "it's going to be such a nice day, I think I'd like to take my horse for a ride this afternoon."

"It is fine weather for it," Bertha said. "Any day now the weather is bound to turn cold. Why don't you do that?"

"I think I will," Joanna replied.

The afternoon was pleasant, sunny with only a slight breeze, and just cool enough to warrant her coat. Seeing her struggling to carry her saddle out of the barn, John jumped down from the rafters of the new addition to give her a hand. While she stood at the gate, he caught her horse and saddled it. When she thanked him, he said, "I'd go with you if I didn't have to work on the house."

"Maybe next time," she said, smiling. On most days, she

would have welcomed the company, but today she was too deeply into her private thoughts to want distraction. She reached over and playfully flipped his hat over his eyes as she rode by him.

Although there was no destination in her mind, she knew where she would eventually end up. She let the little mare have her head, and the horse followed the track along the river from memory of other rides. As usual, they arrived at the same spot as before. Joanna could feel a slight increase in her heartbeat as she approached the little island of willows close to the river's bank. Moments later, her heart almost stopped when she was startled to discover a horse grazing among the willows. Fearful, she started to turn the mare at once, but she hesitated when the horse lifted its head to neigh at the mare. *It was a buckskin.* It looked like Clint's Rowdy, but she knew it could not be. Knowing she should turn her horse back toward home, she could not help but wonder about the horse. And then he appeared, walking from the cover of the trees. "Clint . . ." she gasped, unable to say more, not sure she could trust her eyes.

"I was hopin' you'd ride out this way," he said, and waited for her to cross over the shallow water to the island. "I remember you sayin' this was gonna be your special place."

He caught her as she slid from the saddle. "But how . . . What are you doing here?" she stammered, still finding it impossible that he was actually holding her in his arms. Her face beaming now, she asked excitedly, "Did they let you go?"

"I'm 'fraid not," he replied apologetically. Seeing the puzzlement in her eyes, he hastened to explain.

After he had told her the entire story of his betrayal in the courtroom, she could only sigh in bewilderment, "Oh, Clint . . . what will you do?"

"I don't know," he replied. "They'll be comin' after me again. That much is pretty certain, and if it's Clayton that's comin', he'll be showin' up here for sure. So I guess I'll be headin' for the hills somewhere." He placed his hands on her shoulders so he could look into her eyes. "But I had to come here first to tell you what happened."

"Why didn't you come to the house?" she asked.

"I didn't wanna get your pa and your uncle mixed up in my troubles. That's why I've been waitin' for you out here. I've got no business involvin' you in the mess I've made of my life, but I need supplies and ammunition. I don't have anything but my horse and saddle, and the little bit that was left in my saddlebags. So I need to get some of the stuff I left here. I've been camped here for two days, hopin' you'd show up. I don't wanna just ride in and upset your folks, but I reckon I don't have any choice. Who knows how much time I've got before a lawman from somewhere shows up? But I had to see you again before I leave."

She moved closer, holding him tightly, her head pressed against his shoulder. "Dammit!" she cursed. "I just found you, and now I have to lose you before we've even had a chance. Where will you go?"

"I don't know," he answered. "But maybe if I can keep myself clear of the law, maybe after a while they'll give up, and I can come back for you."

"I'll go with you," she said, without taking a lot of time to consider the consequences.

"No," he said. "I can't do that. I won't do it. We'd be on the run all the time, never knowin' when Clayton or some other lawman would show up. It would be mighty rough livin' out in the wild country." He pressed her close to his chest. "I don't wanna think about you out in the mountains alone somewhere after some sheriff or marshal puts a bullet in me." She started to protest, but he quickly silenced her with a finger on her lips. "I've got to know you're safe here with your father. It's the only way I'll have peace of mind."

"Stay with me here tonight," she pleaded. "I love you." It was the first time she had told him that. A tear welled in her eye as she realized that her one chance for happiness was rapidly dying. "I love you," she repeated, this time in despair as she opened her soul to him.

The words shattered him. He wanted to cry out in protest to the gods that played such vile tricks on miserable mortals. This one woman who held his heart was to be denied him, and he knew that it had to be. "Know this," he said emphatically. "I love you, too, Joanna, and if there's any way to make it happen, I'll find us a place that's safe, and I'll come back for you."

She knew he was right, she could not go with him, but she would have gone with him had he asked her to. They spent the rest of the afternoon on their special island. She gave herself in tearful passion, knowing that it was uncertain when, or even if, she would ever see him again. When finally it was time to go, he helped her on her horse and rode with her until they reached the corner of her uncle's property. He pulled up short of the path to the house. "I don't know how your folks will take it now that I'm a convict on the run again," he said.

"Clint, they know you're a good man, especially my father. He would never turn you away. Besides, you're not asking for anything that doesn't already belong to you. And if you're worried about me, don't. I don't care what they think." She nudged her horse and led the way.

When she entered the house, Bertha was already in the midst of making supper. "I was beginning to worry about you," Bertha remarked. "I was about to send John to look for you."

"I'm sorry," Joanna replied softly. "I guess I just lost track of time."

Usually observant, Bertha was startled when she glanced beyond her niece to discover Clint coming in the door behind her. Standing wide-eyed in astonishment and left speechless for once in her life, she looked to Joanna for an explanation.

"Clint's just come for some of his things," Joanna started. "He's not going to stay." Then while her aunt gaped at her and then at Clint, then back at her again, Joanna explained Clint's unexpected appearance. Before she finished, the men came in from the lower field, equally astonished to find Clint there—overjoyed in young John's case—and the story was repeated, this time by Clint.

As Clint had feared, the situation created some concern for Frederick Steiner. He wasn't quite sure what his Christian position should be in the case of a fugitive from the law. Before, when the deputy marshal had come to the house, and Clint had agreed to return to serve his sentence, Frederick was satisfied that things were in proper order. Now he stood a little uncertain. He would not deny Clint hospitality, but he was not comfortable with it. This was not the case with his brother, Karl. Joanna's father had seen Clint in action when he and his daughter were in grave danger. He had discovered Clint's character in the responsibility he assumed to guarantee Joanna's safety. There was no hesitation on his part; he would help Clint on either side of the law. John's position was already known, but he was too young for his advice to be given serious consideration.

Bertha listened patiently during the second explanation to the men. She watched Joanna's face when Clint told them about the trial in Cheyenne and his decision to escape. Her heart went out to her niece, for her major concern was for Joanna, and she could see no happy ending to a life on the run with a fugitive. As much as she genuinely liked Clint, she felt she must speak against any ideas Joanna might have in mind. "Clint," she finally interrupted, "I understand completely why you did what you did, but if you care for Joanna, you must know you can't take her with you."

"I know that, ma'am," Clint replied. "I wouldn't ask her to."

"I knew you had a good head on your shoulders," Bertha said.

"Well, why don't you women get some supper on the table?" Karl interjected. "The man's probably half starved."

"I could use somethin' to eat," he admitted, "if it's not too much to ask."

"Of course you can have something to eat," Bertha said. "I'm not going to send you off hungry."

"I'm obliged," Clint drawled with a shy little smile in Joanna's direction. "Then I'll be goin' as soon as I get my horse loaded."

"You might as well stay until morning," Frederick said. "It's kinda late to get started tonight."

Joanna gave her uncle a grateful smile, then followed Clint out to the corral while he made his selection of the horses he had left in John's care. His choice was one of the Indian ponies, a pinto, to use for his packhorse. Figuring he would be depending upon his rifle for most of his food, he loaded all the spare ammunition he had. He unrolled a spare shirt and took the money he had left there for safe-keeping, and put it in his packs, along with his cooking utensils and his coffeepot. Then he set the packs beside the stall to be loaded upon the pinto in the morning. Joanna helped with the packs and then walked him back to the house, holding his arm in both of hers.

It was an unusually quiet supper. No one seemed inclined to offer the usual lighthearted conversation so typical at

Bertha's table. It was as if they expected the law to knock on the door at any second. It was a relief for Clint when it was finished and he said his good-byes. Joanna walked to the door of the barn with him and kissed him good night. "Be careful," she said as he left her.

Unable to sleep for most of the night, Joanna finally gave up a little before dawn and went to the window. As she stood staring out into the dark barnyard, she saw a shadowy figure on a horse emerge from the barn, leading his packhorse. Her first impulse was to run to the door to say good-bye, but she hesitated, knowing that it would be easier for both of them if she didn't.

# Chapter 14

Maggie Pitts took a long look at herself in the mirror, then touched her cheek with another dab of rouge. It was getting harder and harder to hide the years that had eroded the youthful appearance she had once thought would never fade. She stepped back to examine the full-length image, turning to study one profile, then turning to judge the other. She squinted critically at the beginnings of a wattle beneath her chin and reached up to pull the loose skin back with her fingers. *Nothing I can do about that*, she thought, *unless I wear dresses cut low enough to distract male eyeballs.* Sighing helplessly, resigned to the facts of nature, she finished dressing, took one last look in the mirror at the completed package, and went into the kitchen.

Times had been hard these last months, and now that winter was approaching, they would be harder still, although, typically, she usually picked up more short-term boarders in the winter, usually lonely men who lived most of their lives in temporary camps, caves, or rough cabins. A week at Maggie's big two-story house, eating in a dining room, and if financially able, enjoying the extra benefits offered by the madam, was their reward for surviving the rest of the year in the wilderness. If the customer was not able to afford the delights of the owner of the house, there were always the offerings of Maggie's cook and housekeeper. Half Irish, half Blackfoot, Corrina was compensated with free room and board, and earned her casual money by servicing occasional drifters.

It had been an equitable arrangement, but Maggie was keen enough to see the handwriting on the wall. She was staring life's advancing years in the face, and her sights were always set on finding her financial salvation. The big house that her late husband had built for her—at the time the finest structure in Big Timber, and still the largest—was now in a state of sad despair and in need of repair. And Maggie's chief assets were her feminine charms and friendly disposition, both of which were losing value every year.

For these reasons, Maggie was particular about her appearance on this early-fall day. Her two new boarders, though rough in appearance, seemed to be flush with money, judging by the size of the rolls they displayed when they paid a week in advance for not one, but two rooms. This might not be the opportunity she hoped for, but it certainly warranted looking into. And not that it mattered, but the big one wasn't that hard to look at. A bath and shave might be enough to make him presentable. The skinny one looked a little too much like a weasel to suit her, but when it came down to her needs, she would make either one do. She had been a prostitute when Frank married her. She was the same now, although she liked to think of herself as a property owner and entrepreneur.

She paused inside the kitchen door to judge the progress of supper. "Corrina, are you about ready to put it on the table?"

"Yes, ma'am," the cook replied. "You can go ahead and ring the bell if you want to. I'm fixin' to carry it in now."

Maggie took a tiny dinner bell from the cupboard, and

walking to the hallway, rang it several times. She then stood at the foot of the stairs and waited until she heard doors opening and boots in the upstairs hallway before returning the bell to its place in the cupboard.

Standing now at the corner of the long dining room table, Maggie greeted her guests as they filed in. "Mr. Smith, Mr. Johnson," she said cheerfully as Ballenger and Yancey pulled chairs away from the table and seated themselves. Not waiting for an invitation to start, both men dived right into the vittles, spooning out platefuls of everything on the table. Corrina, just setting a platter stacked with biscuits on the table, jumped back startled when Yancey used his fork to spear one of the biscuits before the platter was seated.

"Look out, there, missy," Ballenger chortled, "you'll lose a finger or two." He looked at Maggie and grinned. "Ol' Pete's been livin' in the woods too long. We ain't et in such fine trappin's as these for a long spell." Yancey merely grunted, more intent upon his plate.

Maggie answered his comments with a smile as she sat down at the head of the table. Watching the only two guests in the house attack Corrina's steak and gravy, she began to doubt the potential for her long-term salvation. *On the other hand*, she thought while watching Ballenger chewing on a slab of steak held before him on his fork, *if he's rich, he could meet with an early demise*, just as her late husband. Inwardly she shuddered when she thought, *It might be a really rough honeymoon.* Displaying a smile for him, she thought, *Oh well, you do what must be done.*

"How long will you be staying with us, Mr. Smith?" Maggie asked.

Yancey glanced up from his plate long enough to say, "We don't know—depends on things."

Maggie seemed confused. "I thought you were Mr. Johnson," she said.

"Oh . . . well, I am," Yancey replied, caught in the mistake. "Mr. Smith, there, was busy eatin' and I taught him not to talk with his mouth full." Both men roared with laughter at the joke.

Maggie's hopes for future planning drained quickly away as the supper progressed. The rough exteriors should have been warning enough that the two were no more than outlaws, and most likely came by their wealth dishonestly. Now she wished she had not gone to the trouble to put on her best dress to impress these two swine. However, she could still show a profit on the two before they decided to leave town.

His appetite sated, Clell pushed back a little from the table while he sipped another cup of coffee. "That little saloon we passed on the way in here, can a man get into a little card game there?"

"I expect so," Maggie replied. "There's men gambling there most every night."

"And maybe get a little somethin' else?" Ballenger continued, his grin indication enough of what he referred to.

She favored him with a knowing smile. "That depends on how much you can afford. You might be able to get somethin' extra somewhere else if the price is right."

"Like here?" Ballenger asked, enjoying the repartee.

"For the right price," Maggie replied.

"How much would that be?"

"Fifty dollars."

"Fifty dollars!" he exclaimed, then looked at Yancey. "Fifty dollars she says." Back at Maggie, he said, "I ain't ever heard of no whore chargin' that much. You must think a helluva lot of yourself."

"I ain't a whore, so it'll cost you more," she responded, looking him straight in the eye. "And I ain't never had a complaint."

"Is that so?" Clell replied. "Hell, as much as we paid for the rooms, that oughta be included."

"Well, it ain't," Maggie retorted. "If you wanna spend time with a lady, you'll have to pay for it. Otherwise, you can go see one of those hogs that hang around the saloon."

Ballenger chuckled gleefully, fully entertained by the madam's attitude. "Well, darlin'," he said, "I've got the money to buy ten like you. I'll just try you out tonight to see if you're worth fifty dollars." He glanced over at Yancey, who was still stuffing his mouth with biscuits. "How 'bout it, Mr. Johnson, you interested in a go-round with this prairie flower?"

Before Yancey could answer, Maggie interjected, "I don't do doubles. Mr. Johnson can talk to Corrina if he wants to." Yancey shrugged indifferently and continued eating.

Her remark caused Ballenger to chuckle again. "All right, Your Highness, we've got a deal."

"After you take a bath we'll have a deal," Maggie replied. "There's a tub in the washhouse. Corrina can heat some water for you."

"Wait a minute," Clell protested. "Ain't nothin' been said about no bath."

"That's my rule," she insisted. "Don't come to me smellin' like the stable." She felt it necessary to have some measure of control over the obviously rowdy scoundrel; otherwise, she might be the victim of a bruising rough and tumble. If he totally balked at the bath stipulation, she would probably do it, anyway, because she needed the extra fifty badly. She was greatly relieved, however, when he laughingly agreed to terms.

"What the hell?" he roared. "I reckon I can stand up to a bath this late in the season."

\*     \*     \*

Intrigued by the idea of a tryst with a rich man's prostitute, Ballenger presented himself to the washroom where Corrina was busily filling a huge wooden tub with water heated on the stove. Yancey accompanied him, not as a participator, but merely a spectator, his gaze constantly upon the half-breed woman as she came back and forth with her bucket. When the tub was filled, she dropped a washcloth and a bar of soap in the water and left the room saying, "Holler when you need rinsin'."

"Ain't you gonna scrub my back?" Ballenger joked.

"Let him do it," the stoic cook replied as she closed the door.

Enjoying the novelty of it, Ballenger used the soap and cloth to scrape away some of the layers of trail dust and grit. Yancey watched and made warning comments about the dangers of too much bathing and its potential for weakening a man's constitution. Ballenger just laughed at his partner's concerns, convinced that he was strong enough to stand up to any amount of soaking. "Hell, most women do it two or three times a month," he allowed, "and it don't appear to hurt them none."

When he was ready, he called for Corrina and she carried in a couple of large buckets of clean water to rinse him. He stood proudly in the tub while she stood on a stool and poured the water over him. "Now, don't you be jealous of your mistress, girl," he teased, receiving nothing more than a bored grunt in reply. Dried and in a clean robe supplied by Corrina, he was ready to proceed to the madam's bedroom when the maid doused him with some scented water. "What the hell did you do that for?" Clell demanded. "I just took a bath."

"Miss Maggie likes it," was the simple reply.

Shaking his head, hardly believing his partner's willingness to subject himself so blatantly, Yancey remained in the washroom, purportedly to help Corrina empty the large tub. After the water was emptied, he transacted a contract with the stoic maid that was executed right there in the washroom for a sum considerably less than his partner paid for the royal treatment. Following a short period of quick spasms resembling the mating of a pair of rabbits, he walked away satisfied and content to await his partner.

With the definite feeling that he had stepped up into a level of society that he had never experienced before, Clell Ballenger was content. Leaving Maggie's room afterward, he went upstairs to dress, where he found Yancey waiting for him. "Ain't you gonna dip your wick?" Ballenger asked.

"Done done it," Yancey said with a grin. "Been waitin' for you for half an hour."

Ballenger chuckled. "I swear, you could make do with a knothole in a wooden fence."

"If it ain't an ugly fence," Yancey replied matter-of-factly.

"Partner, I could get used to this. I ain't ever been tended to like I was tonight," Ballenger said as he pulled on the same dirty clothes he had ridden in with. "I'm thinkin' I'm 'bout ready to find us a card game."

"That's just what I was thinkin'," Yancey said.

They walked past the stable toward a newly built frame building, the lumber no doubt milled at the sawmill at the edge of the cluster of shacks and tents. "How 'bout walkin' on the downwind side of me?" Yancey requested. "You smell like one of them French trollops."

"It oughta blow offa me in this wind," Ballenger said, already regretting the dousing he had received. "There won't be none of that next time. That's for damn sure."

They stepped up on the small stoop and Yancey opened the door wide. A plank-topped bar ran across the upper end of the room with three tables near the opposite wall, although there was plenty of space for more. The establishment could not have been there very long. New buildings like this one would most likely be appearing more frequently since most of the Indians were now on reservations or had fled to the north.

Walking with the air of one who had recently struck it rich, Ballenger strode up to the bar and addressed the bartender. "Gimme a bottle of the best you got, and don't try to slip any of that cheap stuff in a different bottle by me."

Like most men who met Ballenger the first time, the bartender knew right away that he didn't want any trouble with him or the wiry, sly-looking man with him. Still, he had a reputation to protect, so he responded in kind. "Mister, I don't sell cheap or watered-down stock here. I stand behind the whiskey I sell."

Ballenger responded with a faint smile, amused that the man had gotten his hackles up. "Well, good," he said, "then we won't have no trouble, will we?" He was in a good mood, having decided he was going to hang around the little settlement for a spell. "Who are the three gents settin' at the back table?"

The bartender put a bottle on the bar with two glasses. "The one facin' this way is Tom Pullen, owns the sawmill. The other two, I don't know. They're just passin' through on their way to Bozeman."

"Looks to me like we got us enough to have a little game, partner," Ballenger said to Yancey. "You got a new deck of cards?" he directed back at the bartender.

When Clell pulled out a roll of bills to pay, the bartender's eyes suddenly opened wide. "Yes, sir, gentlemen," he said. "I think they were just wishin' they had a couple more players." He slapped an unopened deck of cards on the counter and escorted the two strangers to the table. "Tom,"

he said to the sawmill operator, "these two gents are lookin'
for a friendly little game of cards."

"That a fact?" Tom replied. "Well, I was just talking to
these two fellows about that very thing. Set yourselves
down."

While Ballenger and Yancey pulled a couple of chairs
over, Pullen glanced at the bartender, who nodded slowly
and cut his eyes over toward Clell. Understanding, Pullen
nodded back and started to make introductions.

Yancey cut him short. "We don't need to know nobody's
name. Just deal the cards and let's play some poker."

"There's a real poker player," Pullen said, laughing. "All
right, then, let's cut for deal."

Ballenger watched the sawmill owner and the way he
shuffled the cards. He'd be the one to watch, he decided. The
other two were a surly pair, drifters. Clell had ridden with
many a man just like them. They most likely didn't have
enough money to stay in the game long.

They started out with a dollar limit, and the first half
dozen hands went along quiet enough. One of the drifters
won a hand, Clell and Yancey won a couple, and Pullen won
one. Pullen suggested they up the limit to five dollars and
everyone agreed. After a few more hands with Clell and
Yancey both doing all right, one of the drifters, a stocky cur
of a man, became dark and brooding as he saw his money
rapidly disappearing. He folded for the second hand in a row
and sat sulking, his eyes fixed on Ballenger, who had just
raised. Glancing at his partner across the table, he quirked
one corner of his mouth in a surly smile. Then he began to
sniff, exaggerating the act like a dog on the scent of something wild. He sniffed in Pullen's direction; then he sniffed
in Ballenger's direction, sticking his nose close up to Ballenger's face. Across from him, Yancey sat back holding his

cards close to his vest, a huge smile spreading across his narrow face, anticipating the fun about to begin.

"Damn if I don't believe it must be the time of month for one of you ladies," the drifter drawled. "Which one of you sweet things is it?"

"I reckon it's me," Ballenger said evenly. He put his cards facedown on the table while the drifter smirked spitefully. In the next instant, the drifter's cheek was split from the corner of his eye to the point of his chin, the result of Ballenger's pistol barrel laid forcefully against the side of his head. He went sprawling from his chair with the big man on top of him before he hit the floor. Again and again Ballenger hammered the hapless man with the butt of his pistol until the drifter finally lay still.

The other drifter started to get up when his partner was first struck, but sat back down when Yancey stuck a gun in his ribs. "Clell gets riled easy," Yancey said. "You'd best keep your seat."

Ballenger got up from the unconscious man, and glaring at the other drifter, advised, "You better drag his sorry ass outta here while I'm still in a good mood." As the battered man's partner struggled to pull him out of the saloon, Pullen started to rake his money from the table, only to receive a menacing stare from the angry man. "Hold on there a minute," he commanded. "Let's see them cards." Pullen turned over two pair, kings and nines. Ballenger turned his cards faceup. "Three fives," he said, and started to rake the money.

"Wait just a minute," Yancey said, and turned over a low straight. Smiling with gratification, he pulled the pot over to him.

"Why, you low down snake in the grass," Ballenger snarled. "You was layin' back all the time, lettin' us do the bettin'."

"Well, gentlemen, it's gettin' late," Pullen blurted nervously. "I expect I'd best be gettin' home." He glanced at an equally nervous bartender. "I think I'll use the back door, Jake. It's closer to my horse."

"Sure you don't wanna hang around?" Ballenger asked. "We could play some three-man poker."

"Thank you just the same, but I expect my wife's wonderin' where I am." He grabbed his coat and hurried out the back.

"We'll most likely be around for a few days," Ballenger called after him. He then turned to Yancey. "Grab that there bottle. I reckon we might as well go, too."

Yancey, having seen a fair share of barroom fights, picked up the bottle. "You reckon one of them jaspers is waitin' outside with a rifle?"

"I would," Ballenger replied with certainty, "if it was the other way around. I expect it'd be a good idea if one of us went out the back."

"I'll go out the front," Yancey volunteered. "I doubt they'll shoot until they see us both come out, especially you. You go around the back and see if you can catch 'em before they can get off a shot." He didn't tell Ballenger that he wasn't worried about getting shot because neither one of the drifters looked like the assassin in his dream.

Just as they suspected, the drifters were lying in wait outside. Yancey had to dive for cover when a rifle shot ripped a sizable chunk out of the door frame only inches from his head. Scrambling on hands and knees, he made it to the protection of the low stoop. Ballenger, sneaking around the building, arrived at the front of the saloon in time to see the rifle blast from the corner of the stable. He immediately returned fire with his pistol. The range was a little too great for accuracy with a pistol, but the repeated fire from Ballenger was enough to surprise the bushwhackers, and they decided not to push their luck. In a few seconds, Ballenger heard the sound of horses galloping away in the night. "Come on, Yancey!" he yelled as he ran after them, trying to load his pistol on the run. A man his size on foot was no contest for two fast horses, so it wasn't much of a contest. The drifters contented themselves with that one shot, and then wisely headed for parts unknown.

# Chapter 15

Deputy Marshal Mack Thompson paused to take a precautionary look at the chuck wagon parked beside Fiddler's Creek. A modest-sized remuda was roped off near the wagon and a couple of men were standing near the campfire. They did not notice the lone rider approaching them from the other side of the creek until he had advanced to within a hundred yards.

"Uh-oh," Percy Johnson said, and hurried to the wagon to get his rifle.

"Who the hell is that?" Floyd Berry asked, squinting in an effort to identify the rider.

"It ain't one of our boys," Percy said, "and I ain't takin' no chances after them last two." He walked over to position himself behind a corner of the wagon. Taking the hint, Floyd took cover at the front of the wagon.

"Hello the camp!" Thompson called out. "I'm comin' in."

"Come on, then," Percy replied, and held his rifle ready to fire at the first indication of foul play.

When Thompson came closer, he identified himself. "I'm U.S. Deputy Marshal Mack Thompson."

Floyd relaxed a bit, but Percy still held his rifle ready before him, watching the stranger closely as he pulled up next to the wagon and dismounted. "Howdy, boys," he said, and pulled his coat open to show them his badge. "Is there any coffee left in that pot?"

"Why, sure, Marshal," Percy replied after seeing the badge. "I'll fetch you a cup." While he pulled a cup from his cupboard, he went on to explain. "Sorry we didn't show you much hospitality, but the last strangers that come into my camp left me with a mighty sore bump on the back of my head."

This immediately snared Thompson's interest. "Much obliged," he said when Percy handed him his coffee. "I'm trailin' two outlaws that I'm guessin' mighta come this way. They held up the bank in Helena."

"Well, I expect you're on the right trail," Percy responded. "It was two fellers that jumped me, and they was ridin' some wore-out horses—stole two of our horses after they sneaked up behind me and knocked me in the head."

"Can you tell me what they looked like?" Thompson asked, already feeling certain that it was Ballenger and Yancey.

"Sure. One of 'em, the one that did most of the talkin', was a big feller with black bushy hair in the back. Had a kinda flat nose, like somebody had slammed a board across it." Thompson nodded. Percy continued. "The other'n was a lanky, kinda skinny feller that didn't say much, but looked like he'd eat your liver if you gave him a chance."

Thompson was certain that Percy had just described Ballenger and Yancey. His description was pretty much the same given by the witnesses at the bank. "That sounds like the two I've been trailin'," he said. "Which way did they go?"

"Yonder way," Percy said, pointing toward the southeast. "They had me hog-tied, but I seen 'em ride off." Then he remembered what Ballenger had said when they first rode up. "They said they was headin' to Big Timber. I don't know if they was or not." He shook his head and added, "I mighta knowed they was bank robbers or somethin'."

"Yep, that they were," Thompson said. "They managed to get away from the sheriff and a posse outta Helena. I guess I was just lucky to scout out this way for 'em." He finished his coffee quickly and stepped up in the saddle. "Much obliged, boys. Thanks for the coffee."

"I hope you catch the son of a bitches," Percy called after him as he rode out past the remuda.

"I ain't takin' another bath, and that's for damn certain," Clell blurted. "It's downright unhealthy for a man to take two baths in four days."

"Then don't come scratchin' around my door," Maggie replied stubbornly. "I don't want you rubbin' your dirt off on my sheets."

"To hell with you and your sheets," Clell shot back. "I ain't takin' no bath, and I ain't payin' no fifty dollars for a ten-dollar tussle with you, either. You done made enough money offa me."

Incensed, but also reluctant to lose the recent source of money, Maggie shot back, "Well, you're not gettin' a free one if that's what you're thinkin'."

"Hell, I ain't thinkin' about a free ride. You're lookin' kinda flabby and wrinkled. Maybe you oughta be payin' me." It was not the money alone that had smothered Clell's flame of passion. He had been eyeballing Corrina more and more, and the half-breed woman looked a hell of a lot younger than her mistress. The fact that it would save him a considerable sum of money was a bonus. He figured like Yancey now, they all looked the same with their skirts up. "You can keep that old thing you're so proud of till it dries up," he said in parting.

"Why, you ol' flat-nosed son of a bitch," Maggie fumed, "I wouldn't let you have no more if you offered a hundred dollars!"

Chuckling to himself, he headed for the kitchen in search of the maid. Finding the kitchen empty, and no sign of the woman out the back door, he went upstairs to look for Yancey. Finding Yancey's door locked, he banged on it and yelled for him.

"What is it?" Yancey yelled back.

"Open the damn door," Ballenger replied impatiently.

"In a minute," Yancey came back. "I'm 'bout finished." True to his word, in a little more than a minute, he came to the door, pulling his trousers up. The door opened and Corrina slipped by him, and hurried down the hall.

"Damn," Ballenger grunted. "That takes care of that." Then he called after her, "I'll be talkin' to you later on this evenin'." He turned back to Yancey. "Get your pants on and we'll go get us a drink and maybe scare up a card game."

Lem Turner had seen the solemn deputy marshal on a couple of occasions when Thompson had passed through the little settlement before. Once he had boarded his horse in Lem's stable and slept in the stall with it. "Yep, Marshal, them four in the corral, the chestnut and that palomino, and the black and the gray belong to two fellers that rode in a few days ago. They're stayin' with Maggie Pitts." In answer to Thompson's question, he replied, "A big man with a flat nose, and his skinny sidekick. Tom Pullen said they pistol-whipped some feller pretty bad in the saloon a couple of nights ago."

"Much obliged," Thompson said, and went on his way, confident that he had caught up with the bank robbers.

His next stop was Maggie Pitts' rooming house where he found the proprietor setting the table for supper. She turned around and gasped slightly when she was startled by the sudden appearance of the gaunt lawman standing right behind her. "My stars!" she exclaimed. "I didn't hear you come in."

He pulled his coat aside to show the badge on his vest. "I'm interested in two of your boarders," he said, "name of Ballenger and Yancey."

"Well, I don't have but two guests right now, but their names are Mr. Johnson and Mr. Smith."

"Are they here now?"

"Why, no. I think Corrina said they went to the saloon a little while ago." She displayed an impatient frown. "That's where they spend all their time when they're not here."

Thompson nodded. "I need to see their rooms."

She shrugged indifferently and led the way up the stairs. "Those two at the end of the hall," she said, pointing.

"You stay out here in the hall," he said as he went past her and entered the first room. It didn't take much of a search to find the money, stuffed in the saddlebags. A clumsy attempt to hide it had been made by cramming some pieces of clothing on top of it. He found much the same in the other room, leaving little doubt that these two were the men who held up the bank. Back out in the hall, he told Maggie to leave the doors closed and not to enter the rooms until he returned. He considered taking the stolen money with him then, but decided it would be safe enough right where it was for a short time. Besides, he had taken a good look, and felt he would be able to tell whether any was missing when he came back for it. The first order of business was to get Ballenger and Yancey in irons. Maggie promised the rooms would not be disturbed.

The two bank robbers were sitting at the back table when Thompson walked in. He glanced at Jake behind the bar when the bartender asked him if he wanted a drink. "Maybe later," Thompson replied casually, and walked back to the table.

They had been sitting there playing two-hand poker while they worked on a bottle of Jake's best, hoping the owner of the sawmill would show up for some cards. Clell, his back to the wall, studied the man walking toward them. "Well, now, maybe we got us somebody to get up a little game of cards," he said to Yancey. To Thompson, he said, "You lookin' for a little action?"

"You could say that," Thompson replied, eyeing Ballenger coldly. "Whaddaya say we start with you two puttin' your hands in the air and standin' up?" he ordered, pulling his Colt .45.

Momentarily stunned, both men sat bolt upright. It was only for a moment, however, before Ballenger recovered from the surprise. "Now, what's the trouble, friend?" he said. "Is this a holdup, right here in front of a witness?" He nodded toward Jake, who was equally astonished.

"Nope," Thompson replied. "This is an arrest for robbin' the bank in Helena." He cut his eyes only briefly toward Yancey, who was starting to shift in his chair. "You'd best get your hands up on the table where I can see them," he warned. "You, too," he told Ballenger. "I'm not gonna tell you again, so if you don't wanna get shot right where you sit, get 'em up there."

"Now, take it easy, there, Sheriff," Ballenger said. "Ain't no sense in anybody gettin' shot. Me and Yancey ain't gonna cause no trouble." He placed his left hand on the table, but before following with his right, he grasped the .44 he habitually rested between his legs anytime he played cards. Thompson had no time to react. Automatically recoiling when the pistol exploded under the table, the bullet striking him in the groin, he was in no position to fire before Ballenger and Yancey turned the table over on him, both men pumping bullets into the doomed lawman as he went down on the floor, his life draining from his body.

"Not today, Sheriff," Yancey hooted excitedly.

Ballenger swung around to level his pistol at the wide-eyed

bartender. "Don't get no ideas about pullin' that shotgun from under the bar, unless you're lookin' to be a dead hero."

"No, sir!" Jake responded, and immediately slapped both hands palms down on the bar.

Ballenger turned his attention back to the dying lawman on the floor. He reached down and ripped the badge from Thompson's vest. "Huh," he grunted. "He ain't a sheriff, he's a marshal." He gave Yancey a disgusted glance. "It might be a smart thing for us to move on."

"Yeah," Yancey replied, "and I was hopin' to stay around here a little longer."

Leaving the marshal's body for Jake to dispose of, they sauntered out of the saloon. Seeing Thompson's horse tied at the hitching rail, Ballenger said, "I don't reckon the marshal has any use for his horse now. We might as well take it with us."

Back at the rooming house, Maggie Pitts was on her knees, rifling through Ballenger's saddlebags. "Gawdamighty!" she squealed. "There must be a million dollars in here!" She hadn't waited long after the marshal left. As soon as Corrina called from the front window that Thompson was out of sight, she had rushed into Ballenger's room to verify what she had suspected. "Look in the other room," she directed her maid. "See if there's anything in the other one's saddlebags." In a few minutes when she heard Corrina's gasp of surprise, she stuck her head out in the hall and yelled, "That marshal has gone to arrest those two. He ain't gonna know exactly how much was in these bags. He didn't take enough time to count it. Take two or three of those little bundles and stuff the clothes back over the rest."

Both women were so busy with the confiscation of this unexpected treasure that they were not aware they had company until the sound of footsteps in the upper hallway caused both to freeze. Caught red-handed with several packets of bills on the floor at her knees, Maggie could only stare fearfully up at the glowering Clell Ballenger in the doorway. She could find no words to defend herself until Yancey came in behind Ballenger, dragging Corrina by the arm. Clell scowled at the half-breed and grunted, "Huh," before walking over to stand directly over Maggie.

"We were just cleaning up your rooms," Maggie whimpered. "We were gonna put everything back."

"I'll bet you was," Ballenger snarled, delivering a sharp backhand that knocked her over on her side. He went immediately after her. "Thinkin' you was gonna steal from me, was you? And I'd never know the difference. Right?" He administered a steady rain of blows as he scolded until her screams of pain turned to pitiful whimpers and she fell limp. Unable to satisfy his anger, he grabbed her blouse with one hand and held her up while he pummeled her with his closed fist.

Again and again he struck until Yancey finally said, "Hell, Clell, she's dead. You done beat her to death."

Half-crazed in his fury, Ballenger turned to look at his partner as if just realizing he was not alone. The rage that had erupted inside him slowly began to ebb like an angry ocean's tide, and he dropped the lifeless body to the floor. "All right," he said, calm again. "I expect we'd best pack up and get the hell outta here." He looked then at Corrina, held firmly in Yancey's grasp. "I ain't leavin' no witnesses," he said.

"I know it," Yancey said, "but I ain't through with her yet. I'm takin' her with us."

"The hell you are."

"The hell I ain't," Yancey retorted.

He and Ballenger glared defiantly at each other for a few moments before the big man backed off. In the moment of calm, it occurred to him that he might have use for the woman himself. "All right," he said. "But you're gonna keep an eye on her. The first time she causes trouble, I'll slit her damn throat." He glared directly at Corrina then. "You understand? The first time."

"I won't be no trouble," the terrified woman quickly pleaded, unable to take her eyes off the mutilated body of her mistress.

"All right, then, pack up!" Ballenger ordered. "I'll go get our horses. While I'm gone, pack all the food and stuff you can find in the kitchen and anything else we might use."

Thinking it best that he went alone to the stable, he walked in just as the owner was hurrying out to see what the gunshots on the other end of town were about. Not expecting to see the big man again after the visit from the marshal, Lem Turner managed to suppress his surprise when Ballenger walked in and said he had come for the horses. It was obvious that the marshal's confrontation with Ballenger and his partner had not gone well for the lawman. He attempted to make casual conversation, but could not accomplish it when facing the outlaw. Ballenger scowled at him when he mentioned extra costs for oats, causing Lem to say, "No extra charge, though. We'll call it even."

When he returned to the house, Clell and Yancey searched for the money they had spent while they were there, especially the fifty-dollar charges for Ballenger's contracts with Maggie. The search was to no avail until Clell's temper erupted again and he started smashing the furniture. It was then that the money showed up in a bureau drawer with a false bottom. At Yancey's direction, Corrina took her pick of the clothes strewn around on the floor and changed into them before Yancey's leering eyes. Just at dark, they rode out, heading east, with Ballenger leading Thompson's horse loaded with food and supplies, blankets and ammunition. Yancey followed with Corrina holding on behind him. Ballenger decided to leave the other two horses, not wanting the bother. They would have preferred to wait until morning, but they could not be certain of the little town's reactions to the killing of the marshal. There was always a chance that somebody might take a shot at them.

When they had ridden far enough to feel safe, they stopped to make camp where a series of gullies broke down to the river. "Might as well stop here," Ballenger said. "It's so damn dark we're liable to break a horse's leg in these damn gullies." When they dismounted, he told Corrina to make a fire and fix something to eat. She quickly did as she was told, fearful of triggering her captors' ire. After feeding them, she submitted to both men's carnal needs without protest. Afterward, she lay bundled in a quilt taken from Maggie's bed and waited patiently until both men were snoring contentedly. Hesitating briefly as she tiptoed between the two sleeping men, she considered the possibility of slipping the revolver from Yancey's holster and shooting both men. The revenge for herself and her mistress would go a long way in repaying the savage pair for their brutality. But the thought of waking them before she could accomplish the deed was enough to prevent her from trying.

Moving quietly then, she tiptoed away from the fire and led the deputy marshal's horse down along the riverbank, afraid to take the time to steal one of the saddles. Once she was sure she was beyond their hearing, she jumped on the horse's back and rode away in the night.

# Chapter 16

Planning to follow the Yellowstone to the far mountains, Clint Conner made his way westward. He opted to avoid most of the infrequent settlements he encountered along the river, riding around the random clusters of tents and shacks of traders and trappers. The occasional farm bore evidence of the Indians' departure as a few brave souls moved in to attempt a living in a land still far from civilized. After camping one night near the confluence of the Yellowstone and the Rosebud creeks, he rode on until he struck another creek, where he came upon two men in the process of building a cabin. Inclined at first to ride around them, he reconsidered, thinking the men looked innocent enough.

"Good day to you," Clint called out as he approached. They were so intent upon their labor that both men were startled.

After quickly moving to stand next to the rifles propped against the knee-high wall of the cabin, they stared back at the stranger for a long moment before one of them returned the greeting. "Good day to you," he echoed, watching him carefully.

The other man, after scrutinizing him and his packhorse

for a few moments, decided that Clint was no more than a lone traveler. "Howdy," he said. "Where you headin'?"

"West," Clint answered.

"Any place in particular?" the man's partner asked.

"Just west," Clint replied, smiling.

Judging Clint to be friendly enough, the first man said, "How you gonna know when you get there?" Then before Clint could answer, he asked, "You new in this part of the country?"

"Yep," Clint replied, "but I reckon everybody out here was new sometime."

The two men looked at each other and laughed. "Step down if you will," the second man said. "We're fixin' to knock off for some dinner. You're welcome to join us."

At this particular time the invitation appealed to Clint. "Much obliged," he said. "I am gettin' a little stiff in the saddle, and a cup of coffee would taste good right now. I'll even furnish the coffee."

It turned out that the men were brothers, John and Julian Tate, and they were the vanguard for two younger brothers who were planning to join them in the spring. "We're figurin' on settin' up a sawmill," John, the eldest, said. "James and Jeremy will be bringin' the sawmill with them." Clint gave his name as Clint Allen, using his middle name for last.

"We're figurin' this is a good spot for a town, what with the steamboats comin' up the river and all," Julian said. "If you're just lookin' for a place to settle down, you might consider this place."

"You may be right," Clint said, "but right now I'm just goin' to see what I can see."

Soon the coffeepot was bubbling, and the Tate brothers fried up some bacon to eat with biscuits they had made that morning. Taking coffee only, Clint spent a pleasant hour with them before bidding them good luck with the sawmill and their town and climbing back in the saddle.

He continued west along the river for the rest of that day until approaching darkness found him at another creek, this one larger than the one the Tate brothers were building on. It seemed an ideal place to make camp, so he turned off the river track and rode up the creek for a quarter mile or so until finding a place that suited him. With plenty of grass for the horses, as well as water and trees for protection, he set about making his camp for the night.

At morning light, he took his time about leaving, deciding to take a better look around him. When he had made camp the night before, there had been very little light to inspect the spot in which he had landed. The abundance of deer sign caused him to consider exploring the creek a little farther, so he saddled Rowdy and loaded the pinto and followed the creek north.

Fairly wide in places, the creek wound its way through hilly prairie land like a great snake, lined with trees and thick brush. With the presence of deer sign everywhere, the opportunity to find fresh meat replaced thoughts of returning to the Yellowstone right away. Before the end of the day, he was rewarded with an easy shot at a young buck drinking at the creek. Clint thought it a good sign, and decided to make his camp on the spot with plans to further explore the creek.

Julian Tate straightened and gazed toward the edge of the cottonwoods. "John," he said, "there's somebody comin'."

John dropped his ax and turned to follow his brother's gaze. A lone rider aboard a strawberry roan was approaching at a slow walk. "I swear, it's gettin' downright crowded out here," he said. "That's the second rider we've seen in two days. I wonder if he's as lost as that other feller."

Deputy U.S. Marshal Zach Clayton had figured on making it to Little Porcupine Creek to camp that night. He made it with a good hour of daylight to spare, but he didn't expect to find two fellows building a cabin there. Seeing no need to be overly cautious, he rode on in and pulled up before the two men eyeing him carefully. "Looks like you fellers have got a right fair start on a cabin," he said.

"We're workin' at it," John Tate replied.

Clayton looked around the clearing, noting the small tent off to the side and the horses hobbled a few dozen yards away. He saw no sign of women or children. Still seated in the saddle, he said, "I'd figured on restin' my horse and camping close to the creek tonight, but I'll ride on a ways."

"What brings you out this way, friend?" Julian asked.

"I'm lookin' for somebody," Clayton replied. "I'm a deputy marshal outta Cheyenne, Wyoming Territory." He opened his coat to display his badge. "Two fellers robbed a bank over at Helena," he continued. "Pretty bad pair, one big with a flat nose, the other one rangy with a face like a weasel. You seen anybody like that?"

"Cheyenne?" John questioned, ignoring the question. "You know you ain't in Wyomin' Territory, don't you?"

Clayton smiled patiently. "I know," he said, "but I started chasin' 'em in Wyomin'. You seen 'em?"

Both brothers shook their heads. "Nope," John replied. "Ain't seen nobody like that. We don't get much company."

"Except for the last two days," Julian reminded him.

"That's right," John said, "you're the second feller passed by here in the last two days. We didn't see nobody for a month before that."

"'Pears like you know where you're goin', though," Julian commented. "That feller we saw the other day didn't rightly know where he was headed." He laughed, then added, "He was a nice enough young feller, though."

The comment struck a chord in Clayton's mind. He had heard a similar remark from Billy Turnipseed about a stranger he had met back at the Belle Fourche. It would be too much of a coincidence, but he felt compelled to ask, "Was he ridin' a buckskin dun?"

"As a matter of fact, he was," John replied. "He a friend of yours?"

"Maybe. How long ago did you see him?"

"Day before yesterday, about dinnertime."

"Remember his name?"

John shook his head. "No, I swear I don't. You remember, Julian?"

"Nah," Julian replied, scratching his head. "Allen somethin' or somethin' Allen. I ain't sure."

Coincidence was piling upon coincidence. Clayton told himself the stranger they had seen was not likely Clint Conner. He didn't figure Clint to be traveling west along the Yellowstone. He felt sure the young man would have headed straight for that young lady on the other side of the Tongue River. Still, it was intriguing enough to encourage him to try to pick up his pace in hopes of catching up with the man, just to satisfy his curiosity. He intended to search through every town, trading post, and collection of huts between here and Bozeman on the chance that Ballenger and Yancey might be running this way. If there was no sign of them by the time he reached Bozeman, he would try Butte and maybe Virginia City. He had a feeling they wouldn't fan out too far from the whiskey mills and whorehouses. They had money to spend. He hadn't figured on Clint, and he didn't particularly want to catch up with him if he was the man these two men had seen. He couldn't resist, however. "Well, I think I'd best get on my way," he finally said.

"You're welcome to light and camp here tonight," John said.

"Much obliged, but I think I'll push on a ways yet. There's a good hour before dark. Maybe I'll see you fellers on the way back."

The Tate brothers nodded good-bye and watched Clayton as he headed west along the river, then went back to work on their cabin. Clayton held his horse to a steady walk, knowing the roan already tired, but he figured it wasn't too hard on him to go a little farther before resting. When dark caught up with him, he made a hasty camp by the river.

The next morning, he did not linger by the fire. Downing the last of the coffeepot, he was soon in the saddle and heading west. Making good time, he crossed Big Porcupine Creek before noon, and continued on toward the Big Horn. Traveling light, and with no packhorse, he was making good time, but the rider the Tates had told him about had too much of a start on him for Clayton to know whether he was catching up or not. Discouraging also was the absence of recent tracks that he could even speculate upon as being those left by Clint Conner.

Three days without sighting anyone brought him to the thriving settlement of Coulson. It had grown a great deal since he had last traveled this part of the country. The recently signed treaties with the Sioux had opened the land along the river to development, and there was already a rush of settlers to claim newly surveyed land for farms outside the town. Clayton was amazed at the new buildings when he rode into the town. A two-story hotel was under construction to add to several saloons, a post office, a general merchandise store, and a telegraph office. Someone had also set up a ferry across the river.

It was the kind of place two outlaws like Ballenger and Yancey might find to their liking. Clayton decided to stable his horse and stop over long enough to keep a watch on the saloons and the large tent he spotted near the ferry landing that was obviously a whorehouse. If Ballenger and Yancey were anywhere in the vicinity, they would most likely show up before long. *I could use a little rest myself*, he thought as he guided the roan toward the stable. *A day or two out of the saddle and a drink of whiskey would go pretty well right now.*

After stabling his horse, he took a walking tour of the town, stopping at the telegraph office first to wire Cheyenne that he was still alive and working. Afterward, he checked the saloons and talked to the bartenders. No one had seen two men matching Ballenger's and Yancey's descriptions. The last saloon he visited was the River House, and this was where he decided to have his drink.

"These two fellers you're lookin' for," the bartender asked, "they friends of yours?"

"Hardly," Clayton replied, sipping his drink. "Have you seen 'em?"

"You a lawman?"

"That's right," Clayton answered.

"What did they do?"

"Well," Clayton replied impatiently, "lately they robbed a bank up in Helena. Along the way, they've murdered and stole all over Nebraska, Kansas, and Wyoming."

"Dang!" the bartender exclaimed quietly. "And you think they're around here?"

"I don't know if they are or not. I'm just tryin' to find out. Have you seen anybody that fits that description?" Clayton was beginning to lose his patience with the man.

"Ain't that somethin'," the bartender said, shaking his head in wonder. "So we've got law in town now. I didn't even know that. How long have you been here?"

"Jesus Christ, man!" Clayton exploded. "I'm not the local law here. As far as I know, there ain't no law in Coulson. I'm a U.S. deputy marshal out of Cheyenne, Wyomin', and I'm tryin' like hell to find two outlaws that might be headed this way."

"Cheyenne? That's a helluva ways from here, ain't it?"

"It ain't far enough," Clayton replied, his patience shot. He tossed the last of his whiskey down and promptly walked out.

As he reached the door, the bartender called after him, "I think them two fellers mighta been in here night before last."

Clayton stopped abruptly, his hand on the doorknob. He turned about and returned to the bar. "What's your name, mister?"

"Sam Crowder," the bartender replied.

"Well, Sam, help me out here. All right?" When Sam nodded, Clayton questioned him extensively about the appearance of the two men he had seen, their behavior, and how much money they had spent.

"Oh, they was well-heeled," Sam said, "flashin' money around, all night. They had a good time for theirselves. I kinda hated to see 'em leave, but they was gettin' the itch— the big feller, especially—to go down by the river to Sophie's." He shook his head and chuckled just thinking about it; then he abruptly frowned at Clayton. "And you think them fellers might be the same ones that robbed a bank in Helena?"

"Maybe," Clayton allowed. "I can't say for sure till I find 'em."

"Well, I hope you're wrong. Them fellers spent a lot of money in here. I've been lookin' for 'em to come back ever since."

"Yeah, they're a lovable pair, no doubt about it," Clayton said, and left the bartender still shaking his head in wonder as he walked down toward the river and Sophie's tent.

\* \* \*

"A lawman? Well, I've done business with more'n a few lawmen," Sophie Beasley said, smirking, "but I don't give no discounts to lawmen or lawyers."

"I ain't a customer," Clayton informed her. "I'm here on business. I wanna ask you a few questions about a couple of your recent customers."

"I don't talk about my customers," Sophie insisted. "How long do you think I'd stay in business if I talked about my customers?"

"Have it your way," Clayton said with a shrug of his shoulders. "I was hopin' to save you some hurtin'. These two I'm lookin' for have killed a couple of women like you." He thought he was lying, unaware of the recent fate of Maggie Pitts. His bluff worked, however.

Sophie's face suddenly took on a serious look, and she paused to let his comment sink in as she thought about the imposing bulk of Clell Ballenger. "Well," she reconsidered, "I get paid by the hour," she said, "talk or wrestle, I get paid for my time."

"I got no money for prostitutes," Clayton said, and made motions as if about to leave. "I hope, for your sake, you ain't one of the unlucky ones that has to deal with Clell Ballenger."

Her face blanched at the sound of the name. "Clell!" she exclaimed. "That was the big fellow's name. The other one was Pete. They didn't offer no last names, and I didn't ask for any."

"Now we're gettin' somewhere," Clayton said. His normally slow pulse quickened a bit as he realized that he might be close to Ballenger and Yancey. "Do you know where they went when they left here?"

"I don't know where they went, but they said they was comin' back in a day or two."

"Good," Clayton said. "I appreciate your help." He started to leave.

"Wait a minute!" Sophie blurted. "Ain't you gonna stay around to protect me? I don't wanna do no business with a pair of murderers." His warning had taken deep effect upon her.

"Don't worry," he assured her. "I'll be watchin' for 'em." Then he grinned. "I was just japin' about them killin' whores."

"You son of a bitch," she growled as he left.

After two days of hunting and exploring along Big Porcupine Creek, Clint decided to return to his original plan to follow the Yellowstone west. Impatient now to reach the high mountains he had always longed to see, he pushed on over rolling, tumbling prairie that seemed to stretch endlessly away from the winding river. A day and a half's travel brought him to the confluence with a river he guessed to be the Big Horn, based upon the description he had received from John Tate.

The last few mornings had been quite chilly, even though the days were still mild, comfortable in fact. But the cool mornings were fair warning that the mild afternoons would be few in number from now on. Winter was never far away on the high plains, a fact that caused him to seek the protection of the mountains even more, and preferably in time to build a suitable winter camp. With these thoughts in mind, he welcomed the sight of a small trading post on the south shore where the Big Horn joined the Yellowstone. When he first spotted it, he wasn't certain it was, in fact, a trading post. There was no solid structure, house or log cabin. Instead, a tipi, painted with tribal symbols, sat before a small corral with a rough shed for a barn. There was a board attached over the entrance to the tipi that proclaimed JIM

CROSS—TRADER. It did not show promise of a permanent business. It was enough to engage Clint's curiosity, however.

As Clint approached, a strapping bear of a man emerged from the tipi, dressed in buckskins and Indian moccasins. His hair, dark with streaks of silver, was worn long, and tied with a single strand of rawhide, so that it lay across his back like a great mane. His full beard was solid black except for a streak of white running from each corner of his mouth, giving the appearance of two long fangs. Though demonic at first impression, his face transformed to one of welcome as soon as he smiled and greeted Clint.

"Good afternoon, friend," he said. "My name's Jim Cross. Step down and rest yourself a spell."

"Afternoon," Clint returned, pulling Rowdy up before the tipi. He threw a leg over and stepped down. "If your sign means what it says, I'll be needin' a few things."

Jim's smile widened, displaying teeth whiter than Clint had ever seen before. "Well, if I've got what you're needin', I'll do my best to skin you properly." He laughed heartily at his joke. "What is it you're a'needin'? I've got some flour and coffee beans, dried beans and salt, if it's food you're wantin'."

"What I'm lookin' for is somethin' to keep me warm. Winter's comin' on and I need somethin' more than the wool coat I'm carrying."

Jim Cross nodded his understanding, then stepped back and took a sidelong look at Clint's packhorse and the few mule deer hides tied across his packs. His expression was not one of great expectation. "What have you got to trade?" he asked. "If you're thinkin' about a bearskin coat or somethin', them hides there ain't hardly enough to get you a sleeve."

"I've got three hides," Clint replied. "I need to keep one

of 'em. So I can trade two, but I've got a shotgun, some rifles, and a couple of pistols to trade, too."

Jim's eyes lit up at this. "Well, now, that's different. It sounds like you and me can talk some trade. Hold on a minute." He turned his head slightly toward the tipi. "Spring Flower, come on out here and make us some coffee." He turned back to Clint, his smile still in place, and said, "We might as well have a little somethin' to warm our bellies while we talk." He paused a moment while a slender Indian woman emerged from the tipi and went to the fire to fetch the coffeepot. "This here's my woman, Spring Flower, full-blood Crow. Come on inside and we'll see what we can do for you."

Clint followed the huge man inside, noticing the rifle propped next to the flap where the woman had evidently stood covering her husband until sure that Clint was intent only upon trading. On one side of the lodge, he saw a bed and some cooking utensils. The rest of the tipi was filled with stacks of furs, kegs of molasses, barrels of flour, sugar, beans, and other supplies. Clint was taken aback at the sight of so much merchandise packed inside the small dwelling. He turned to Cross and commented, "You're gonna need to build you a house."

Cross laughed. "I know it," he said, "and I'll do just that when I make up my mind if I'm gonna stay here or move on to someplace else. I ain't sure if this is a good spot or not. Riverboats don't come up this way like they used to. Folks say the railroads will be comin' before long. I might pack up my wares and head farther north." He laughed again. "Hell, you're only the second man I've seen this week. Another feller rode by day before yesterday, and he didn't need nothin'."

He reached over and pulled a fur coat from a stack of various furs. "Now, here's the very thing you're lookin' for," he said, shaking out the heavy bearskin coat and holding it up before him. "Try this on. It'll keep you warm when it gets so cold piss freezes." While Clint tried the coat on, Cross stood back a step to watch. "That what you're lookin' for? Spring Flower stitched that coat. She's got some deerskin shirts and britches you oughta take a look at, too. 'Course I need to see what kinda guns you're lookin' to trade."

Expecting old and worn-out weapons, Jim Cross opened his eyes just a touch wider when Clint pulled a Henry rifle out from under the deerskin. He hoped Clint hadn't noticed the sparkle in his eyes when he saw the rifle, but the young man's wry smile told him his reactions had not escaped Clint's notice. "I reckon there ain't no use in beatin' around the bush on this," Cross admitted. "This weapon looks to be in fine shape. I'd have to shoot it to know for sure." Clint opened one of the packs and produced a box of .44 cartridges. He took out three and handed them to Cross. Cross loaded them in the magazine and cocked the rifle. Then he walked toward the riverbank and picked a cottonwood on the low bluffs on the other side as a target. An interested observer, Clint watched. He had never fired the rifle himself. It had belonged to one of the men who tried to jump him when he, Joanna, and Karl were camped at the Tongue River.

The huge man fired three times at the tree, placing all three shots in a pattern roughly the size of a chair seat. He brought the rifle down and examined it again. "Pulls a little to the left," he said.

"Damn little," Clint replied, knowing Jim was working up a trade. "I expect that rifle's worth the price of that bear coat and then some."

"Maybe," Cross said, scratching his beard and pretending to give it a lot of thought, "if you throw in that box of cartridges."

"And you throw in that buckskin shirt your wife is holding over there," Clint replied.

Cross laughed and conceded, knowing he could exact a greater price for the rifle from the Blackfoot Indians. And so it went. They drank coffee and ate food that Spring Flower cooked over her fire. At the end of the day, Cross had acquired the Henry rifle, with ammunition, a shotgun, two pistols, and a single-shot Springfield rifle. In addition to the bearskin coat, Clint gained a fringed buckskin shirt and pants, and rid himself of the weapons he had no use for. Cross definitely got the better deal, but both men were happy.

At Jim's invitation, Clint made his camp there that night. After talking late with the jovial trader, he retired to his blankets, feeling confident that he was now ready to wrestle old man winter in the mountains. He did not go to sleep right away, however, as he lay there thinking about his plans to find a place to hole up for a while until lawmen gave up looking for him—at the same time wondering how he would be able to stay away from Joanna for very long. It was during moments like these, alone at night, when he let his confidence slip a little, and he wondered whether there really was any future for him on the path he had chosen. The image of Billy Turnipseed surfaced again in his mind.

# Chapter 17

"Whaddaya say we move on back upriver?" Pete Yancey suggested as he emptied the dregs of his coffee cup on the ground beside him. "I'm gettin' pretty damn tired of sleepin' outside when I've got plenty of money to buy me a hotel room."

Clell Ballenger grunted as he reached under him to remove a small rock that had begun to bore into his behind. "Maybe you ain't heard," he said sarcastically, "but there's a bunch of folks wearin' badges lookin' for us upriver."

"Hell, I ain't talkin' about goin' back to Helena or Butte, no place like that. Why don't we ride on over to Virginia City? Ain't nobody over that way knows us." He shifted his lean body around to find a more comfortable position. "Now, that's a proper city for two gents like us. They got saloons and hotels and whorehouses that ain't tents. Besides, I expect they've gave up lookin' for us by now."

Ballenger gave it some thought. It did seem pointless to have a bundle of money if you couldn't spend it the way you wanted to. He kind of liked Coulson, though. It would suit him just fine if they had finished the hotel they were building. There were plenty of saloons for drinking and card playing, and Sophie, down by the sawmill, seemed to satisfy his needs in that department. Still, the thought of Virginia City, with a much greater array of pleasure palaces, was tempting. "Maybe you're right," he finally replied. "I am gettin' tired of campin' by this river. Hell, let's go to Virginia City. If they do send another marshal after us, we'll take care of him like we did the last one. I tell you what, let's go to the River House for a drink, and one more round with ol' Sophie, and we'll start out for Virginia City in the mornin'. Whaddaya say?"

"It by God suits me," Yancey replied enthusiastically. Never one to pass up an opportunity for a physical encounter with a willing woman, he nevertheless would just as soon have started to Virginia City right then.

Deputy Marshal Zach Clayton spent most of the day trying to watch the town as inconspicuously as possible, first from one end of town, and then from the other. He rode out of the quiet settlement after noon and scouted along the river and various creeks in search of a camp. It was all to no avail, and he began to fear that the two outlaws had decided to move on to another town. After cursing his luck for missing the notorious pair yet again, he turned his horse back toward Coulson.

He was well familiar with the horses the two outlaws rode, and there were none matching their description tied at any of the several hitching posts in town. Walking the dusty street, leading his horse, he checked every saloon, ending up at the River House.

"Well, I see you came back to see us," Sam Crowder said when the marshal walked in the door. "You need a little drink of whiskey?"

Clayton thought it over for a moment before deciding. "No," he said, his mind still on whether to hang around the town another day or to move on to the next one. "Have you got any coffee?"

"Yeah, I've got a pot on the stove over there. I made it first thing this mornin', so it might be a little stout about now."

"Hell, that's all right," Clayton said. "I like it a little burnt." Suddenly feeling tired, he took the cup Sam offered and took it over to a table when another patron walked up to the bar. Ballenger had told the bartender they'd be back. Clayton knew that didn't necessarily guarantee their return, but they might return, so he decided to wait for a while. If they had left town already, it was going to be another chore to find them, not knowing whether they went east or west.

He could see a cluster of buildings ahead as he guided Rowdy around a series of gullies that ran to the river. In the distance, he could see the faint outline of a range of mountains. The sight made his heart quicken as he realized that he might reach them in a day or so. He had planned to avoid towns of any size, like the one he could see ahead, but Rowdy's left front hoof had somehow managed to loosen the shoe and Clint wanted to fix it as soon as possible. So in that sense, he guessed it was lucky he came to a town.

The stable's owner and blacksmith were one and the same, a cheerful fellow named Farley James. He was shoeing a chestnut Morgan when Clint pulled Rowdy up in front of the stable door. Giving Clint no more than a glance, Farley continued nailing a new shoe on the Morgan's hoof until it was finished; then he dropped the hoof to the ground and straightened up to greet the stranger.

"How do?" he said. "You needin' somethin'? Stable or smithy?"

"Howdy," Clint replied. "I think my horse is gettin' ready to throw a shoe."

"Well, let's take a look," Farley said. "Just let me put this horse back in the stall." He led the chestnut to a wide stall in the rear of the stable and put him in with another horse. He returned and lifted the leg indicated by Clint. "It's loose, all right. It's pretty worn, too. If all of 'em are this worn, it wouldn't hurt to replace 'em all."

Clint was not surprised. "I expect they are," he said. "And I expect you might as well replace 'em."

"What about your packhorse?" Farley asked. "Is he in the same fix?"

"He's an Indian pony. He ain't wearin' no shoes."

Farley grunted his disappointment. "All right, then," he said, "I'll get right on it. You can stand around and wait, or leave 'em here and come back in about an hour."

"I reckon I'll wait," Clint said, and stepped back out of the way.

He watched for a while until he became bored with it, and then walked back through the stable toward the corral behind, always interested in horses. Near the back door, he passed the stall Farley had led the Morgan to. He glanced at the horse, just noticing the palomino in the stall with him. He paused for a moment to admire the showy palomino, then started to walk on. He stopped and went back to the stall, a startling thought frozen in his mind. Looking harder at the two horses—a chestnut Morgan and a palomino—he muttered, "The Goddamn world ain't that small." Taking a closer look, he noted the faces of the two horses, the palomino with a white race, the Morgan with a white star. *Ballenger and Yancey!* He was struck dumb for a second or two, unable to believe that he had crossed their path again, but he was certain he correctly remembered the horses the notorious pair rode.

He quickly walked back to the front of the barn. "Those two horses in the back stall, who do they belong to?"

"I don't know," Farley replied, "two fellers ridin' through town."

"One of 'em big with a flat nose?" Clint asked. "The other one tall and kinda skinny?"

"I couldn't say," the blacksmith responded. "I was gone to dinner when they brought 'em in. They left 'em with Edgar. He's the boy that helps me out around here. Edgar didn't say nothin' about what they looked like. They gave him a twenty-dollar bill and said to shoe 'em, they'd go get a drink and come back for 'em. So I shoed 'em."

Clint didn't say anything more for a long moment while he considered the possibility that this was merely a coincidence. But what if it wasn't? *Hell*, he thought, *it's mighty long odds. Most likely it's not the same pair.* Feeling the probability that the horses belonged to someone other than Ballenger and Yancey, he nevertheless considered riding out of town to avoid the improbable encounter. His curiosity got the best of him, however, and he decided he had to see for himself. "Your boy didn't say where the two of 'em went for a drink, did he?"

"Nope," Farley replied, pausing in his work to wonder now about Clint's profound interest in the two men. "I doubt he asked, but the closest saloon is Sam Crowder's place." He pointed toward the south end of the street. "The River House."

"I'll be back for my horses," Clint said as he drew his Winchester from the saddle sling. "Maybe I'd better pay you now. I might be in a hurry when I come back."

"Maybe you'd better," Farley said, dropping Rowdy's hoof and wiping his hands on his apron. It seemed like the smart thing to do, judging by the stranger's questions and the way he checked his rifle.

While Clint talked to the smithy, Zach Clayton sat sipping his bitter coffee at a back table in the River House. It wasn't long, however, before his patience ran out on the waiting as well as the overcooked coffee. Finally he got up and went to the bar, where Sam was busy cleaning shot glasses with a rag that looked as if it had been used on the floor. "Those two men I asked you about," Clayton said, "did they give you any idea when they might be back?"

"Them two?" Sam replied. "Hell, they was already in here 'bout thirty minutes before you came in."

"Why the hell didn't you say so?" Clayton roared.

Sam appeared truly astonished by the question. "You never asked," he responded.

Thoroughly disgusted with the halfwit, Clayton came close to going over the bar after him. "I've been sittin' back there waitin' and all that time you coulda told me they'd already been here. I've got a good mind to . . ." He stopped short of threatening the man's life.

Sam backed away from the bar, confused by the sudden outburst, and concerned for his safety. "Well, damn," he said, "they just went down to Sophie's—most likely still there—ain't been that long."

Wasting no more time with the simple bartender, Clayton charged out the door. Pausing only long enough to draw his rifle from the scabbard, he ran toward the river, leaving his horse tied at the rail. When he got to the sawmill, roughly fifty yards upstream from the long tent that served as Sophie's place of business, he ducked inside the shed that housed the steam engine. The mill was standing idle with no one in the engine shed or the long shed where logs were stacked, awaiting the saw.

Making his way around a stack of recently sawn boards, he knelt on one knee while he studied the entrance to Sophie's, taking note of the fact that there was no back entrance. He was not sure the information just gotten from Sam Crowder was, in fact, accurate. There were no horses tied at the front of the tent, and from the point where he knelt, he couldn't see the other side. He remained there for a quarter of an hour, waiting to see whether anyone came in or out. Finally when patience began to ebb, he decided to make his move and assume Ballenger and Yancey were both inside.

Running in a slight crouch, his rifle ready to fire in an instant at the first sign of a target, he covered the ground between the sawmill and the tent quickly. Pulling up beside the front flap of the tent, he paused a moment to catch his breath and listen before slipping inside.

There was no one in the front part of the tent that served as Sophie's parlor. Stepping carefully on the board floor so as not to make a sound, he moved across the tiny room to the curtain that served as a wall between the parlor and the bedroom. Having been there before, Clayton knew that there were only three compartments in the tent. The third was Sophie's kitchen. From the sound of labored breathing, he knew that Sophie was in the midst of a business deal. A moment later he heard conversation that told him he had run his prey to ground.

"Damn you, what the hell's the matter with you? You look like a scared rabbit," a gruff male voice complained. "If you don't loosen up and give me the ride I paid for, I'll take my money back."

"I'm sorry, Clell," Sophie pleaded fearfully. "I'm doin' the best I can." On the other side of the curtain, Clayton could well imagine why Sophie was tense. He was to blame.

"By God," Clell said, "you was a helluva lot more worth the money last time."

There was one question in Clayton's mind now: *Where is Pete Yancey?* He automatically took a quick look over his shoulder to make sure there was no one behind him. He heard the woeful voice of Sophie again as she pleaded, "Don't, Clell, you're hurting me." It was enough to make

Clayton decide to move in before the woman was hurt badly. He would have to take the chance that Yancey was not with Ballenger.

In one swift move, he thrust the curtain aside and burst into the room, and immediately knew he was a dead man. There was no one on the bed. Grinning wickedly at him on the other side of the bed, Ballenger stood in nothing but his underdrawers, one arm around Sophie's neck, holding her before him as a shield. With the other hand, he aimed a pistol at the surprised deputy marshal.

"Well, if it ain't my old friend, Deputy Zach Clayton," Clell drawled smugly. "This time it looks like I got the jump on you, don't it?"

"Hello, Ballenger," Clayton replied. "Where's that other cockroach you ride with?" Still reeling from the shock of walking into a trap, he realized that the only reason he was not dead was the cruel outlaw's fondness for gloating. He quickly considered the odds of getting off a shot without hitting Sophie, but decided there was not much chance for one in a lethal spot. The best he could do was to hit him in the arm or leg, and Clell would simply shoot him for his trouble.

Answering Clayton's question, Ballenger said, "Yancey? Oh, he's around here somewhere, probably asleep in the kitchen. He always gets sleepy after he's had a tussle with a woman." Without taking his eyes off Clayton, he called, "Yancey! Come see what I caught sneakin' in the tent." There was no response to his call.

Knowing the only chance he had was to keep the gloating monster amused, Clayton attempted to jape him. "I gotta admit that was pretty slick. How the hell did you know I was out there?"

Ballenger responded with a bellow of a laugh. "Got you dead to rights, didn't I?" He was almost gleeful in turning the tables on the deputy. "Sweet ol' Sophie here needs a thicker curtain. When the sun shines through that open tent flap, it throws a shadow on the curtain. You just happened to come in when I was just fixin' to get down to business." Irritated then that Yancey had failed to respond, he turned his head toward the kitchen curtain and yelled louder, "Yancey! Wake the hell up!"

Clayton didn't hesitate. He figured it was the only chance he was going to get. When Ballenger turned to call Yancey, he gave Clayton a target for one shot. Though only half his face was exposed, when he turned back to face the deputy, Clayton fired his rifle. The bullet caught the huge man in the jaw, ripping through his mouth and out the other cheek. In shock, Ballenger staggered backward, releasing Sophie. He tried to return fire, but was off balance enough to spoil his aim. The result of his shot was a bullet hole through Clayton's coat just below the armpit. He didn't have time for a second shot. Clayton dropped to one knee when Sophie fell to the floor, and cranked three more slugs into Ballenger's chest, causing the huge man to release his pistol and drop to his knees. He remained on his knees long enough to mutter, "You've kilt me." Then he fell face forward on the floor.

"I reckon," Clayton replied, and immediately turned his rifle toward the kitchen curtain, expecting shots from Yancey. But there was no sound from that quarter.

With no more than a glance at the terrified woman, Clayton edged over toward the curtain, mindful of the surprise he had received when he came from the parlor. When Sophie's sobbing became distracting, he growled, "You ain't hurt. Put your clothes on and be still." With still no sound or motion from the kitchen, he decided it was now or never, so he grabbed one end of the curtain, and with one violent move, he ripped it halfway across. At the same time, he knelt again with his rifle ready, only to confront an empty room. He stood frozen for a few moments, staring at a gaping rip in the outside canvas where Yancey had hastily fashioned a rear exit to Sophie's tent.

In full flight, Pete Yancey was running for his life, having just been startled from a sound sleep by a sudden eruption of rifle fire that sounded as if it were right under the chair he dozed in. When the gunfire rattled his slumber, his first instinct was to escape. Without knowing who or how many had attacked Ballenger, he stumbled away from the kitchen table and sliced a hole in the back wall of the tent with his skinning knife. His one objective at the moment was to gain the protection of the sawmill.

Back in the tent, Clayton peered through the opening Yancey had cut in the back wall just in time to see the outlaw scurrying over a pile of logs. There was no shot, but he took it anyway, hoping for some luck. The slug ripped a chunk from a log, but Yancey got away. Knowing he couldn't afford to let him escape to take cover in the town, Clayton plunged through the tear in the tent, faced with the prospect of making it across the fifty yards of open ground without getting shot.

Running as fast as he could while trying to zigzag to present a more difficult target, he felt a rifle slug kick up dirt beside his foot. It told him that Yancey took the shot while still running. In a matter of seconds, he reached the cover of the log pile Yancey had escaped behind. Breathing hard, he paused to consider his next move. Looking beyond the logs to the saw shed, he could see very little cover available to Yancey. Then, too late to get off a clear shot, he caught a glimpse of the rangy fugitive as he ran toward the general store. "Damn!" Clayton cursed. There were too many places in town that offered Yancey the opportunity to wait in ambush.

\* \* \*

Inside the River House Saloon, Clint was talking to Sam Crowder. Sam was in the midst of answering Clint's questions about the two strangers recently in his saloon. Before he could, however, the sound of gunshots rang out from the direction of Sophie's. Both men ran outside, looking toward the river. As they stood there puzzling over the shooting, a man ran around the general store and stopped at the corner of the building, obviously preparing to ambush someone.

Clint felt a cold sensation grip his stomach. The man looked like Pete Yancey, but Clint was not certain. Regardless, Yancey or not, he was apparently waiting to shoot someone chasing him. Clint cocked his rifle and started walking toward the store. So intent upon the person chasing him, Yancey was unaware of the danger behind him. With his pistol ready, he peeked around the corner, waiting. When within a dozen yards of him, Clint called out, "Yancey! Drop it!"

Yancey's reactions were lightning fast, but his aim was high as he whirled around and fired. His bullet went through the crown of Clint's hat, knocking it off his head. Any other time, Yancey would have been fast enough to have gotten off another shot, maybe two more. But this time, when he spun around, it was to confront the face he thought he had seen in his dream, the clean-shaven, youthful face with the single lock of hair dropping across the forehead. The shock caused him to freeze long enough for Clint to fire back. No one could know of Yancey's fateful dream in which he thought he actually saw the bullet that killed him, but in that fatal instant, Clint's rifle slug slammed into Yancey's forehead, dead center.

The last two shots, right between the store and the saloon, caused the unwise outpouring of people from other buildings, anxious to see what had happened. Clint, his heart still pounding from the near-death encounter, backed away slowly, uncertain of what he should do, if anything. He had just killed a man, but it was certainly good riddance. His uncertainty was short-lived, however, because Zach Clayton suddenly appeared around the corner. *I should have known it was Clayton*, he thought.

There was no choice other than to run. Seeing that Clayton was distracted by the discovery of Yancey's body, Clint turned and hurried toward the stable, passing curious citizens of the town as they ran to the scene of the shooting. He met Farley James, as the smithy ran from his barn.

"What happened?" Farley yelled when he saw Clint.

"Feller got shot," was Clint's simple reply. "I need my horses."

"In the front stalls," Farley called back over his shoulder as he ran toward the street.

# Chapter 18

"What did he look like?" Clayton asked Sam Crowder.

"Hell, I don't know," Sam replied. "I mean, he was a fairly young feller, clean shaven, 'bout your height, I reckon, maybe a little more husky."

"Did he give his name?" Clayton pressed, having dealt with Sam's inane testimony before.

"Nah," Sam replied, and shrugged it off. "I never asked him." Then a spark of thought lit his eyes. "He was mighty interested in this feller and the other'n, though. Asked me all kind of questions about 'em."

"I know his name," one of the spectators volunteered and stepped forward. "I own the stable and blacksmith shop. I shoed his horse about an hour ago. His name's Allen. At least, that's what he said it was."

Clayton almost smiled. "Allen, huh? Was it Clint Allen?"

Farley shrugged. "Maybe," he said.

"You know where he is now?" He asked the question knowing that it was useless.

"He took off," Farley answered, "got his horses and left, not thirty minutes ago."

"Damn!" Clayton cursed, knowing he had been this close to sewing up the entire affair. Half an hour's start, he was tempted to just forget about Clint Conner, alias Clint Allen. *Instead of arresting him, I ought to give him deputy's pay for killing Yancey.* The fact was not lost upon him that Clint had probably saved his neck again. To further complicate things, he had two bodies to take care of as well as retrieving what bank money they still had. He had no intention of hauling Ballenger and Yancey all the way back to Cheyenne. "Is there a doctor in town?" he asked. When told that there was not, he asked, "What about an undertaker?"

"Elmer Brady usually takes care of that," someone replied. "He's the barber."

Clayton turned to find the barber at his elbow. "Are you Brady?"

"Yes, sir," Brady replied. "I can take care of him for you. You want a plain pine box? For a little more money, I can fancy it up a little."

"There's another body down at the whore's tent," Clayton replied coldly. "I don't give a damn if you just dig a hole and throw 'em in it. The territorial governor ain't likely to pay for a fancy coffin for the likes of these two." He turned back to the stable owner then. "You got their horses?" When Farley replied that he did, Clayton told him he'd meet him at the stable in a few minutes. Turning again to Elmer Brady, he said, "I need you to write death certificates for the two of 'em."

"Death certificates?" Elmer replied. "I don't know nothin' about no death certificates. Around here, if we put 'em in the ground, folks assume they're dead."

Clayton maintained his patience, even though Clint's lead was increasing with every wasted minute. "I need verification that the two of 'em are dead, since I ain't toting no bodies back with me. It doesn't have to be an official certificate. Just write it out on a piece of paper, date it, and sign it as undertaker."

"I don't even know their names," Elmer protested, not overly fond of having to bother with paperwork.

"I'll give you the names," Clayton said, his patience exhausted.

After searching both bodies, Clayton picked up the death certificates and went to the stables, where he collected the weapons and saddlebags with the remainder of the money stolen from the bank in Helena. He decided to take Ballenger's chestnut Morgan to carry the extra baggage, leaving the showy palomino in Farley's care. With matters taken care of in Coulson as well as could be expected, Clayton was at last ready to go after Clint. It would have been easy to let the fugitive go, but Clayton knew that he had to follow him to put an end to the affair.

"I don't suppose you've got any idea which way he went when he left here," Clayton said to Farley.

"Well, no," the smithy replied. "Like I said, I was on my way to see what the shootin' was about. But I expect I can find his tracks easy enough." Without hesitating, he walked out to the front of the barn and started staring at the many hoofprints in the dust. Almost immediately he stopped and straightened up. "There you go," he said. "That's him right there."

"How the hell do you know those tracks are his?" Clayton asked, somewhat skeptical.

"Easy," Farley answered sheepishly. "I hadn't finished filin' down those new shoes before I ran up to the saloon." He pointed to the tracks. "See that burr on that shoe? And there's another'n on that one there." He looked up at Clayton proudly. "And if that ain't enough, there's the tracks of that Indian pony he's leadin' that ain't got no shoes."

Clayton couldn't help but smile. "That oughta be enough," he said, "if I can catch up to him before those burrs wear off."

\*   \*   \*

With no real destination, Clint rode north, away from the river, pushing Rowdy hard, knowing that somewhere back there, Clayton would be coming after him. The farther away from the river he rode, the rougher the terrain got as he made his way through treeless expanses of uneven prairie. As he rode, periodically looking back over his shoulder, he questioned his decision to kill Pete Yancey. In truth, he had not planned to shoot Yancey. He had just thought to prevent him from ambushing someone. As he heard his horses' labored breathing and reasoned that he had to rest them, he thought it might have been better if he had let Yancey shoot Clayton. Now he was left with three choices: ambush, surrender, or run. Since he had no intention to surrender, and no desire to ambush the deputy marshal, he was left with no choice but to run.

The immediate problem, however, was his tired horses, so as soon as he came upon a small creek, he dismounted. While the horses drank, he climbed up to the top of a low mesa and looked back over the way he had come. There was no sign of anyone on his trail so far. From now on, he decided he'd better take more pains to hide his tracks. The prairie he looked out upon was broken with many low hills and grass-covered ravines like the one his horses were now grazing in. Since leaving Coulson, he had ridden straight north. It might be best if he veered from that course. It was time for another decision.

The mountains he had seen in the distance when he arrived in Coulson were to the west. His initial intention had been to gain the safety of those mountains and hide out until he felt it safe to return for Joanna. But it seemed that his destiny had been written to cross trails with Zach Clayton no matter where he went. He had made up his mind that he would not be taken alive by Clayton again to be returned to prison. And the thought of being eventually tracked down and killed in the far mountains without seeing Joanna again was not one he could accept. The woman was on his mind almost constantly.

His decision was made. He had met only one woman in his life whom he knew he truly loved, and his existence seemed empty without her. After the horses were rested, he would turn to the east. If he was lucky, he might lose Clayton. If not, he was determined to see Joanna once more before he faced the deputy to kill or be killed. He sat Indian-style on the mesa for over an hour, watching the empty prairie before he went back to the horses and started out again, this time to the east.

Although the tracks were easy to identify, it was not always easy to find them, and a fair amount of time was spent before Clayton detected a consistent trail to the north. It was obvious to the seasoned tracker that the direction taken was not selected with any thought other than running as fast as possible. Once Clint settled on a definite direction, Clayton found it easier to track him, following the most sensible path through the rolling prairie, and stopping less often to look for tracks to verify the trail.

Looking ahead at a low plateau, he wondered how far Clint would run, looking for sanction in that direction. It would be a hell of a long way before reaching terrain that he couldn't track him in. Coming to a creek running through the bottom of a ravine, he stopped to water his horses. *Looks like he stopped here to rest his horses*, Clayton thought. Examining the prints, he tried to guess how far ahead Clint might be. *No more than a few hours*, he thought. Following the tracks out of the ravine, he stopped and smiled to himself when he saw the trail bend to the east. *Downfall of many a young man*, he thought, remembering other occasions when he had cornered fugitives who could not stay away from their lady-loves. It was a reasonable bet that he wouldn't need the tracks to know where Clint was heading.

The chase continued for most of a week, crossing Big Porcupine Creek and the Little Porcupine. Clayton traveled long days, from first light until dark, but he could not shorten the distance between him and the fugitive. He was determined to run Clint to ground now. He had spent too much time in closing the case, and he was anxious to see it end. Consequently, when day after day ended without sight of the man he trailed, Clayton grew impatient to the point of irritation, resulting in a stronger determination to run him to ground. He knew, however, that the chase was nearing an end when he made his camp for the night with less than a day's ride from Frederick Steiner's farm. He would start out in the morning with no need to follow tracks. He was certain of the trail's end.

One-half a day ahead of Clayton, Clint sat in the saddle watching the house from the wagon track that led along the Yellowstone as darkness fell over Frederick Steiner's farm. Now that he had ridden Rowdy to the point of faltering, he hesitated to ride the final yards. What if Joanna had changed her mind about going with him? Maybe it was not right for him to take her. He knew it might break her father's heart to see his daughter ride off with an outlaw, maybe never to see her again. One might argue that, if he truly loved Joanna, he would turn around now and take his trouble elsewhere. Finally he told himself that he was going to have to make up his mind, and knowing she was only a few dozen yards away, he could not turn away.

Joanna Becker took her apron off and left it on the back of a chair. For the most part, the supper dishes were done, except for the cups that were still being used to finish the last of the coffee. Her father and her uncle were still sitting around the table swapping stories about their youth, much to the entertainment of her cousin John. Aunt Bertha had retired to her bed with a headache.

Joanna stood and listened to the two men for a few moments before deciding to go out on the porch for a breath of air before finishing the cleanup. "You'll be giving that boy some ideas," she said, laughing as she spun on her heel and started for the door.

Outside, she pulled the door shut behind her and walked to the edge of the porch, where she stood to breathe in the cool night air. Gazing up at a clear moonless sky, she smiled at the canopy of stars so far away, yet seeming so bright in the crisp fall air. As her eyes became more adjusted to the dark, she let her gaze fall to the path before the house, and suddenly gasped as a dark figure on a horse slowly took form.

Immediately alarmed, she had started for the door when his voice stopped her. "Joanna," he said as he dismounted.

She recognized his voice at once. Turning back toward him, her heart threatening to burst from her breast, she gasped, "Clint?" hardly believing it could be him. In a moment of unbridled joy, she hurried from the porch, her feet barely touching the ground as she flew into his arms.

Holding him as if he might disappear as suddenly as he had appeared, she pressed her face against his chest. Joyful tears rolled down her cheeks as she cried, "I thought I might never see you again."

"I thought I could stay away, but I couldn't," he confessed openly. "I love you, Joanna. I had to come back."

"I prayed you'd come back soon, and if you did, I promised myself I wouldn't let you leave again without me." She reached up to kiss him.

His lips found hers in an embrace of two souls crying out for each other. When at last they parted, he placed his hands on her shoulders, holding her at arm's length while he confessed. "I shouldn't have come here, Joanna. Zach Clayton is comin' on behind me. I don't know how far back, but I know he'll be comin'." He told her about the killings at Coulson. "I can't seem to get that man off my trail. Everywhere I go he shows up, so he's bound to show up here sooner or later. Clayton's a smart man. He knows I'd have to come see you one more time."

She felt as if her heart was being wrenched from her bosom. She didn't think she could stand to see him leave again without her, but she understood why he would not want to endanger her while he was on the run. She shook her head in indecision. "Oh, Clint, will we ever be together? Maybe it was not meant to be." Then she stepped back and said, "You must be hungry. Come inside and I'll fix you something to eat."

"No, I don't think that's a good idea," he said. "It's best if your folks don't know I'm back."

"They'll start to wonder what happened to me if I don't come back," she said.

"I know. I'll ride over to that little island by the river and camp there tonight. If you can get away in the mornin', meet me out there. But don't tell anybody where you're goin'."

"I'll be there," she said, "right after I give them their breakfast. Aunt Bertha's gone to bed, sick with a headache, so I'll probably be fixing breakfast by myself."

They embraced again, and then he said, "You'd best go on back inside before somebody comes lookin' for you."

She kissed him lightly again. "Good night, darling. I'll come to our special island as soon as I can."

* * *

The next morning Bertha was not as fragile as Joanna expected her to be. The two women cooked breakfast for the men as usual, but there seemed to be something different about Joanna's attitude. Bertha noticed that her niece appeared to be impatient, and when Joanna commented that she wanted to take her horse for a ride this morning, Bertha said, "Go on and go. I'll finish up the dishes." Then she paused to watch Joanna as she hurried to rid herself of her apron. "You'd best wear your coat. It's chilly out these mornings."

"I will, Aunt Bertha," Joanna replied as she grabbed her coat from one of the pegs by the door.

Her aunt raised an eyebrow as the door closed, and announced to herself, "If I didn't know better, I'd think that young man was still here." Her niece had not gone for a ride since Clint left.

Not wishing to bother the men who were clearing some brush down by the stream, Joanna saddled the little mare and led her out of the corral. Stepping up in the saddle, she encouraged the horse to lope down the path and swing out on the wagon track by the river. She could feel the joyful flush upon her cheeks caused by the frosty morning air, oblivious of the man leaning against a cottonwood next to the river, or the horse standing below the bank.

"Well, good mornin', missy," Zach Clayton muttered as he watched the young lady guide her horse along the river trace. Waiting until she had created a sizable lead, he then descended the low bank, stepped up in the saddle, and, matching Joanna's pace, started out after her.

Before he saw her, Rowdy alerted him that someone was coming. He moved up through the willows until he could see the trail that wound along the bank. With his rifle raised and ready to fire, he waited until the rider appeared. It was Joanna riding one of his Indian ponies, the little mare that she had adopted for her own. His heart quickened as he low- ered his rifle and ran to meet her.

She urged her horse into the shallow water and crossed over to the little island where he stood, ready to catch her in his arms as she stepped down. Their embrace was long and passionate, and would not have ended so suddenly but for the voice behind them.

"I hope I ain't interruptin'," Clayton said.

Clint cast Joanna aside and reached for his rifle on the ground only to confront Clayton sitting on his horse, his own rifle trained on him. "Now, see, there you go again," Clayton said. "Every time I see you, you're pointin' that rifle at me, and I've already got mine aimed right about your gut. So why don't you just lay that weapon back down where it was and we'll talk?"

"I can't do it, Clayton," Clint replied emphatically. "I got railroaded the last time I listened to you, and I ain't goin' back to that prison. I reckon you're gonna have to shoot me."

"No, Clint!" Joanna begged. "He'll kill you!"

"Better listen to her, Clint. You ain't no killer. Besides, I didn't come here to talk to you. I rode all the way over here to talk to this young lady." He smiled at Joanna. "Good mornin' to you, ma'am. I came to bring you some bad news. There was two men shot dead over in Coulson last week, both fugitives from the Wyoming Territorial Prison. I got their names right here on a death certificate— Clell Ballenger and Clint Conner. I recollect you had some interest in Conner. I'm sorry to have to bring you the news of his untimely death, but I thought you'd wanna know."

He put the papers back inside his coat pocket and slipped his rifle back in the saddle sling. "I guess I'll be goin' now.

I've got a long ride back to Cheyenne." He smiled at Clint. "You young folks carry on with what you were doin' . . . Mr. Allen."

He turned his horse and climbed up the bank, and then he was gone.